HONOR BOUND

WITCH BORN BOOK 1

C.J. ARCHER

WWW.CJARCHER.COM

CHAPTER 1

1583 - London, England

*L*awrence Shawe burst through the apothecary shop's door with far more vehemence than usual. Considering he never undertook any activity that required enthusiasm on his part, it was enough to distract Isabel from her herbs. She glanced up from the jar she'd been filling with dried juniper berries to glare at him but the look on his face dampened her temper. His cheeks were flushed and his hat sat lop-sided on his silver-streaked hair. He'd certainly exerted himself on this occasion. Indeed, he might even have been running.

"What is it, Lawrence?" Isabel asked. "What's happened?"

"Someone tried to poison the queen."

She dropped the handful of berries onto the workbench. "Dear God, how awful! Is she all right?"

Lawrence nodded and squeezed his finger and thumb into his eye sockets. When he drew them away again, he no longer looked exercised, just exhausted. His reddened eyelids sagged like old porch roofs over his blue eyes and even his clothes, usually so fastidiously tidy, had creases. Creased clothing equated to utter disarray in Lawrence's book.

As physician to Her Majesty Queen Elizabeth, Lawrence would take a poisoning attempt on her life very seriously. Any threat to her health was a direct threat to not only his career, but perhaps even his life if he failed to save her. As the only son of Isabel's aged employer, she had a vested interest in Lawrence's wellbeing, and therefore Her Majesty's health too.

"Perfectly all right," he said. "Lady Manningham, however, is quite ill." He crossed the rush-covered floor of the small apothecary shop and stood beside her at the workbench. He picked up a berry and rolled it between his thumb and fingers until it crumbled. "Her Majesty's Gentlewoman of the Privy Chamber ate the poisoned sweetmeats intended for the queen." He snorted out a laugh as he sniffed his fingers. "Silly woman. I've told her on numerous occasions her taste for sweet foods will be the death of her."

Isabel didn't think the joke terribly funny considering the circumstances. Nevertheless she breathed a sigh of relief over the queen's condition. "Is there any remedy you require for Lady Manningham? You're welcome to anything from the shop, of course. Your father would wish it."

He sprinkled the crushed remnants of the berry onto the bench and dusted his hands. "How is Father today?" he asked.

"The same." She sighed deeply and swept up the crumbs with her bare hands. "His limbs ache and he's confined to his bed most of the time, but he still insists on personally greeting his favored clients." She smiled. Old Man Shawe, as everyone affectionately called the apothecary, would rather die than give up his work entirely. Even so, his ill health meant Isabel now ran the shop and the Shawe household since Lawrence lived elsewhere. She dealt with customers and suppliers, servants and apprentices. She prepared remedies, dispensed advice and kept the accounts. Old Man Shawe was apothecary in name only—and a well-known name at that, bringing new clients from all over London—but she included him in all the decisions out of courtesy. It was the least she could do for the man who had helped her at a most desperate time.

"Have you been massaging a hot poultice of comfrey into his limbs?" Lawrence asked.

"Every morning and night."

"Yes, but with vigorous strokes. Like this." He took her arm and rubbed his thumb along her sleeve with far less pressure than was correct. "The massage itself can be more soothing than the poultice." He used gentle, low tones as if speaking to one of his ill patients. She wondered if he spoke to the queen that way, in and out of bed. Or so the rumors went.

Isabel pursed her lips to stop the wicked smile threatening to betray her thoughts. "Yes, Lawrence," she said, withdrawing her arm. "I am caring for your father as best as I can."

"I didn't mean... I'm sorry, I..." He blushed, turning his milky cheeks rosy, then tried to hide it by dipping his head. "Forgive my rudeness. I know you're giving Father the utmost care. I wouldn't entrust his health to anyone else." He smiled an apology and at that moment Isabel could see why so many women found him attractive. He was only a little taller than her but still handsome for a man past his fortieth year. With his good looks, pleasant manner and a favored position at court, the widower was considered a catch by many women.

Isabel wasn't one of them. She liked Lawrence well enough, but he meant nothing more to her than a friend and fellow scholar of medicines. And as her employer's son, she was as much indebted to him as to his father.

"Forgive me?" he said, with a raise of his eyebrows.

"There is nothing to forgive." She moved towards the door at the back of the shop which led to the rear storeroom and the stairs up to the living rooms. "Do you wish to see your father?"

"Yes but I can only spare a moment. There is much to be done at Whitehall."

"Of course. Poor Lady Manningham. Has the villain been caught?"

"Not yet. Burghley and Walsingham are investigating."

"I suppose you're here because you need a tonic."

"And to see your pleasant face." Although his words were playful, he wasn't smiling. In fact, his gaze had turned alarmingly tender.

Isabel laughed in an attempt to rescue them both from a potentially humiliating situation. "Then I'm sorry to disappoint, as I'm sure my face is hideously red from spending all morning beside a bubbling cauldron."

He lifted one shoulder as if shrugging off the tension that had threatened to engulf them. "But still a pleasing sight, nevertheless."

"You're too charming for a humble apothecary's assistant, Lawrence," she chided. "Go use it on one of the ladies at court."

He leaned back against the bench, smiling. The moment of tender seriousness had passed and Isabel wondered if perhaps she had imagined it.

"Not a single one of them can match you," he said.

"Now I know you're teasing me. There are many beautiful women at court. And some very eligible ones who I'm sure harbor a secret admiration for a handsome physician."

"I'm not merely talking about external beauty, Isabel, although you certainly have that."

She had been wrong. Laurence was merely attempting a different tactic. She quickly rounded the long counter which doubled as her workbench and scanned the earthen jars shelved above it. "If you tell me what was in the poison, I can provide you with something to counteract Lady Manningham's discomfort," she said, returning to a safe topic. "I assume she didn't ingest a large dose, considering she is still alive."

"Fortunately she merely nibbled on one of the poisoned sweetmeats. I left her in Doctor Lopes's capable hands," he said, referring to Her Majesty's chief physician. "She's taken a purgation but there is not a lot more to be done except perhaps a soothing tonic to settle her stomach. Ah, horehound." He pointed to a labeled jar on the lower shelf.

Isabel unstopped it and carefully poured some of the liquid into a phial. "It should ease her pain somewhat."

He took it and thanked her. "Add it to Whitehall's account."

"I'm sure your father would want me to give it to you without charge, particularly if it's intended for Our Sovereign's lady."

"He would but I insist you charge the palace the full amount."

Isabel reached under the counter and pulled out the accounts book. She dipped the quill in the ink and wrote down the quantity and price. "Now, was there anything else or would you like to see your father?"

"Ye-es." He pocketed the phial. "Isabel." He looked up and a sense of foreboding crept over her. "My real reason for coming here today was to warn you to be alert. Someone from Whitehall will probably want to ask you and Father some questions."

The sense of foreboding turned to dread. She should have known that her past would one day find her. "What sort of questions? What has the poisoning got to do with us?"

"I could smell the poisons used in the sweetmeats."

"And?"

"Hemlock, henbane and monkshood. This is one of the few apothecary shops in London that sells all those ingredients."

She tensed. "They all have legitimate purposes if used in their correct dosages. And we keep them in the locked storeroom. I'm the only one allowed to dispense them. Besides, there must be other apothecaries who sell those three herbs."

"I know of only five."

Isabel picked up the jar of horehound and tried to replace the stopper but it didn't seem to fit no matter how hard she tried to force it. "Stupid thing," she muttered, casting it aside.

Lawrence passed her another stopper. "I think this one belongs to that jar." Concern made his angular features even sharper. "Don't be nervous."

"I'm not nervous," she said, willing the hairs on the back of her neck to flatten.

"This has nothing to do with your father," he said.

Papa. Poor, dear Papa, seven years in his grave and still unable to rest in peace. "I know." But would the authorities agree? When they discovered her connection to him she would become their main suspect. And a capable investigator would surely discover it.

Well, she would just have to hope for an incapable one. "Papa was innocent." The words slipped out from habit. It seemed she had been thinking them, if not saying them, every day for the last seven years.

Lawrence said nothing. Since his mother's death, he was one of only two people in Isabel's new life—as she thought of her years living in London—who knew her background. His silence was damning.

"I must see Father." He caught both her hands in his. "Be careful what you tell the authorities when they come."

"Of course," she managed to whisper through her tight throat.

He left through the rear door and his footsteps retreated up the stairs to Old Man Shawe's room. Too distracted to work, Isabel looked out the window at Bucklersbury Street and wondered what an official from Whitehall would look like. Whoever he might be, he would wear finer clothes than the merchants, tradesmen and servants going about their business in the muddy apothecary's street. She was sure she would know him when she saw him.

It had begun to rain, scattering people forced to be out on such a bleak February day. Some retreated indoors while others sheltered beneath the overhanging upper stories of the grocery and apothecary shops lining the street. Isabel thought one or two might make use of her warm fire, but none entered. The rain would keep trade slow that afternoon but she didn't mind. There was much to be done.

She pulled the rickety ladder out from the gap between two sets of shelves and picked up the jar of juniper berries from the workbench. The bottom two rungs groaned under her weight. It seemed Fox hadn't got around to fixing them yet. She would have to have another word with him, and this time she would make sure he knew the consequences of avoiding his duties. If Fox couldn't take orders from her instead of Old Man Shawe then he would have to seek an apprenticeship elsewhere.

She frowned at the layer of dust on the top shelf and considered wiping it off. But the jar grew heavy and since no one except herself and Fox would ever see the dust anyway, she decided to leave it. She heaved the jar up but there wasn't enough space for it on the shelf. The entire row, every single jar, needed to be moved along. That meant returning the jar she held to the workbench, shifting the ladder down to the end then climbing back up and shuffling the other jars one by one then retrieving...

For a fleeting moment, she considered using her powers to move the jars, but she forced the instinct from her mind. She hadn't used her witchcraft since that fateful day six years ago and she wasn't about to start now.

With a sigh, she descended the ladder, resting the jar on her hip like a baby. The front door to the shop opened and she was about to call out to the customer that she would be only a moment, when he spoke first.

"Let me take that for you."

That voice...

She looked down into the face she hadn't seen for six long years. And dropped the jar.

He caught it, although she suspected it was unwittingly done because someone who looked as shocked as he did couldn't consciously work their body with such quick finesse. She should know. Her legs felt as stable as water and she gripped the ladder tighter to stop herself from falling. She certainly wouldn't attempt the next rung yet. Making an ungainly descent in front of the man she hadn't been able to banish from her dreams would be too horrible.

"Isabel?"

"Nick." She was sure she said it out loud but she couldn't hear it so she said it again. "Nick." His name felt strange on her tongue.

"It is you," he whispered, his dark gaze lifted up to her. As if his legs had grown weary, he sat down heavily on the stool provided for customers near the workbench. "Oh my God," he said. "It is you."

Taking very careful steps, she slowly descended the ladder. When her foot touched the second last rung, a loud crack shattered the thick silence. Isabel fell to the floor in an undignified heap just as her husband, Nicholas Merritt, rushed to her side.

"Isabel, are you all right?" He knelt and touched her shoulder.

For a brief moment the connection recalled shared memories —of affection, passion and finally of pain. It was this last that made her shake him off. That and her embarrassment.

"I'm well." She got to her feet unaided and smoothed down

7

her woolen gown wishing she could smooth away her erratic heartbeat as easily.

"Are you sure you're not hurt?" he asked. "You landed rather awkwardly."

"I'm fine!" Good Lord, this was not the way their reunion was supposed to happen. It was supposed to involve her being perfectly serene and looking her prettiest, and Nick groveling.

He didn't grovel. He didn't say anything. He was so close she only had to reach out to touch his hair. The power of his presence, something she'd always found enthralling, sucked her in. She gripped the bench at her back to stop from flinging her arms around him and doing the groveling instead.

"Isabel." He spoke so quietly she had to strain to hear him. "Christ!" he said with sudden vehemence. He dragged a hand through his hair but said nothing else.

She turned away because seeing the shock on his face made her feel more insecure than she had in a long time.

"Am I so awful that you cannot even look at me?" he demanded.

Her breath escaped in a whoosh and tears stung the back of her eyes. She must look at him. If she wanted to put him from her mind once and for all, she must first face him. She waited until her vision cleared, then slowly turned around.

He looked the same, and yet so different. He still had the boyish face she held so dear in her memory, and although he was yet to laugh, the twinkle in his eyes and the dimples in his cheeks were only a smile away.

But the boy had become a man since she'd last seen him. It was as if a sculptor had chiseled a little of the youthfulness away to reveal a harder, leaner and even more handsome face. A small furrow at the bridge of his straight nose and a few lines around his eyes and mouth only enhanced his new masculinity. There was power and intensity in his features and stance where before there had been only carefree frivolity.

She wondered if her appearance had altered as dramatically in the last six years. His expression gave no indication as he studied her. Under the scrutiny, Isabel resisted the urge to straighten her skirts and check that her cap hadn't slipped in the fall.

"No," she said at last when she felt certain her voice wouldn't falter. "Not awful at all." Far from it.

She marveled that he was still so tall, something she had not expected. She had thought he would not seem so big since she had grown up so much since leaving him. She had been wrong. He towered over her like a solid, impenetrable wall as he had always done.

They stood like two strangers, warily watching each other, until Isabel could stand it no longer.

"How did you know where to find me?" she asked.

He frowned at her. "I didn't. I wasn't looking for you. I just walked in...and here you are." He sounded like a man awed by a wondrous magic trick.

Magic. The reminder of the vile thing behind their separation sliced through her like a knife.

Then his words sank in. He hadn't been looking for her. The fact that his admission hurt meant time had healed nothing, and she had not changed as much as she thought.

"Yes," she said. "Here I am."

"They said you had gone to Cambridge," he said. "I tore that city apart looking for you." His voice rose from a flat monotone to a pitch that grated her raw nerves. "If I'd known you were in London..." He shook his head, still staring at her.

He had been searching for her. The ache in her heart lessened. "You wouldn't have found me. I'm not Isabel Merritt here."

"Camm?" he asked, referring to her maiden name.

She nodded.

"My God," he said. "It's really you." His laugh was more of a maniacal bark.

Maybe he'd gone mad. Perhaps the scheme he'd become involved in after their marriage, the cause of his long absences, had affected his mind. She edged away from him.

"No!" He caught her face in his hands with a delicacy at odds with his tone. "Don't move." His skin felt rough on her cheeks but then he caressed her with his thumbs and she thought she had never felt anything so soft in her life.

"Isabel," he murmured.

His gaze held hers and before she could sever the connection, he captured her mouth in a fierce kiss. Some distant part of her wanted to struggle but the rest of her wanted to drown in his soft lips and his warmth. It wasn't like the kisses of old. They had always been passionate but never so powerful. It was as if every emotion he had experienced in the intervening years had surged to the surface and clashed in this single searing kiss.

His hand pressed against the back of her head, holding her in place, but he needn't have bothered because she didn't want to go anywhere. She had dreamed of this kiss for six years and she wasn't going to end it yet. Not when it sent a rush of heat through her, nourishing her starved body, filling a hole she hadn't known existed.

But after only a few short moments, he pulled away. "I'm sorry," he said, breathing hard. "I shouldn't have done that." He ran a hand through his hair and turned away. "I wish I hadn't." Regret echoed through his hollow voice.

She hugged her arms over her chest to try and contain her shaking. That kiss had been a mistake. It had ignited something she had thought mastered. Something deep within her, a primal, timeless need.

"But I couldn't help it," he continued. "I mean, look at you! You're here, you're real, you're not dead and I've been living in the same city as you this whole time!"

He had thought her dead? "Yes."

His eyes narrowed. "Yes? Is that all you have to say to me after six years?"

His acrimony stung. "Yes," she said again, because it truly was all she could think of saying. Her thoughts tumbled about and she couldn't possibly form a coherent sentence from them.

He scoffed and strode to the door but didn't open it. Instead, he stormed back, half turned, shook a finger at her then grunted and strode away again. With his back to her, he placed a hand against the wall and looked down at the floor. "Well, Wife, do I get an explanation? Are you going to tell me to my face this time that you have a lover?" His head turned to one side as if he couldn't face what was on the other. "I suppose you have children—"

"No!" She took a step towards him but stopped. "There are no children and no lover. There never has been." And never will be.

"Don't lie to me, Isabel. You did enough of that in our first two years of marriage."

"I have never lied to you!" She crossed the room and stood where he could see her. "Not once, Nick. Whereas you lied to me every time you went away. Every time you told me you had business in London, every time you wrote telling me you would be home soon and forever. So do not accuse me of lying because your conscience is hardly clear on that score."

Nicholas had never seen Isabel look so angry, or so beautiful. It was quite a formidable combination and stirred something inside him. Her face may be flushed from her anger and the heat of the fire, and her hair had fallen out from the cap to brush against her cheek, but she was the most amazing woman he had ever set eyes on. Even more beautiful than he remembered, something he had not thought possible. Her upturned nose was still the same, the honey color of her hair unchanged and the slimness of her figure, but there was something about the way she had walked towards him just then and spoken her mind. The girl he had married wouldn't have said it quite that way, used that tone, or moved with such determination. Nor would she have thrust out her chin, such an adorable chin too, or held his gaze.

As he looked away, too ashamed because she was right and he had lied to her over and over, he had to admit that the girl he married had changed. She had become a woman.

He turned back to her again, her words ringing in his ears. "No lover? But the Forster lad..." He remembered the name because he had searched Canterbury for her under Merritt, Camm and Forster thinking she might have taken her lover's name.

"Forster? Your mean Jacob Forster? He was a nice boy, but hardly someone I would take to my bed."

"How would I know what sort of man you'd take to your bed?"

"If you were around more you would."

Nicholas had the sickening feeling that he was to blame for Isabel's leaving all along. Even so, he had to persevere. Had to know, even if it meant heartache deeper than anything he'd ever experienced.

"They told me you and the Forster boy had run away to Canterbury together," he said dully.

"Then they were wrong."

"So it would seem." He felt almost weak with relief. She had no lover.

"I suspect Jacob Forster and I had the unhappy coincidence of leaving Newport at the same time. I'm sorry you thought I left you for another man. I didn't." She thrust out her chin again, not sounding sorry at all.

Nicholas straightened. "Then why did you leave?"

She turned away and busied herself with the herbs laid out on the bench. Being an apothecary's daughter, she had always been interested in medicines and herbal remedies, but he had never thought to find her working as a shop girl. Not the wife of Nicholas Merritt. Sir Nicholas now.

"There are too many reasons to go into here and now," she said.

"Then when and where? I have a right to know what...what I did wrong. Was it my absences?"

She sprinkled some dried leaves into a mortar and crushed them with a pestle using far more force than necessary. No doubt the leaves gave off a powerful odor but he couldn't distinguish it amidst the jumble of other pleasing scents emanating from the cauldron bubbling over the fire.

He was about to press her for an answer when the door at the rear of the shop opened and a man entered.

"Isabel, I—" The gentleman spotted Nicholas and stopped. "Forgive me, Sir, I'm sorry for interrupting." He bowed and turned to Isabel, frowning at the tension in her face. "Are you all right?"

He must be someone of considerable wealth to have a pearl earring and velvet cloak, but what concerned Nicholas more was that he called his wife—his wife—by her first name. Not Mistress

Camm or whatever, but Isabel. By rights, the only man alive who should be calling her that was himself.

"Perfectly fine," she said, although anyone who knew her would detect the sharp edge to her voice and know that everything was far from fine.

"Is this man bothering you?" The gentleman drew himself up to his full height, still several inches shorter than Nicholas, and gave him a glare meant to convey superiority.

Nicholas had to applaud her friend for trying. With his soft hands and slight stature, he was clearly not used to being cast in the role of protector. He looked out of his depth trying to intimidate. But, more importantly, the dandy was prepared to do it. For Isabel. Nicholas knew what that compulsion felt like. He was prepared to do anything for her too. If only he knew what she wanted.

"He... I...," she stuttered, her face slowly reddening. It seemed she wasn't prepared to tell the newcomer that her husband had found her, or indeed that she had a husband. "We were just..."

"We were just discussing my terrible case of..." Nicholas searched for a suitable ailment.

"Flaccid erectus," she said.

His eyes widened as he glared at her. She responded with a sly smile. "Not exactly flaccid," he said, "more...crooked."

"Whatever is wrong with your yard, be sure to listen to Isabel," the gentleman said, relaxing his stance a little. "She's one of the finest apothecaries in London. As physician to the queen, I employ her herbal remedies on occasion and have found them to be most beneficial. Your condition should clear up in no time if you follow her instructions. Good day, Sir. Isabel." He nodded to them both then left the shop.

Isabel blew out a breath.

"Strange, I don't seem to recall there ever being a problem with my yard in our relationship," Nicholas said. "But I didn't see your departure coming, so I might be wrong on that score too."

She slumped back against the bench as if suddenly deflated. "Nick—" She broke off and rested her head in her hand.

He reached for her, but dropped his arm at the last moment. "I'm sorry," he said. "This has been a trying time for us both."

She nodded. "Let's at least be civil to one another."

"Of course. But tell me, who was that man?"

"Lawrence Shawe. My employer's son. He's a newly appointed physician to Her Majesty."

"A little informal with his address, don't you think?"

She glared at him. "What he calls me is not your concern. So what did you come here for? A remedy?"

"Remedy? Yes. Of course. I have...a sore throat."

"A sore throat? Then why didn't you say so when Lawrence was here? It might have saved you some embarrassment."

Because Nicholas didn't think of it then. "I wouldn't be embarrassed if you hadn't given me an erection problem."

"It suited my mood at the time." A faint smile played at her lips. It faded and she turned her back to him. He watched as she mixed three different powders together then packaged them up and handed it to him. "Dissolve this in a cup of red wine and gargle it three times a day. If the ailment continues then come and see me next week."

"I'll be back tomorrow."

"Tomorrow is Sunday. The shop won't be open."

"I know."

He opened the door and left without turning back to look at her even though every part of him wanted to. As he walked down Bucklersbury Street he tried to sift through his emotions and set them aside so he could think clearly.

But the only clear thought he had was that he had found Isabel. After all his searching, he had uncovered her by pure chance. No, not chance. Not exactly. He almost laughed at the irony but there was nothing humorous about it. The very thing that had kept him away from her for long periods after their marriage was the same one that had brought him to her now. Spying.

CHAPTER 2

*N*icholas waited until the maidservant left, closing the door to the Earl of Ashbourne's private study behind her. Then he turned to his good friend and superior sitting across from him. "I have to be reassigned," he said.

Richard Savoy, Lord Ashbourne, lifted his dark eyebrows and leaned back in the chair. He stretched out long legs and massaged his old thigh injury, a sign that he was delaying his answer. Nicholas's announcement must have come as a surprise. "You know that's not possible. Our agents in Rheims are uncovering fresh plots all the time, and the Scots queen herself is suspected of being behind some of them. You are our best agent, although a little unorthodox at times," he added with a rueful smile. "Walsingham is thanking his good fortune that you're in London now. He trusts you to sniff out the guilty party in this latest incident against Our Sovereign."

Nicholas had expected opposition. Living agents weren't allowed to merely walk away from assignments, although he personally knew of two. Of course, both were dismissed because of the severe disabilities resulting from their work. Nevertheless he had to keep trying. "You could take over, Ash."

Ashbourne grunted and rubbed his thigh again. "Ever since that damn Spaniard used my leg for target practice, Walsingham has wanted me behind a desk." The short bark of bitter laughter was at odds with Ash's normally jovial nature. "Besides, Walsingham wants you." He threw up his hands in mock surrender. "I tried to tell him you're more trouble than you're worth but he insisted."

"He'll change his mind when he hears why."

"Let me guess," the earl said with a barely contained smile, "one of your female admirers is related to the suspect, or perhaps married to him. No, better yet, she is the suspect! A little advice, Merritt," he leaned forward conspiratorially, "if you actually bed the girl instead of making excuses, you might wind up the investigation quicker."

"I get the feeling you're not taking me seriously, Ash."

The earl's eyes twinkled with mischief. "I told you, Walsingham won't care if your mother is integral to the plot, you won't be reassigned."

"Not even if she's my wife?"

"Your mother?"

"The suspect!"

Lord Ashbourne's smug smile finally vanished. But instead of firing questions at Nicholas, the earl reached for his cup of wine. He drank the entire contents in one gulp, something he only did when he and Nicholas set out to get drunk together before a mission.

He slammed the empty cup down on the desk beside him, rattling the quill resting in the inkwell. "You found her?"

Nicholas blinked. Although he'd never mentioned his marital woes to his friend, he should have known Ash would be aware of the saga. No doubt he had made it a priority to find out everything about the agents under his command.

"I stumbled across her only a few hours ago," Nicholas said. "She works for one of the apothecaries suspected of supplying the poison. Shawe."

Ashbourne rifled through a pile of papers on his desk until he found the one he wanted. "Our information says Shawe is bed-ridden and his assistant, Isabel Camm, runs the shop. Is that her?"

Nicholas nodded and rubbed his tired eyes. He had come directly from Bucklersbury Street to Ashbourne House on the

Strand, taking the long route to give himself time to think. But the only coherent thought he could form was that he had found Isabel and that he needed to discover why she had left so he could fix it. He couldn't do that while investigating her or her employer.

He wasn't about to make another mistake like that again.

"This has been a shock for you," Ash said.

Nicholas stood and crossed the floor to the window, disturbing the rushes and causing whatever scent the house-keeper used to freshen them to fill the room. Isabel would know the herb in an instant.

He liked the view from the earl's third floor study. It usually had a calming effect. But not today. Like the neighboring manors, Ashbourne House backed onto the Strand with the grand front overlooking the elaborate knot garden stretching down to the river. He could just make out the private landing stage through the trees where Ashbourne's mother and sister, wrapped in furs against the cold, alighted from a barge. A servant balancing armfuls of parcels followed them as they progressed up the path towards the house.

"I thought her...lost forever," he said to his reflection. "I had given up hope of finding her some time ago after a thorough search." No, not hope exactly. In all the last six hellish years, he had never allowed himself that luxury because hopes were easily shattered He had been living on a fragile cliff since Isabel's departure, waiting for it to crumble into the tumultuous sea beneath him. No, he had not hoped, until the moment he had walked into the apothecary shop expecting to find a cantan-kerous old man guilty of treason and found Isabel.

"Her presence is going to cause a problem," Ashbourne said.

And didn't Nicholas know it. "That's why I can't continue the investigation."

"You have to." Ash stood and joined him at the window. Nicholas sensed his friend's body stiffen at the sight of his mother and sister crossing the courtyard adjoining the house. "I'll inform Walsingham when I dine with him tonight, but I doubt he will say anything different. There simply is no one else with your unique ability to access a suspect's world."

17

"But the conflict—"

"Might provide you with the perfect opening." Ash rubbed his chin in thought. "You could use this opportunity to befriend her colleagues, investigate them without raising her suspicions. She'll think you're merely trying to re-establish ties."

That was exactly what he didn't want to do. If Isabel learned of his plan... He already had so much to feel guilty for, he didn't want to give her another reason. "Do I have a choice in this?"

"Not unless you want to incur Walsingham's wrath."

And thereby the queen's. "Very well. But I should warn you, she's innocent."

Ash raised one eyebrow. "How do you know? What did you learn earlier?"

What had he learned? That Isabel was as bewitching as ever, and that she didn't have a lover. He still felt weak with relief at that. "Not a great deal. Is Lawrence Shawe being watched?"

Ash nodded. "I don't think he's got anything to do with this incident. His credentials and reputation are outstanding. But you spoke of your wife's innocence. What are you basing that on?"

Heat flared inside him and Nicholas clenched his fists against the instinct to hit out. He turned slowly and glared at Ash. "She's. My. Wife," he forced out through a tight jaw. "I know her."

The earl's mouth formed a grim line. An ordinary man would have felt threatened by someone of Nicholas's size struggling to contain his anger, but Ash didn't flinch, didn't even blink. "And how well do you know her after...how many years?"

"Six. But that's irrelevant—"

"Do you know why she left you? Wasn't there talk of another man?"

"No! I mean, yes, there was talk, but she assured me there was no one else. I believe," he said, flexing his fingers, "that she wasn't happy with my long absences soon after our wedding. I think." Something he planned on finding out for sure in the morning.

"She didn't see enough of you so she decided to do the very thing that would ensure she saw even less of you?" Ash grunted. "My friend, I know something of women and I can assure you that is the least likely reason for her departure."

Nicholas turned back to the window. Ash had a point. So if it wasn't his absences, then what?

A sickening thought struck him. Maybe she knew the specific reason for his disappearances at that time.

"Continue to investigate her as well as the other apothecaries on our list," Ash said. With a sweep of his arm, he indicated the mess of papers and unopened correspondence on his desk. "Now, I have work to do."

Nicholas made to leave but Ash stopped him with a firm grip on his shoulder. "Don't worry, Merritt, she'll understand. But don't explain your position yet. Not until this investigation is over. Then you have my permission to divulge whatever is necessary to mend your relationship."

It didn't matter how much permission his superiors gave, Nicholas would never admit anything to Isabel. If she didn't already know, then telling her about his spying would only make matters worse between them. She was a clever woman. If he explained his absences following their marriage then she would make the connection between himself and her father's arrest.

And that would surely end any chance of reconciliation.

* * *

SUNDAYS WERE SUPPOSED to be a day of rest. A day for attending church and conversing with friends, and for quiet reflection. Isabel's reflections were anything but quiet. Nick had crept back into them. After years of trying to forget his face, of trying to forget his touch and smile, he was back at the forefront of her thoughts.

Usually she would see to Old Man Shawe's needs after church then spend the afternoon visiting the other apothecaries and their wives. If the weather was particularly wintry, she would merely sit in front of the small second floor parlor's brazier and read one of her herbals until it became too dark to make out the words.

But not today. Unable to even concentrate on the familiar Turner's Herbal, she snapped the book shut and crossed the shop floor to the window. The sign hanging above the door flipped back and forth in the wind and Fawkner's dog barked incessantly as it always did on blustery days. Without the constant stream of customers, Bucklersbury felt more like a sleepy village street than a busy London thoroughfare. Only a handful of people braved the conditions, heads bent into the wind, their gloved hands clamping hats in place. Nick wasn't one of them.

Instead of retreating to the parlor, Isabel had remained downstairs once Old Man Shawe was settled with his stew and ale. She'd given the servants the day off and Fox had not returned from church (a usual state of affairs since his girl had left him), so she was alone with only her bedridden employer upstairs. It wouldn't be long before he succumbed to his afternoon nap.

Isabel returned the book to the shelf and attempted to do some work instead. She tipped out an Angelica root from an airtight jar onto the counter then began carefully slicing it. After a few minutes, the repetitive task calmed her taut nerves and the warmth from the fire made her sleepy.

"Hello, Isabel."

She whipped round and the knife slipped, cutting her finger. She gasped, not so much from the sting but from the surprise at Nick's sudden appearance. "I didn't hear the door open."

He shrugged. "You must have been intent on your task. I thought you didn't work Sundays."

"Since I had to stay here to wait for you, there wasn't much else to do," she said with more tartness than she intended.

Nick removed his hat and cloak and hung them on the hooks near the door. "I'm sorry to disrupt your day."

He didn't look at all sorry. He remained near the door, his gaze taking in the shelves, the jars, the fire and the back door which she'd closed to keep in the warmth. It gave her a few moments to study him in return.

Overnight, as she tossed in her bed, she had wondered if he really was still handsome or if the shock of their reunion and her longing to see him had clouded her perception. But looking at him again, big and broad but with a lithe grace, she realized it was no illusion. He had the sort of face that made women take a second look as he passed and a physical presence that could intimidate if he chose. The shop seemed smaller with him in it. And hotter. So much hotter.

The throb of her cut finger drew her attention. A stripe of blood marked the tip. She concentrated on healing it, but with Nick drawing her attention, progress was slow. His gaze returned to her and she dropped her hand, hiding it behind her. She didn't want him to see the cut. She wanted to appear confident and sophisticated, not a skittish girl startled by her own husband.

"You're bleeding." He pointed to a smear of blood on her skirt where her finger must have brushed against it.

So much for sophisticated. "It's nothing."

"Let me see." He stepped closer and held out his hand, palm up like he expected her to hand over her finger as if it were detached.

She kept it behind her. "I said it's fine, just a little cut. I'll tend to it later." He was so close she could smell his masculinity even above the ever-present aroma of herbs that filled the shop. Or maybe it was the memory of his smell, so familiar that her imagination had conjured it up again now that he was within touching distance.

"Since you appear to be here on your own, you might have trouble tending to it one-handed. Let me help you," he said in a low voice that slid across her skin like silk. At her hesitation, he shrugged. "Have it your way. But you're probably dripping blood all over the floor."

Which she'd have to clean up. With a sigh, she held out her finger. The streak of blood had become a rivulet, steadily dripping onto the rushes. Nick retrieved a handkerchief from his doublet pocket and wrapped it around the cut. His free hand uncurled her other fingers which she'd balled into a fist. She could have resisted, probably should have, but his touch disarmed her with its tenderness.

He didn't look at her but focused on her hand like it was the most important thing in the world. His thumb traced the creases of her palm and a tiny tremor rippled through her. He must have felt it too because he looked up and their gazes connected.

The blue of his eyes blazed wildly, like a man not in complete control. She had seen that look before. During the two years after their marriage and before her departure he had looked at her that way whenever he returned from one of his long absences.

Desire.

Isabel felt it too. The need and the ache, deep inside, suppressed for so long. She closed her eyes and silently begged him to touch her elsewhere, everywhere. Her arm perhaps, or her cheek or throat. She had always loved the way his tongue caressed the sensitive flesh there.

But he stayed with her hand and unwrapped the handkerchief. He pressed her finger to his lips then drew the tip into his mouth.

Isabel gasped as desire swelled within her.

Nick planted delicate kisses down her injured finger to her palm then drew her hand up to his face and pressed it to his cheek. His breath warmed her flesh as his lips brushed her wrist.

"Oh, Isabel." His murmur caressed her, arousing her body from a deep slumber. It felt good to be touched so intimately by a man. No, not any man. By Nick. Her husband.

The man she left for a very good reason.

She snatched her hand away and stepped back. Nick's own hands dropped to his sides like sinking stones and he straightened. His eyes, dark and hooded, studied her. His chest rose and fell as rapidly as her own and she knew he was trying to swim through the thick pool of lust to reach the surface and normality. Just as she was.

"Now that," he said with a crooked smile, "was interesting."

Isabel pressed her back against the workbench. "Don't," she said.

"Don't what?" His look was all boyish innocence.

"Don't try to charm me. It won't work this time."

"Charm you? Do you find me charming?"

Everyone found him charming. "This..." she held up the hand he had been paying so much attention to, "...is not helping matters. You said yesterday you wanted to talk to me, so let's get it over with."

"By all means, let's discuss why you left me. I admit to a certain amount of curiosity."

She blanched at the bitterness threading his words, so unlike him. But understandable, she had to remember. No doubt he had become a topic for gossips overnight in Newport, the village bordering his Kent lands. It would have been humiliating for any man, but especially for one from a respected family such as his. The son of a knight is not usually the sort to be abandoned by a wife, especially since he was so well liked. He must have resented the attention it brought him. He must resent it still.

"I've waited a long time to find out." His body stiffened as if bracing against a blow. "Tell me, Isabel, why did you leave?"

She had practiced the words over and over but they still came out in a rapid tumble. "You were always away and I was tired of being alone not knowing where you were or what you were doing."

He didn't look in the least bit surprised. "You weren't alone. You had my mother and sister."

She snorted. Some company those cold fish were for a young wife. If they weren't ignoring Isabel then they were plotting of ways to rid themselves of her. In the end they had got what they wanted, much to Isabel's frustration. It still made her blood boil to think they had won and that Nick was none the wiser and never would be.

God, she hoped he never found out the real reason for her departure because that would mean the old crow had broken her promise and told him his wife was a witch.

And Isabel couldn't bear it if he knew. To see the disgust in his eyes when he looked at her, the loathing and perhaps even fear. If he didn't throw her out of the house altogether, he would simply have ignored her. A far worse fate to be sure. She would have become insignificant to her husband, no better than the lowliest servant. No, even the servants received a nod from Nick when they crossed paths.

She had pictured it all in her mind before she made her decision to leave—Nick exiting the room when she entered, the sneering tone in his curt words if he spoke to her at all, the disregard for her opinion. She knew how it would be.

It was the same way her father had treated her mother when her powers came in.

Isabel had decided she couldn't live like that. She would rather never see Nick at all than see him hate her. So she had made the hardest decision of her life and left him. He might resent her for it, but she knew it was for the best.

Except she hadn't counted on him finding her.

And now she must lie to him to keep her secret.

"I sent you letters twice a week telling you what I was doing," he said.

She tipped her chin. "Yes, and every single one contained lies. I know you weren't where you claimed to be."

She could determine the point at which he decided not to deny it by the way his face relaxed then reddened. "How?"

She swallowed. "I, I had you followed." Actually she'd found him using his glove as a talisman but that too was her secret. "When you claimed to be in London, the man I hired wrote telling me you were in Hampshire."

He frowned. "I didn't notice anyone."

"He was discreet."

"If I didn't spot him between Kent and Hampshire then he was not only discreet he was invisible."

"Stop trying to change the subject. The fact is, you lied to me."

"And that's why you left? Without confronting me first?"

"Would you have admitted what you were doing?"

He looked down at the floor. "It's not as simple as that." He suddenly lifted his gaze to meet hers. "There was no other woman, if that's what you think."

She gripped the bench at her back to steady herself and watched him for several seconds, trying to determine if he was telling the truth. But then she had to look away because his gaze was so intense it almost unraveled her.

No other woman.

It shouldn't matter, not now, but it did. It mattered very much.

"Then what were you doing in Hampshire that you had to lie to me about it?" she asked when she had regained a measure of composure.

"Business. Nothing that concerns you."

She stiffened. It appeared he hadn't changed. He still didn't want her sharing every part of his life. "I was your wife, your business does concern me. Perhaps if you'd told me..." No, it wouldn't have changed anything and it wouldn't be fair to let him think that it would.

"Not was, Isabel. You are my wife." He stood close, his body like a wall in front of her. He leaned down and for a heart-stopping moment she thought he would kiss her, but instead he whispered in her ear. "And as your legal husband, I am perfectly within my rights to take what is mine."

She knew he was trying to fluster her to break down her defenses and get her to admit her true reason for leaving, but he seemed to have forgotten that she wasn't the sort to be easily intimidated. Not by him. She knew Nick, and frightening he wasn't. At least not to her.

"And as your legal wife," she whispered back, "I will give it." She heard his breath catch then the hiss of it escaping. Trying to contain her satisfaction, she turned her face and brushed a kiss against the corner of his lips. "But that is all you will get from me," she added as a little shiver of excitement rippled through her. This was her Nick in all his magnificence and she wasn't going to let him go without first sating the suppressed ache that kept her awake at night. It might not be fair, for either of them, but being fair was the last thing on her mind. The sweetness of his kiss and the heat of his body conspired to undo her and shake her resolve. She wanted to touch him, feel his big hands all over her, caressing, exploring. She no longer cared why Fate had brought them back together or what would happen afterwards. There would be time to decipher it all later.

Desire pulsed through her and she pressed her body into his to feel more of him. He kissed her lightly then drew back. Frustrated, wanting his lips on hers again, she closed her eyes and put her arms around his neck.

"Your room," he rasped, gripping her hips to hold her back. "Where?"

"Up...stairs," she said, breathless.

She took his hand and pulled him through the back door and up two flights of stairs.

"The old man...?" he said.

"Will be asleep by now." She led him into her bedchamber and closed the door. "We have the place to ourselves."

She pushed him back against the door because the bed seemed too far away, and unfastened his hose from his doublet. She had to touch him, feel him inside her before she went mad. When she freed his erection they both gasped. He was thick, ready. She touched the tip with her thumb, smearing a droplet around the smooth skin, smiling a little as he sucked air between his teeth. She stroked him, thinking about the countless times she'd touched him there then not thinking about anything at all except that he was with her and it felt so good, so natural, so right.

She reached down with her other hand to cup him but he pulled it away. "Patience, my angel," he murmured. "It's been a long time and I don't want this to end yet."

But she didn't want to be patient. She wanted him inside her now before she changed her mind and ended the delicious, foolish liaison. She let go of him and lifted her skirts. He helped her bunch them up around her hips then he reached down and rubbed her until she melted like butter. She groaned, clinging to him, wanting him inside her yet not wanting him to stop.

"More," she managed to whisper into his doublet. The smell of the fine woolen cloth and their mingled desire filled her nostrils, heightened her need for him. And she needed him right now because six years without his nimble fingers, his sensual touch, his hardness, was too long.

He thrust a finger inside her.

Oh! She sank her teeth into his doublet as her blood surged, pulsing through her like a flood.

He inserted a second finger. She gasped and ground down onto his hand, wanting him deeper. Her body tightened like a coil, pressure building with the heat inside her. Every nerve was sprung, ready to unwind, to bring sweet release. And then waves engulfed her, shattering her like glass. Her shout, muffled by his doublet, surprised her but didn't stop her from seeking his erection.

Still trembling, she guided him into her. He felt good—big and thick and familiar. He groaned loudly then picked her up, his hands beneath her rump, and pressed her back against the closed door. She wrapped her legs around his hips and tried to draw him in deeper but he held her in place.

"Wait," he said, his voice so hoarse she didn't recognize it. "I want to savor—"

"No. Can't...wait." She wriggled to get into a better position, finally pushing him further in.

He groaned again. "Isabel," he muttered against her lips. "My Isabel." He thrust into her, slowly, impaling her against the door. Then, as if he suddenly ran out of patience, he picked up speed and adjusted his angle and—

Oh! She kissed him harder, relishing the taste of him, the feel of him, wanting the moment to go on forever. "Yessss," she hissed, arching into him.

His kisses hardened, became hungrier and she returned them eagerly. Their entwined bodies moved to a wild, basic rhythm. The thud of her heart against her ribs matched it. She'd forgotten how magnificent he could be, and how her body reacted to him, to this. It was more powerful than any magic she possessed.

"Oh Nick," she cried into his chest.

As if in answer, his muscles tensed. He swelled inside her and with a roar that seemed to come from somewhere deep, he climaxed.

She clung to him until his shuddering ceased. Then she lowered her legs and stood on the floor which felt anything but stable. He looked at her with eyes the color of twilight storm clouds, his lips swollen from her kisses, his breathing labored. Although he didn't speak, she could tell from the way he searched her face that he wanted to know what their love-making had meant to her.

With her heart in her throat, she turned away.

CHAPTER 3

"*I* don't suppose this means you'll return home to Kent with me," Nicholas said, refastening his breeches. He had wanted to lie with Isabel on the bed for a while and relish the hum of satisfaction vibrating across his skin, but she didn't go anywhere near the bed, staying instead by the door.

"This," she said, adjusting her skirts, "changes nothing." She spoke primly, without meeting his gaze. No doubt she was attempting to appear composed but she failed miserably. Her face remained flushed and her fingers shook as they smoothed the woolen garments. Did that mean her words were a lie? God he hoped so.

Despite what she'd said, he couldn't help smiling at her. She was so fresh and beautiful and yet more vulnerable than she had been downstairs in the shop. Whether that meant she still cared for him, he couldn't be sure, but she certainly still cared for his love-making. That, at least, was something.

"Then I'll send for your things," he said. "You should have your own possessions—"

"No!" She looked up sharply. "I don't want them."

"You should at least have your clothes, Isabel. You are the wife of a knight, you need to dress appropriately."

Her eyebrows rose. "You've been knighted? What in Heaven's name for?"

Not exactly the response he'd imagined these long years. "Services to the realm." He was treading very close to the truth, but fortunately she didn't question him further or he might have to lie outright. Perhaps she thought he had been befriended by the queen because of his extensive lands, like his father before him.

"Congratulations." She sounded flat. "You're progressing in the world."

"I suppose."

"I don't want my clothes or anything else from your house."

"It's your house too. Your home."

The flush in her cheeks faded and her lips formed a tight line. "My life is here now and I have all that I need."

This wasn't going well at all. "You are my wife—"

"So you keep reminding me, Nick. But your sudden reappearance doesn't change a thing."

"You still haven't told me what that thing is, Isabel." He couldn't keep the frustration out of his voice. It was like trying to shimmy up a greased pole, almost reaching the top only to slide back to the bottom. "At least tell me why you left," he said.

"I have told you. Your long absences—"

"Have nothing to do with it," he finished for her. Why did she persist with that lie? "You see less of me now than you ever did then," he said, borrowing a line from Ash. "So there must be another reason."

She turned away and opened the door, her back straight as a rod. It seemed she wasn't prepared to give him an answer yet. But he would find out, whatever it took.

He left her bedchamber and returned downstairs to the shop, very aware of her following. He knew she was close enough to touch but he didn't know how he knew. He just did. "I suppose you chose to become an apothecary's assistant because of your father," he said. "He was a very capable apothecary, I believe." If only Samuel hadn't used his knowledge to aid his treacherous friends he might still be alive and famous for his remedies, instead of dead and infamous.

Isabel nodded numbly when Nick turned to look at her once they re-entered the shop. She still felt annoyed with herself—and alarmed—after succumbing to his formidable charms, but she couldn't deny that her body felt refreshed, alive. But what else had they awoken by giving into their urges?

"Being his only child, Papa taught me well," she said, trying to keep the tremor of nervousness out of her voice. "Master Shawe remembered me and offered me employment when I arrived here."

"You knew Shawe before you came to London?"

The fire had died down to a few glowing embers but the room remained warm. Isabel moved towards her workbench and began to clear up the Angelica root she'd been cutting. When she saw the bloodied knife, she remembered her cut finger. Looking down, she noticed it was almost healed, something she didn't think possible without concentrating on the task. It seemed she could still learn a thing or two about her powers. Considering she didn't use them often, that wasn't surprising.

"He and Papa were both apothecaries in Winchester." She kept her back to Nick because looking at him, still flushed from their love making, made her want to pull him close again. And that was definitely a bad idea. "Rivals and yet friends at the same time. After I left to marry you, Papa saw fewer patients and lectured more. Old Man Shawe took on most of his patients." Her father preferred books and experiments to people so it suited him. Shawe was the opposite. He loved the art of herbs and healing and would help anyone, from whores to the gentry. To him, it was all about making people feel better, but for her father, the notoriety of being the first to discover a new remedy was what kept him in his study until late.

That and his avoidance of her mother.

After Isabel married and moved away, her mother had written to tell her his moods had become darker and he barely even acknowledged his wife anymore. The letters had pleaded with Isabel to visit them in Winchester and talk to him but Isabel had remained at Lyle Hall, Nick's ancestral home in Kent. She had already tried speaking to her father before her marriage but with no result, and once her own powers came in, she hadn't wanted to see him at all. If he had snubbed his wife, what would he do to his daughter? It was best he didn't know she was a witch too.

But Nick knew about the letters, about her father's work and her mother's anguish. Isabel had told him everything during their first two years of marriage. Almost everything. He had not just been her husband but also her only friend, so far from home. Which only made his constant desertions, and his subsequent lies, so much more painful.

"And Shawe took you on, no questions asked?" Nick persisted.

She shrugged. "He knew I had married and I'm sure he wanted to know what had happened to my husband but he never asked. He needed an assistant after his wife became too ill to help and I needed a roof over my head. It was a mutually satisfying arrangement."

He said nothing, but she could feel his presence close behind her. Something unseen seemed to zap between them when he was near. "You could have taken some money," he finally said, voice low. "Or some of your jewels. There would have been no need to find work."

She spun round and fixed him with a glare. "I didn't want your money, your jewels, nothing from there." She didn't say "from home" because she no longer thought of it as that. She never really had. And if she had taken money or jewelry, imagine the uproar from his mother! The old crow would've reported her to the local Justice of the Peace quicker than she could cry thief. Anything to sully her daughter-in-law's reputation and obtain an annulment so her son could marry someone more appropriate, preferably with a title and fortune.

Speaking of which...

"So you never decided to seek an annulment?" she asked, forcing the question out despite her reluctance. Did she really want to know the answer?

He had been watching her outburst with a quizzical frown which deepened at her question. "Annulment? It's a bit late for that don't you think?"

"I'm sure a valid reason could be found with the right amount of money." Anything could be bought, even annulments after two years of marriage. It might prove to be surprisingly easy since they'd had no children.

"I didn't want an annulment!" He swore then apologized for losing his temper. Ever the gentleman.

And just like that, everything changed. She wanted to know more. Needed to know more. "So no one ever suggested you get one?"

His gaze lost some of its intensity then finally dropped to the floor. "Of course people did. But I refused."

The front door to the shop opened and Fox entered. The apprentice glanced from Isabel to Nick then back again. "Everything all right, Mistress?" he asked, nose twitching like a rat smelling danger.

"Perfectly, Fox. Sir Nick...olas was just leaving." She almost laughed at the strangeness of his new title but checked herself. It wouldn't do to allow anyone to know of her familiarity with Nick, especially when she had a feeling he would be around a great deal more in an attempt to reacquaint himself with his conjugal rights. Something she must avoid. "He couldn't wait until tomorrow for his remedy." She handed Nick a phial of chickweed ointment which a customer had failed to collect the day before. "Rub this on the affected skin twice a day and the rash will disappear within the week."

"Most kind," he said wryly. He pocketed the phial then left with a meaningful glare that told her he hadn't finished his interrogation.

When Fox disappeared upstairs, Isabel leaned heavily against the workbench and rubbed her temple. Lord, subterfuge was tiring. Or perhaps her exhaustion stemmed from the frenetic love-making. Their beautiful, vigorous, stupid love-making.

She pinched the bridge of her nose and squeezed her eyes shut. Why had she given in to him after barely a few minutes alone in his presence? It seemed her body had a will of its own when it came to Nick. Silly, silly girl. Any more of that and he might discover what she was trying to hide. If her body could heal without her knowledge, what else might she do without thinking? Throw him against a wall the way she had his mother on that fateful day?

No, next time she would be more alert. She had to be or she risked losing more than her secret—she risked losing her heart to him all over again.

* * *

NICHOLAS TURNED west out of Bucklersbury and walked past several shops until he realized he should have turned east onto Poultry to go home. It seemed he hadn't fully regained his senses after losing them the moment he entered Isabel's shop. Thankfully he'd had enough presence of mind while she was distracted by the apprentice to scan the labeled jars. None contained any of the poisons used in the latest plot against the queen but that didn't mean they weren't kept in the storeroom. The closed door he'd noticed near the stairs was the most likely location since it was easily accessible from the shop. He would have to think of a way to see inside it next time without raising Isabel's suspicions.

He groaned. As if he didn't feel guilty enough about her father, now he had to spy on his own wife. He pulled his long coat closed against the sharp sting of the wind and shook his head at the preposterous situation he had gotten himself into.

If Isabel found out about either investigation, she would never forgive him. Or worse, she would hate him. He was quite sure she didn't already since she had taken him to her bed so quickly. No, not her bed, her door. He laughed out loud at the memory of her eagerness to have him, equaled by his own willingness to be had.

Two women walking in the opposite direction eyed him suspiciously and he tipped his hat. "Beautiful day."

Neither answered but he didn't care. The sky hung low and gray, the wind railed like a bitter old shrew and the mud and dung from the street clung to his hose but he felt happier than he had in years. Thank God Isabel hadn't turned virtuous.

He laughed again then suddenly sobered because the encounter hadn't been funny. Amazing, exhilarating, better than he imagined, but not funny. The aftermath had been even less so. Instead of begging him to take her back as he'd hoped, she'd been distant, cool. Maybe she was confused as to what their love-making meant for their relationship. He certainly was.

Or maybe there was another explanation. Maybe she regretted it.

* * *

PULLMAN'S APOTHECARY shop was vastly different to Isabel's. It contained not a single book and the smell was not as pleasant. The dead animals hanging from the ceiling probably had something to do with that. Nicholas recognized a tortoise, two different kinds of fish, an eel and the leathery skin of an alligator. There were also several creatures he didn't recognize and wasn't sure he wanted to find out what they were.

He scanned the labeled jars on the shelves behind the counter and tried not to breathe too deeply as he waited for the apprentice to fetch his master. Unlike Isabel's, the jars weren't organized alphabetically and seemed to be in no particular order. That, and the poor handwriting, made his job slower and he just managed to read all of them when the door at the rear of the shop opened.

A small man with a bushy ginger beard and eyebrows strode in, an enquiring smile almost disappearing beneath all the hair. "Sir Nicholas is it? I am most honored to have your esteemed presence grace my humble shop." He ended the sentence with a short bow. "How may I help you, Sir?"

Esteemed? He was a knight, not a duke! Nicholas had decided to use his real name for his enquiries. In previous investigations, he had pretended to be a petty thief, an earl and everything in between, but sometimes just being himself worked best. This was one of those occasions. If Isabel noticed him visiting several other apothecaries in and around Bucklersbury Street, it was wiser to use his own name in case she grew suspicious and made her own enquiries.

He hadn't seen her yet. But he would soon. The anticipation made him want to rush the interview, but he had to force himself to concentrate on the task and the little man studying him with intense yellow eyes.

"Is there somewhere we can talk privately?" Nicholas said to the apothecary. "It's just that my needs are somewhat..." he glanced at the apprentice, an exact copy of Pullman but with only a patchy sprinkle of facial hair.

"There is no need to be embarrassed Sir, my son is perfectly discreet. Now," he spoke softly and stepped closer, "is it something of a, ah, sexual nature? Perhaps your staff is not performing as it should? Is it sleeping like a kitten when it should be roaring like a lion?"

What was it about apothecaries and erection problems? Pullman was the third to make the suggestion, including Isabel herself in jest.

"It's something of a poisonous nature. I need a substance to kill the rats in my warehouse."

"Poison? Oh." Pullman sounded disappointed. "In that case, come with me. We keep them under lock and key."

The shop was similar in layout to many Nicholas had visited on Bucklersbury, including Isabel's, with the storeroom near the stairs out the back. Nicholas watched as Pullman withdrew a large key from his long gown and inserted it into the door.

"These poisons must be valuable," Nicholas joked.

"Valuable? Oh, no no no." Pullman pushed open the door to reveal a small room crowded with more jars, strange animals, and spare parts for the distillery. "We are required by the City authorities to keep them safely locked away. And I always do as the authorities suggest."

That's not what Nicholas had heard. His sources had told him that of the five apothecaries who stocked the poisons used in the latest attempt against the queen, Pullman was the most lax when it came to dispensing them. He never asked the customer why he needed the dangerous substances and for a fee he would forget to write down the purchase in his record book. The other apothecaries on Nicholas's list had varying degrees of security with Shawe's being the strictest about who they dispensed their poisons to.

"So every time you sell these poisons you have to come out here?" Nicholas persisted. "How tiresome."

"It is, it is," Pullman said as he climbed the ladder.

C.J. ARCHER

Nicholas noted the location of the three jars containing monkshood, hemlock and henbane. "And you're the only one who can unlock this room? But what if you weren't here today? I'd have to go to another shop."

"Not so!" Pullman sounded offended as he climbed back down, a jar under his arm. "My son has another key, as does my other apprentice. One of us is always around. No no no, there's no need to go to my competitors. A bunch of quacks," he scoffed, "especially down at Shawe's."

"Shawe's?" Nicholas followed Pullman back into the shop where the apothecary proceeded to measure out an amount of the pre-prepared poison into a phial. "I heard they had a good reputation." It was true. Over the last two days he'd questioned his landlady, her maid and several inn keepers and all had recommended Shawe's for herbal remedies. Apparently "the pretty shop girl," as the maid called Isabel, had a cure for anything and sound advice to go with it. Her only complaint was that she didn't sell love potions.

Before he handed over the phial, Pullman asked for payment. "Now all I have to do is register the sale," he said, indicating his large accounts book. When Nicholas didn't comment and the silence began to stretch, he added, "Of course, anyone can come here and read the register to see who has been sold what. And the authorities are very concerned about the sale of poisons, particularly in these troubled times. In fact," he leaned forward, "I've heard a recent attempt on Our Gracious Sovereign's life has led to a secret investigation by the Privy Council."

News traveled fast in some circles. Interestingly, Pullman was the only apothecary Nicholas had visited to mention the plot. It may not mean anything except that he was the stupidest of the lot to be giving away such information to a complete stranger.

"How much would keep my name off that register?" Nicholas asked.

"A crown."

"That much!"

Pullman gave him a benign smile. "As I said, there is an investigation going on."

"That's not my concern." Nicholas slapped his hat on his

head. "I only want to poison a few rats. Go ahead and register my name. Make sure you spell Merritt with two R's and two T's. Everyone gets that wrong."

"Very well," the apothecary said, writing in his book. "Is there anything else, Sir?"

Nicholas hesitated then said, "Do you sell love potions?"

Pullman's face lit up. "Of course!" He turned to his jars and pulled out a large one labeled Caraway Oil for Lovers. "This is the best in all of London. It has the highest success rate." He began pouring the liquid into a phial then stopped. "But if you require it to make a woman fall in love with you, I cannot recommend it."

"Then what is the point? Is it a love potion or not?"

Pullman chuckled. "No no no, you don't understand. This love potion ensures that the woman who consumes it will stay with her husband. Or lover," he added with a wink. "It ensures they do not stray."

Nicholas cleared his throat. "Keep pouring."

The apothecary did as ordered, smiling the entire time, then handed the phial to Nicholas. "It's also useful for flatulence, stomach ailments and preventing theft."

Nicholas studied the phial. "Theft?"

"If you rub some of the oil on an object it won't be stolen. The same properties in the caraway that prevent a woman, or man, from straying prevents the object also from disappearing. It's a most useful potion."

"Indeed." Nicholas pocketed the phial and thanked the apothecary.

"Are you sure I can't interest you in some ground unicorn's horn?" Pullman said. "I've just received some from my supplier so it's very fresh."

"Unicorn's horn? For the rats? Or is that a love potion too?"

The apothecary dropped his gaze to Nicholas's groin. "Your staff."

Nicholas stalked towards the door. "My staff works perfectly. Good day."

He strode down Bucklersbury towards Isabel's shop

wondering how many men had asked her to cure their erection problems. The only cock she should be thinking about was his.

If he had anything to do with it, she would be doing more than just thinking about it later. Perhaps he could entice her back to the rooms he rented after dining at the Four Feathers. Although judging by her reaction after their encounter against her bedchamber door, it would take all his powers of persuasion to get her to agree.

"Good day, Sir. How is your yard today?"

With his thoughts still on Isabel and her bedchamber door, it took a few moments for Nicholas to realize the man blocking his path was speaking to him.

"My what?" he asked, looking down into the face of the man he'd met at Isabel's two days earlier. Lawrence Shawe.

"Your flaccid member," Shawe said in a voice loud enough that anyone walking past would have heard.

"Fine, thank you," Nicholas said, silently cursing Isabel's quick witted response that day.

"Good, good. My father has the best remedies in town." Despite his serious tone and friendly manner, Nicholas had the feeling Shawe was enjoying himself.

"Yes, his assistant was most helpful in...alleviating my condition." Nicholas flashed him a smile.

Shawe's jaw slackened. "I, ah, well, that's good I suppose." He squared his shoulders and tugged the fur collar of his cloak in a way that was intended to draw Nicholas's attention to the fine garment. "What was your name again?"

"Merritt."

Shawe frowned. "That sounds familiar." His mouth twisted as he thought. "I'm good with faces so I would recognize you if I had seen you before the other day. Are you a friend of Father's?"

"I've never met him." Nicholas kept his face passive and his body still as he watched Shawe try to remember. No doubt he had heard somewhere that Isabel had married a Merritt. Perhaps when Old Man Shawe first took her in, he had explained her situation to his son, mentioning her marriage, and the matter had never been spoken of again.

Shawe shook his head. "No, I can't recall. Perhaps I'm confusing you with Wherrett or Perrett."

Nicholas flexed his fingers and relaxed. "Tell me, you're a physician for Her Majesty, are you not?"

Shawe straightened. "I am."

"So you would know about this latest plot? I hear she has been poisoned," he added when Shawe just blinked back at him.

The physician glanced around them then stepped closer. "Where did you hear that?"

"Pullman the apothecary let it slip," he said. "Quite easily I might add."

"And what were you doing speaking to that quack about Her Majesty's health?" Shawe seemed to be more offended that Nicholas had visited another apothecary than shocked at hearing the news was out. Probably he knew it was impossible to keep such gossip inside palace walls.

"I was buying some rat poison from him and he offered to keep my name out of his register. For a fee. He says the City authorities take a dim view of people who buy poisons."

"He did, did he? And what were you doing buying poisons from him when you could have bought it from my father's shop?"

Ah, good, the conversation was leading exactly where Nicholas wanted it to. "I didn't know your father sold poisons. I was given Pullman's name by a neighbor so I went there first."

"Well, he does. The assistant you have already met could have helped you if only you'd asked. She has the key to the storeroom where the poisons are kept."

Nicholas raised one eyebrow. "The only key? What if it was lost?"

"Isabel is very careful. She doesn't lose things."

Only husbands and only on purpose.

"You are heading to my father's shop now, I see?"

"What makes you say that?" Nicholas asked cautiously.

Shawe tipped his chin up, looking pleased he had guessed correctly. "You are only a few steps from the front entrance and you were walking in that direction."

Well deduced. "I wanted to see your father's lovely assistant again." Nicholas decided to stay with the truth this time. "Tell me, is she married?"

In the few heartbeats it took Shawe to answer, the still air hung heavily around Nicholas's shoulders. The sounds of people going about their business on Bucklersbury Street seemed to fade to a distant hum.

"She was once," Shawe finally said. "I don't know what happened to the husband."

"Does she have any male callers?"

The physician's eyes narrowed. "What business is it of yours?"

I'm her husband, Nicholas wanted to say. But he refrained because it wasn't what Isabel would want at this point, nor would it suit his purposes. When his investigation concluded, however, he would tell everyone she was his.

"No business of mine," Nicholas said lightly. "But I do find her most enchanting. I thought perhaps I could see more of her, but I wanted to know what my competition was like."

"Your competition? She is not a prize to be won at a country fair. She is a wonderful, caring, generous woman and deserves better than men like you who think a wink is enough to woo her."

It seemed Nicholas's competition was standing right in front him. He wanted to tell the puffed up toad that he'd skipped the wooing stage and gone straight to tumbling but he bit back his retort and managed a laugh. "Well said, Shawe, well said." Nicholas slapped him on the shoulder. "Shall we go see her? Perhaps she has something else for my member today."

"I thought you said her remedy fixed it?"

"Yes, but today is another day, is it not?" He laughed at Shawe's splutter and steered the physician towards the shop.

* * *

ISABEL HAD EXPECTED to see Nick again, but not so soon and not with Lawrence. Not that Lawrence looked pleased about it. If his top lip curled any further it would disappear up his nose. Nick must have said something quite distressing to rile the usually calm doctor. Whatever it was, Nick himself must have found it amusing because he was laughing.

She turned back to two of her regular customers warming themselves by the fire. Meg and Anna, whores who frequented the shop at least once a week, had just purchased salves on credit for bruises which Isabel suspected their whoremaster had inflicted. Isabel handed them the pots but both were too intent on gazing at Nick and Lawrence to notice.

"Who's he then?" Anna asked loud enough for the gentlemen to hear. She shrugged one shoulder so her coat slipped off to reveal a large amount of breast jiggling over the top of her loose bodice. Although she didn't look up to see, Isabel assumed Nick was watching. One of the men, probably Lawrence, clicked his tongue.

"A customer," Isabel said.

"Mighty handsome brute." There was no chance Nick couldn't have heard that—Anna practically shouted it across the room. "Tall and dark too, just my type."

"They're all your type," Meg said with a roll of her eyes. The quieter of the two, Meg looked weary and drawn of late. When Isabel had first met her, the young girl used to take pride in her appearance, but lately her face paint looked like it had been slapped on carelessly, her wig was often askew and her clothes were little better than rags. Having always had a soft spot for her, Isabel worried that something was wrong. Perhaps it was related to the bruising. She had been about to ask when the two men had entered.

"Come on, Anna," Meg said, tugging her friend's sleeve, "we'd best go or Biggin will give us a what-for."

Isabel squeezed Meg's arm. "Stop by again soon and we'll talk," she said quietly so no one else could hear.

Meg smiled. "Thanks, Izzy, I will." She hooked her arm through Anna's and dragged the bigger girl towards the door.

"Bye, Handsome," Anna said to Nick, blowing him a kiss as she passed. He smiled and winked back at her. "And bye, Doctor Shawe. Maybe next time you can give me a real thorough check up."

"I doubt you can afford my fee," Lawrence said without looking up from the gloves he held.

"But I'll wager you can afford mine." Anna's tinkling laughter followed the girls out the door until it swung closed.

"Really, Isabel, I don't know why you allow those harlots in here," Lawrence said. "They're degrading the shop's reputation."

She shrugged. "They're paying customers." Sometimes. "And I enjoy their company." She said it to get a reaction out of Nick who hadn't stopped smiling since his arrival, but it was Lawrence who spluttered an objection. "Now what can I do for you, Sir?" she asked Nick before Lawrence could lecture her on the suitability of the company she kept.

Nick approached the counter and leaned on it. "I seem to have the same problem with my member again. Could you prescribe your unique remedy again? It worked wonders yesterday."

"Two days ago," she corrected quickly. Good grief, it was as though he didn't care if Lawrence guessed what had happened between them!

He grinned at her, the two dimples puncturing his cheeks in a most irritating way. Her stomach fluttered as a sickening thought occurred to her—what if Nick had already told Lawrence he was her husband?

"Physicians prescribe," Lawrence cut in, "apothecaries dispense. Isabel may I see you out the back, please."

"Yes!" she said, relieved to be out of Nick's compelling presence.

Isabel ordered Fox to leave his task in the storeroom and mind the shop while she spoke with Lawrence. Once they were alone, she turned to her employer's son. "You look flustered," she said. "Is something wrong?"

"That man..." Lawrence shook his finger at the door leading to the shop, "...bought some poison off Pullman!"

Isabel chewed her top lip to stop it lifting in a smile. "Do not concern yourself. A lot of people go to Pullman for poison. He has a reputation for being lax with his record keeping. But his other remedies are a swindle. He's been investigated by the

Grocer's Company a few times but they haven't been able to prove anything that warrants throwing him out of the guild."

Lawrence shook his head, dislodging his hat. "You misunderstand. I'm not concerned that he went to Pullman's, but I am concerned that he bought poison. You see, I saw him go into two other apothecaries before Pullman's and he bought poison at each of them."

"How do you know?"

"I went in and asked."

"Lawrence! It is none of your business what...that man buys or who from." She was surprised he had followed Nick in the first place. Whatever for? Jealousy?

He glanced at the closed door. "Don't you see the coincidence, Isabel, with the recent poisoning of Our Supreme Sovereign?"

She chewed her lip, considered the idea for a moment then dismissed it. Nick might have secrets but he was no traitor. "Just because he bought poison doesn't mean he used it on the queen. There are many legitimate reasons for buying poison. Perhaps he has rats."

He clicked his tongue and shook his head. "Actually I was thinking more along the lines that he's the one investigating the attempt on her life. Why else would he go to more than one apothecary to buy poison?"

Isabel laughed then suddenly stopped. The idea wasn't so ridiculous. It explained the real reason Nick had walked into her shop and her life two days ago. He was investigating her, or Shawe's in general. Good Lord, how extraordinary!

Well, she was no traitor and if he knew her at all then he would know that, despite her family history.

"Perhaps he works for the Queen's Coroner," she said, thinking out loud. "They usually investigate such matters."

"Only if someone died. Lady Manningham is as pale as a corpse at the moment, but she is recovering."

Isabel stared at the door. "Then the Privy Council must have employed him." But why Nicholas in particular? She reached for the door intending to find out but Lawrence caught her hand.

"Be careful with this stranger. He seems to like you, but I

suspect he intends investigating Father's business by getting close to you." His thumb rubbed along her knuckles. "Don't tell him anything."

Isabel withdrew her hand. "Lawrence, there is nothing to tell. We stock the poisons but so do several others in this street." He looked a little offended so she gave him a smile then thought of something that might cheer him up. "Perhaps you could stay for a while. I prefer not to be alone with him in case I say something I shouldn't." More like in case she did something she shouldn't, like drag Nick upstairs and tumble into bed with him.

"I can only stay a short while then I have to return to my patients. With everything going on at Whitehall, I've been neglecting my regular practice of late."

Then Isabel only had a short while in which to get rid of her husband.

* * *

NICHOLAS TRIED TALKING to Fox the apprentice but the boy didn't seem to know too much about Isabel's life outside the shop. When a customer entered, he abandoned his questions to concentrate on his other investigation.

With Fox's attention drawn to the customer, Nicholas roamed freely around the shop. He already knew where the poisons were kept and that Isabel had the only key to the storeroom but that didn't mean she was the only one with access. Fox himself had been in there minutes earlier. What about the servants? And how bedridden was the old man? The fact that he had been a friend of Isabel's father put him right at the top of Nicholas's suspect list.

The coincidence was too strong to ignore. Damn it, why did he always have to be the one investigating people close to Isabel? He leaned against the bookshelves and silently cursed Ash, Walsingham and every other agent he could think of for not being available to take over.

With that off his chest, he checked the book titles. One in particular, an Herbal, was entirely free of dust, unlike its neighbors. He removed it from the shelf and flipped through the well-thumbed pages. He was about to return it when he noticed the corner of one page had been turned over as a marker. He opened it at that page and a loose sheet of paper fluttered to the floor. Nicholas picked it up and read it.

Your courage in this life will be rewarded in the next.

It was signed S. de B.

Nicholas frowned. What did that mean? And who was S. de B.?

He replaced the paper and was about to close the tome when the text on the open page caught his eye. It contained a recipe for developing a lethal concoction using the exact three poisons that Doctor Lopes had found in the sweetmeats intended for the queen.

CHAPTER 4

"*L*awrence told me you bought poison off Pullman," Isabel said to Nick when she re-entered the shop. It was all she could think to say since Lawrence was within earshot.

Nick returned the book he'd been reading to the shelves. With surprise she noticed it was Turner's Herbal. Perhaps he was reading up on poisons.

She went cold. What if Lawrence was right and Nick was investigating her.

"Yes," he said, holding up his hands in surrender, "and I'm sorry if that offends you. I've already been chastised for not coming here. Next time I want to kill some rats, I'll think of you first."

"I'm sure you will. And I wouldn't go to Pullman for anything of a more...personal nature," she said, keeping her voice low so the other customer couldn't hear. "His remedies generally don't perform the miracles he claims they do."

"He did try to sell me some ground unicorn's horn," he said. "I declined."

"A wise decision. I hear it's nothing more than the crushed teeth of whatever poor creature wandered into his shop the week before. He didn't try to sell you a love potion too, did he?"

Nick crossed his arms. "No. I don't need a love potion."

She wondered if that was said for her benefit or Lawrence's, hovering at her side like a trusty hound. "Of course, N—, ah, what was your name again, Sir?"

"Merritt. Nicholas Merritt." He bowed. "At your service, m'lady."

She blushed. With her being the wife of a knight, he was entitled to address her that formally, but it felt strange, particularly in front of Lawrence who would have noted it. "Mistress Camm will do fine."

When Nick had told her he'd been knighted, it had struck her as odd at first, since it appeared he'd done nothing of worth to deserve it except own a large part of Kent. But if he was in fact working for the crown, it made sense. Perhaps he'd performed a commendable deed for Her Majesty in a previous investigation.

The customer left and Fox coughed to get her attention. She dismissed him with a nod and replaced him behind the counter. "Now, would you like more ointment?" She had to think what for. Although he'd claimed he had a sore throat, she now realized that was probably a ruse to cover up his investigation. Besides, Lawrence thought he was there for an entirely different problem. "Did the last treatment not help?"

Nick leaned against the counter and looked at her, a half smile playing around his mouth. "Oh, it helped. But it wasn't enough. Not nearly enough."

Good Lord, he still had a mischievous streak as wide as the Thames. "Stop it," she muttered under her breath.

"Only if you agree to see me tonight," he whispered back.

Lawrence approached the counter. "Give the man his remedy, Isabel, so he can be on his way. We wouldn't want to keep you," he said to Nick.

"I'm in no hurry."

Isabel tried hard not to roll her eyes. It was like watching a battle of wits and wills. Knowing both men as she did, she could guess which one would win. "Lawrence, could you fetch me Turner's Herbal. I need to look up a different combination of herbs since the last remedy didn't work well enough on Master Merritt."

Lawrence seemed reluctant to move away but in the end he

shrugged and walked over to the bookshelves. Not quite out of earshot, he probably thought he could overhear their conversation just as easily from there.

With his back safely turned, Isabel glared at Nick. Go, she mouthed.

He shook his head and reached for the pen near the accounts book. He dipped it in the ink and wrote in the corner of the book: Midday Four Feathers Bishopsgate. He raised his eyebrows at her.

It was clear he wasn't leaving until she agreed so she nodded. After all, she could always not turn up. But then he'd probably return to the shop tomorrow and she certainly didn't want that. Not with Lawrence already behaving like a mother cat on the prowl.

Lawrence returned with the book and Isabel made up an ointment loosely based on the ingredients given then handed it to Nick.

"Thank you," he said, pocketing the phial. "As always, you've been exceptionally helpful. I'll recommend your establishment to all my friends."

"That's quite all right," Lawrence said, "there are enough regular customers for Isabel and Fox to handle already."

Isabel frowned at him. Why would he say that?

"Perhaps your father needs to employ more staff," Nick said.

"Thank you for your advice." Lawrence crossed the floor and opened the door. He stood to one side and made an after-you gesture with his hand.

Nick took the blunt hint. With a cheerful bow to Isabel and a tip of his hat to Lawrence, he left.

"Why did you say that?" Isabel said to Lawrence after he shut the door. "We always need more customers. Paying ones, as you often point out." Although Old Man Shawe had built up a shop with an excellent reputation for service, he tended to be lax about payment. Many of his customers paid in kind, with poultry or other livestock or by offering a service in return. Those who paid with coin generally added the expense to their list of owed monies and paid only when they could afford to, or wanted to. It meant there was often a shortage of funds in the household and Isabel frequently went without wages to make ends meet.

Whenever she brought the issue up with Old Man Shawe, he would dismiss her with a wave of his hand. "We'll manage," he'd say. "We always do."

"Yes," said Lawrence, "but do we want that sort of customer? If that man is intelligencer as we suspect, then he is little better than a liar and a scoundrel." He had a point about the lying. "What we want is the nobility," Lawrence continued. "I doubt that disrespectful rogue would know a single knight, let alone an earl."

If only he knew. His mistake should have made her laugh but Isabel couldn't even summon a smile. She sighed and wondered about the people Nick did associate with in London. Was his circle of friends any different to when he was living in Kent? She couldn't recall anyone there that he was particularly close to, except his older brother before the accident. When Walter had died so soon after their father it had devastated Nick. Looking back, Isabel considered that to be when their own troubles started. Instead of becoming closer to his wife in his grief, Nick had become more distant, literally and figuratively.

Isabel bit her lip to stop the welling tears from spilling. Taking a deep breath, she touched the message Nick had left in the accounts book. The ink had dried so she turned the page and began ruling columns on the fresh sheet. It wouldn't do to let Lawrence see the message, just as it wouldn't do to let him witness the turmoil Nick's presence created within her.

* * *

"YOU NEED to find out who her associates are," Ash said, pouring wine into two cups.

"That's why I've invited her here," Nicholas said, accepting his cup. He sat on a bench seat across the table from Lord Ashbourne in the Four Feathers inn on Bishopsgate Street. They often met there because it was a cheerful little place close to Nicholas's London lodgings and a long way from Ash's mansion. The earl preferred the long walk to clear his head before facing the Dragon, as he called his mother.

"Here?" Ash asked. "At the Four Feathers?"

"Yes."

"And your wife has agreed to come?"

"Yes."

Ash looked impressed. "How did you manage that? I thought she hated you."

"She doesn't seem to hate me," Nicholas said, unable to stop smiling. No, she certainly didn't, although Isabel was a little reluctant to be reacquainted with him. But that wasn't the same as hating, that was merely...feminine nerves. "I have my considerable charms to thank for that."

Ash snorted. "I think your so-called charms have got you into more trouble than they have got you out of it."

Nicholas laughed as his gaze flicked past the other patrons to the door. The large dining room was growing crowded, mostly with members of the Leathersellers Company and the remnants of an audience who'd watched a play staged in the yard earlier. Partitions had sprung up between the dining tables in an attempt at privacy but did nothing to stifle the hum of conversations rising and falling like waves lapping the shore. There was no sign of Isabel but it was still early.

After hastily suggesting the inn as a meeting place, he'd begun to have second thoughts. An inn, no matter how clean or respectable, was no place for the wife of a knight to enter alone. Perhaps he should have offered to escort her from the shop. Somehow he didn't think she'd agree to that.

Nicholas drained his cup and Ash topped it up from the jug. "So do you plan on doing more than just speaking to her tonight?" Ash asked.

"Now that would be telling."

"That would also be highly unethical." Ash leaned across the table and fixed Nicholas with a stern glare. "She's your suspect," he said, voice low. "Don't jeopardize this, Merritt. I'm your friend and I'm warning you, Walsingham expects a result."

Ash rarely spoke with so much seriousness let alone with barely veiled threats. Walsingham must be exerting a great deal of pressure on him to close the case. Nicholas felt sorry for his friend but there was little he could do to speed up his enquiries. And keeping Isabel out of his bed wasn't an option.

"Did you tell him about my conflict?" he asked. A few days ago, Nicholas wanted someone else to take over, but now he wasn't so sure. Another investigator might think Isabel guilty and take appropriate action, whereas he knew she was innocent and so continued to investigate other suspects—despite, and even because of, the evidence he had found in her herbal.

"He knows of your marriage, yes. It changes nothing." Ash twisted his wine cup between his thumb and finger. "Tell me, why did you ask me here tonight? Somehow I doubt it's for my elegant manners or pretty looks."

"Pretty? Ha! Definitely not."

Ash touched the small white scar slicing through his eyebrow as if he knew it marred his otherwise handsome face. "I assume there's something amiss with the case?"

Nicholas leaned forward so that only a few inches separated them. "It's about my wife. And her father."

"The traitor? What of him?"

Nicholas winced. The word grated like a saw across his skin, even after all this time. Perhaps it was because he associated his father-in-law's crime with the beginning of the end of his own marriage and happiness. "Something about his case and this one makes me uneasy."

"You don't think there's a connection, do you? Other than your wife, I mean."

"I'm not sure. It's certainly an unlucky coincidence for Isabel."

Ash hesitated slightly before saying: "Most people would not think it a coincidence."

Anger flared but Nicholas dampened it. "Most people don't know her like I do. She's not guilty." Of that he could be sure. More or less. "She's got a good heart and wouldn't step on a snail if she could help it."

"What if she can't help it?"

Nicholas didn't like where Ash was heading. "Meaning?"

Ash looked down at his empty cup. Loud laughter peppered

the general hum in the dining room but Nicholas barely noticed it. "What if she is compelled by her beliefs to do something?" Ash asked. "Perhaps she believes removing the queen will be good for the country, or perhaps she believes she does God's work—"

"She's not a papist. She's not even overly pious, and she admires the queen."

"People change."

True. "But something doesn't feel right about this. First her father, now Isabel. It's too...convenient."

"Are you doubting her father's innocence now?"

"No. Do you know much about his case?" Nicholas asked, swallowing the rest of his wine.

"A little, but tell me what you know."

Nicholas suspected his superior knew more than "a little" but obliged him anyway. "Samuel, my father-in-law, had both the means and the opportunity to administer the poison. He was visiting court at the time. The queen herself invited him to discuss his theories and remedies with her physicians. He had considerable notoriety, having written a book on herbal cures. On the morning after the unfortunate incident, a concoction of the deadly poisons was found in his room. The night before, he'd had a conference with Her Majesty and could easily have slipped some of it into her wine."

"Is that when you became involved?" Ash asked.

Nicholas nodded. "I'd been married about six months. My father and older brother were not long in their graves and I was still coming to terms with their deaths and my new responsibilities. Walsingham contacted me and informed me I would be assuming my brother's role in the intelligence network. My first case was to investigate my own father-in-law." He rubbed a hand across his forehead, wishing he could bury that time once and for all. "I tried to refuse it, but there was nothing I could do. As you know, Walsingham can be...convincing."

Ash snorted. "Go on."

"Through my investigations, I learned that Samuel moved in some highly dangerous circles. He met with men who were known to Walsingham's agents. Many of them were educated," intelligent men and I suspect Samuel's initial contact with them was purely scientific and innocent. But the relationship must have moved beyond discussions of the New Sciences at some point." He shook his head. "I think they used him, manipulated him into doing their dirty work for them."

"What happened to them?"

"Nothing," Nicholas said bitterly. "There was no proof of their involvement and Samuel wouldn't confess. They're still free. He died in jail awaiting trial." He shook his head, trying to dislodge the painful memories. It still haunted him—Samuel's despair, Isabel's and her mother's distress and Nicholas's own involvement in the terrible saga.

"Don't blame yourself," Ash said.

"I don't." And that was the truth, mostly. His hands had been tied. He'd undertaken the investigation believing he would exonerate Samuel. It had torn him apart when he'd discovered his father-in-law's guilt instead. He'd known it would spell the end of Samuel, and of Nicholas's own wedded bliss with Isabel.

"You need to see if any of your father-in-law's associates have been in touch with your wife," Ash said.

Nicholas thought telling Ash about the note he'd found in the herbal would do no one any good, least of all Isabel. "Or with the person who is setting her up."

Ash raised an eyebrow. "I think there's more here than you are going to tell me today." He clapped his friend's shoulder but didn't let go. His grip tightened. "But I trust you to do the right thing."

"She's innocent," Nicholas said again, as much to himself as to Ash.

After a long moment, Ash's grip lessened. "If you believe it, then so do I."

Nicholas watched the earl for any sign of sarcasm but could detect only sincerity. "However I think she's keeping a secret from me."

Ash frowned. "That may have nothing to do with this case. Maybe she's not telling you about a lover."

"Thanks. That makes me feel so much better."

Ash drained his cup and stood. "I must go. But before I do,

you should know the man in the hooded cloak over there has been watching us."

Without looking in the direction he was referring to, Nicholas nodded. "Spotted him earlier. He entered right behind me, took that seat and has been casting glances our way ever since. I haven't seen his face yet."

"Should have known you'd be a step ahead of me in this game. Take care, Merritt."

"I don't need to. There won't be any danger," Nicholas said, lightly. "I've been discreet in my investigations. That fellow is probably just a footpad and will attempt to rob me as I leave."

Ash scoffed. "I meant be careful with your wife. I think you're in grave danger of falling in love with her. And that would be a tragedy for me. I'd miss these drinking sessions."

Nicholas stood and slapped the earl on the back. "Then you'll just have to find a woman of your very own."

Ash grunted, turned, and nearly walked straight into Isabel. She looked him over quickly then smiled the way she did at her customers.

Ash apologized and bowed. "Good evening. You must be Lady Merritt."

Isabel glared at Nicholas. "I suppose I am," she said, her smile tightening at the edges. "But then so is Nick's mother so to avoid confusion, please call me Isabel. And who are you?"

"Just call me Ash."

"Actually, he's Richard Savoy, the earl of Ashbourne," Nicholas said.

It was Ash's turn to aim an unconvincing smile in Nicholas's direction. He shrugged it off. Isabel should know what kind of company her husband kept nowadays. He'd come a long way since she left him and it wouldn't hurt to let her know it.

Ash opened his mouth to speak but Nicholas cut him off. "And he was just leaving."

With a shrug and another bow, the earl left.

"Well, it seems Lawrence was wrong," Isabel said, taking Ash's seat and removing her gloves. She was dressed simply in a green gown, unadorned with jewels or embellishment of any kind. Her golden brown curls were pulled up tightly beneath her hat, showing no evidence of their soft bounce. Nevertheless, she was the most beautiful woman in that room and every man there had noticed her. Heads had turned when she entered, and even now some still glanced her way.

Nicholas did his best to ignore them. "Shawe? Why?"

"Let's just say he would never have guessed that you're friends with an earl. Mind you he doesn't know you've been knighted."

"And I prefer to keep it that way." He signaled for Nelly, the landlord's wife, to bring more wine.

She must have been waiting for his sign because she already had a bottle in hand and wasted no time reaching them. She gave him a wink behind Isabel's back and he regretted not meeting his wife elsewhere. Somewhere he wasn't known.

"Hello, Nicky, got a lady friend with you today?" Nelly said, placing the bottle and another cup on the table. She was a large, plain girl with a ready laugh when she was happy and a vicious temper when she wasn't. Fortunately for her husband's business, she was usually in good humor.

"Isabel is my...apothecary," he said.

Nelly grinned. "Lucky your apothecary's a woman then, eh?" She turned to Isabel. "You want to watch this one. He can talk a maiden out of her hose and into his bed without raising a sweat."

"I don't doubt it," Isabel said. Her face was blank but there was a note of danger in her tone.

Nicholas quickly ordered two trenchers of the inn's roasted pork and watched with growing unease as Nelly left to serve the hooded man.

"She was joking," he said to Isabel without taking his gaze off Nelly's mysterious customer.

"About the maiden or the sweat?"

The man kept his hood low while he spoke to Nelly. It appeared he wasn't going to let Nicholas catch even a glimpse. "Both," he said, turning his attention to pouring the wine.

"In six years?" She lifted her cup to her lips but didn't drink. She gave him a skeptical glance over the rim. "It's all right, Nick. I hardly expected you to remain celibate. It's none of my business anyway," she added quickly before sipping.

He got the feeling from her blush that she cared more than she was willing to admit. Good. "My wife is the only woman I've bedded since my wedding day. Nelly was just having a bit of fun. She's like that."

"You obviously know each other well," she said, studying the table cloth. "Which means you must come here often. Is it near your lodgings?"

"I have rooms around the corner within a grander residence," he said. "Although my landlady and her house have fallen on hard times."

"I'm surprised we haven't crossed paths in the last few years." She sounded so cool, like a new acquaintance rather than the woman who knew him better than anyone. She still didn't look directly at him.

"I'm rarely ill," he said. "I've no need for an apothecary."

Finally she glanced up. "That reminds me, how is your sore throat? Recovering nicely?"

He tried to determine if she was teasing him, if she knew his illness was a ruse, but again he couldn't determine anything from her closed face. It used to be easy to know what she was thinking, but it seemed she had learned to control her expressions.

"Thank you for coming, Isabel," he said to avoid entering into a discussion in which he'd need to be very careful.

"You make it sound like I had a choice."

Her sudden annoyance surprised him. "You did," he said. She was the last person he had any hold over—hadn't their history proved that? He could in no way force her to meet him than he could have made her stay six years ago. Of that he was certain.

"Is that what you think?" she said, choking back a laugh. "The way I see it is, if I hadn't come, you would be back in the shop this very afternoon. And tomorrow and the day after and every day until I agreed to see you." She cornered him with a frosty glare. "Is that not so?"

She was entirely correct of course, but he felt no inclination to yield the point. Instead, he smiled and reached across the table and touched her hand. Her long, fine-boned fingers had the telltale signs of a shopkeeper—ink stains, roughened tips and short nails. He wondered if they would smell like the herbs in her shop. He wanted to know. Desperately. He lifted her hand to his lips.

He stopped before he kissed it. Frowning, he checked her fingers. No cut. He glanced at her other hand but there was no cut on that one either.

"That's amazing stuff!" he said.

She snatched her hand away. "What is?"

"Whatever salve you used on the cut. It's completely healed. Not even a mark."

"There is," she said, without showing him. "But it's faint. And stop changing the subject. That's twice now. I asked you if you would have left me alone if I hadn't come here today."

"You're quite correct," he said with a shrug. "I would have returned to the shop. However I like to think there's another reason why you're here."

Isabel squeezed her hands together in her lap. She tried to keep her gaze steady on her husband, but he was so arrogantly confident that she dreaded what he was about to say.

Because he had most likely guessed the real reason why she had gone to the Four Feathers to meet him.

He leaned forward and gave her a crooked smile. "Because," he whispered, so low she had to lean forward herself to hear him over the noise, "you want me."

After the briefest of moments in which her blood turned to a thundering torrent between her ears and her face grew hot, she managed to regain her composure. She threw her head back and laughed.

"Don't fool yourself, Nick. That brief encounter was...refreshing. Thrilling even. But it was no more than that."

His smile broadened. A knowing, clever smile. "If you say so," he said, sitting back, not taking his bright blue eyes from her.

She swallowed a mouthful of wine then swallowed the rest. When she returned the empty cup to the table, he was still smiling. Damn him. It had been bad enough that he'd noticed her cut finger was healed, but to have him know that she ached for him was too irritating. And dangerous. Because if he knew, he'd do everything he could to lure her into bed.

She didn't have enough defenses to resist him.

"Tell me," she said, shoving aside her desire and focusing on distracting him, "why were you asking several of my fellow apothecaries about poison?"

CHAPTER 5

*I*sabel had the satisfaction of seeing Nick shocked. The moment was fleeting but there was a definite tightening around his lips and a paling of his complexion.

"I went to Pullman's for rat poison," he said.

"And what about the others?"

One side of his mouth lifted in a crooked smile. "Jealous I didn't come to you?"

"Call it what you like, Nick, but I want an answer."

He leaned back and stretched out his long legs, brushing the hem of her skirt with his feet as he did so. He opened his mouth just as Nelly arrived with two trenchers of pork and vegetables so instead of answering, he said, "Ah, smells wonderful as usual, Nell. And your timing is perfect—I'm starving."

"Yes, perfect," Isabel echoed with as much enthusiasm as she could muster.

Nelly winked at Isabel. "Keep a man well-fed and he'll never stray, that's what I always say. Works for my Jebediah." She nodded at an enormous-bellied man talking to a diner. He didn't look like he could stray anywhere in a hurry.

"Thank you," Isabel said with a wink back at Nelly. Perhaps if she got this woman on side, she could learn some things about Nick. Like who he met in the inn and how often. "I'll bear that in mind. I wonder if it works in reverse—starve a man and he'll leave."

Nick frowned at her. She smiled back.

Nelly leaned down, causing her considerable bosom to strain against her bodice. "When I want to get rid of my Jebediah, I'll let you know."

After Nelly left, Isabel waited until Nick had finished his meal before she broached the subject again.

"Are you going to answer me," she said, "or will you find something else to distract you?"

He sighed and pushed his empty trencher aside. "There's nothing sinister going on if that's your concern. I was merely pricing the rat poison on offer at several different apothecaries. Pullman had the best price so I decided to buy it there."

He was lying. She couldn't say how she knew it, she just did. Too tired to hear any more excuses, she stood and gathered up her gloves.

Nick sprang up too. "Where are you going?"

"Home."

"So soon? I thought we'd talk for a while and then..." He shrugged.

"And then take what is legally yours?" she finished for him. She didn't wait for his answer, but strode away.

Nelly handed Isabel her coat at the door. "Enjoy your afternoon," she said with a chuckle and a lascivious glance back at Nick who was paying Jebediah.

Outside, the cold air stung Isabel's eyes and burned her cheeks. She hunched into her coat and walked off down Bishopsgate Street, leaving the muffled sounds of the inn behind her. The sun hung pale and sickly over the buildings, valiantly bathing the paved street and the impressive houses lining it in wan light.

"Isabel! Wait!" Nick caught her arm and she stopped. She could have shrugged him off, probably should have, but she didn't want to make a scene in front of the passersby hurrying to be out of the cold. So she told herself.

"Isabel, what's wrong? What did I say?" His voice sounded

strangely disembodied in the still, cold air, like a player upon a stage.

She shivered and instantly wished she hadn't because he rubbed his hands up her arms to warm her. His touch made her skin tingle beneath the layers of clothing and longing tugged deep down. Flushing, she remembered why she had really come to the Four Feathers. He was right. She wanted him. Every part of her desired him, ached to feel more of his touch.

"You're cold," he said. He must have been cold himself, having left his coat behind at the inn in his haste to leave.

She pulled away and began walking again, trying hard to stop shaking. He stepped in front of her. She tried to maneuver around him but he blocked her way. Giving up, she glared at him.

He glared back. "I'm not moving until you tell me what's wrong," he said.

"You'll freeze out here without a coat. Go back and get it."

"No." His lips flexed into a mischievous smile and he crossed his arms. A challenge albeit a teasing one.

"All right then, I'll freeze out here. Move!"

"Come here and I'll keep you warm." His smile widened. He seemed to be enjoying the banter, and that annoyed her even more.

"Fine! I'll tell you what's wrong. You're lying, Nick. Just like when we were married."

"Are married, Isabel," he shot back, the smile vanishing. "Are, not were."

A gasp echoed through the stillness. It didn't come from Isabel or Nick, but somewhere in the shadowy recesses of the nearby buildings.

Nick shoved her behind him. "Who's that?" he called out. "Show your face."

No answer.

"Maybe it was just a rat," Isabel said, trying to peer past Nick's bulk without luck. "Or the wind."

"There is no wind." He began to turn towards her when a cloaked and hooded figure flew out of the shadows like a bat from a cave. The metal of a blade flashed in his gloved hand.

"Nick!" She flung her hands up in an instinctive move. Power surged down her arms to her palms, its heat bursting from her fingertips like sparks.

The knife veered off course. It had been heading straight for Nick's heart but missed and would have struck his arm if he hadn't side-stepped out of the way. The sudden movement caused him to lose his balance and nearly topple into her, distracting her from doing more than merely deflecting the dagger.

The knifeman paused, grunted then ran off. Righting himself, Nick chased after him but stopped only a few paces away.

"Go back to the Four Feathers," he ordered her. "Wait for me there." He took off again.

Isabel watched as the hooded attacker rounded a corner with Nick in pursuit. With her heart pounding and her throat dry, there were many choices Isabel could have made. In the end, she made the hardest one—she did as she was told.

* * *

NICHOLAS HAD CHASED after many shadowy figures in his time but none so swift or nimble as this hooded knifeman. If he hadn't been so familiar with the city's laneways he would have been hopelessly lost, but he recognized many of the livery company halls and other landmarks. Once they crossed over Thames Street he knew they were heading down to the river. Unless his quarry intended to take a wherry across to Southwark, Nicholas had him—the lane ended at the water stairs.

The sunlight seemed to avoid the narrow, muddy lane with its houses packed side by side as if propping each other up. Nicholas had to follow the sound of his quarry's footsteps and rely on occasional glimpses of the cloaked figure. Twice he stumbled over dark objects that could have been sleeping dogs or drunks or merely rubbish.

Nicholas silently cursed the man for taking so long to be caught. All he wanted to do was go back to Isabel and finish the day the way he'd intended it to end—with her in his bed. But now he had to chase down the hooded figure—the same one who'd been watching him in the inn.

When the lane suddenly ended at the river bank, the attacker halted at the top of the water stairs. The cries of the watermen drifted across the stillness but none waited at the stairs. Unless the knifeman intended braving the freezing water there was no way out.

Got him.

The man sank under the overhanging porch of a nearby building, disappearing into the shadows. Nicholas slowed to a walk and drew his rapier.

"I have you now," he said. "Show yourself."

A grunt that could have been either laughter or an exertion of effort came from the attacker. Then the door behind him opened and his billowing cloak was momentarily silhouetted by the glow cast by a brazier before he disappeared up a flight of stairs.

A woman and children screamed. "Whoa!" a man shouted. "What you think you're doin'?"

Nicholas ran inside and up the stairs to a chorus of more screams. A woman pulled her two young daughters close and her husband, a short man with a face like a bloodhound, stepped in Nicholas's way.

"Get out!" the man bellowed, swinging his fist wildly.

Nicholas dodged it. "Sorry," he said. "Just passing through." He ran towards the window where the cloaked figure had climbed through and hoisted himself up. He poked his head out just in time to see a boot descending. He ducked and it skimmed his forehead before disappearing onto the roof.

"Get out of my house!" roared the owner. "Or I'll call the constable."

"No need. Sorry again." Nicholas sprang up and caught onto the overhanging roof beam. Below him, the man waved a fist, cursing.

Nicholas climbed the steep roof then skidded down the other side on his rear. The houses were so crowded together that those not actually joined were nearly touching anyway, making crossing from one roof to another quite easy. It was their steep pitch that made the chase difficult. Up ahead, the cloaked figure climbed the next roof. When he slipped and slid down into the deep valley between them, Nicholas saw his chance. He dove for the man's foot but the boot kicked him in the chest, winding him.

Bloody hell! He stood again just as his attacker scrambled up the roof and disappeared over the ridge. Nicholas followed him up and down two more roofs until he saw the man stop ahead. He looked down, glanced back at Nicholas, then jumped.

When Nicholas reached the same spot, he realized why the man had hesitated. The gap to the next roof was too wide to jump across. He peered over the edge to the street below, half expecting the other man to reach up and grab his leg. But there was no one there.

He frowned. Where had he gone? A high scream gave him the answer. Nicholas lay on his stomach, grabbed the frame of the open window below and somersaulted through it. He was met with another scream. He glanced at the woman sitting on the enormous bed not even attempting to cover her bare breasts.

"This here's a respectable house!" she shouted at Nicholas. "We don't take customers through windows. If you want servicing go see May downstairs and wait your turn."

The lump of blankets beside her sneezed.

"God bless you, Sir," Nicholas said. With a quick bow to the woman he added, "My apologies, I've been most rude. But could you find it in your heart to forgive me and tell me which way the hooded man went?"

She snorted then pointed at the door on the opposite side of the room. He thanked her and headed through it into the adjoining room where he was greeted by another naked woman, this one standing by the fireplace and definitely alone. He would have tipped his hat but he'd lost it some time ago.

"Good evening, ma'am, but did another man come through here? He would have been hooded and puffing."

Her full lips pouted at him and she cupped her heavy breasts in offering, teasing the nipples to points. "Come lie with me and I'll tell you. No charge for a han'some gentleman like yerself."

"Thanks, but not right now. In a bit of a hurry." He produced a coin. "The other man...?"

Shrugging, she took the money. "Downstairs."

He winked at her then followed the direction of her nod through the door and down the stairs. In a front parlor room, a large, heavily made up woman with bright orange hair put a hand on her wide hip and gave him a glare. He'd expected to be chased away with a broom at the very least so the reception was a pleasant surprise.

"Another one," she said with a click of her tongue. "My girls are respectable, you hear."

"Very respectable. Especially the one in the first room at the top of the stairs. The other gentleman, where did he go?"

The woman he assumed was May, nodded. "Rushed past me like a storm, he did, without even a word of apology."

Nicholas apologized, twice, then ran out the door as she called after him, "Tell all your friends about us. I'll take off a shilling if there's more than five."

Finding himself back in the lane, Nicholas ran towards Thames Street and scanned left and right. The knifeman had disappeared. He cursed under his breath and wanted to hit something but since the nearest object was a passerby, he hailed him instead.

"Have you seen a hooded man running past here?" Nicholas asked. "The friend I was just dining with left behind a purse of money which I'd like to return."

The lad, dressed in the blue gown of apprentices, stretched out his hand. "I'll find him and see he gets it."

Nicholas dangled his own purse over the open palm then snatched it up again. "No, I'd like to speak to him. As I said, he's a friend. Did he come past?"

The lad shrugged. "Nope. Weather's keeping everyone indoors today. It's quieter than an ugly shrew's bedchamber round here."

Nicholas thanked him and headed back towards Bishopsgate Street and the Four Feathers. His frustration cooled in the crisp air and he decided to think of other matters. Other, more enticing matters. Isabel.

He might as well attempt to talk to her again, although he'd had little success so far. It seemed she wasn't willing to tell him the real reason why she left. But he had to keep trying or how could he fix the problem?

To get her talking, he either needed to gain her trust again or get her at a moment when her defenses were at their weakest. As he saw it, there was only one way to achieve both of those aims at the same time. Bed her. He smiled. If that resulted in a very pleasing evening—or several—then that was an additional benefit to his scheme.

The thought kept him warm all the way back to the Four Feathers despite the cold and the absence of a coat which he'd left behind at the inn. At the door, he hesitated. After the long chase, he was in no condition for seducing women. He probably smelled of sweat and the contents of a pot thrown out a window that had splashed against his legs as he ran past. With a sigh, he pushed open the inn door and looked towards the table he and Isabel had shared. It was empty.

"She's gone," Nelly said.

Nicholas blinked at her. "Gone? Alone? Where?"

"Yes, yes and I dunno." She shrugged then handed him his coat. "Thought you'd come back for this."

He took it and thanked her. As he turned to go, she said, "She waited for a while but gave up. You were gone a long time."

He supposed he was. He put on his coat and headed home. It wasn't until he noticed the shops closing their doors that he realized he had been gone a long time. Feeling a little numb after the chase and from the disappointment at not seeing Isabel again, he unlocked the front door of Mistress Plunkett's house and crept past the parlor where his snoring landlady had fallen asleep in a chair by the fire. He headed upstairs and opened the door to his study.

And froze.

"You're back," Isabel said.

He stared at her until he realized he was staring then removed his coat and flung it onto a nearby chest. She sat in his favorite chair by the fireplace, her feet outstretched towards the warmth. She'd freed her hair and it hung in loose curls over her shoulders, just the way he liked it. Her cheeks were flushed and the flames reflected in her eyes danced seductively.

He found he was staring again and forced himself to look around the room. Apart from the presence of his wife and a bottle of wine and two cups on the table, nothing seemed out of place and he thanked his cautious nature that made him always keep the big oak chest locked. If Isabel had gone through the papers in it she would have learned of his spying, and that would have been disastrous.

"How did you know where I live?" he asked, sitting in the chair beside her. He too stretched his booted feet towards the fire, so close to hers they could have touched if he turned the toes a little to the right.

She handed him a cup, already filled with wine, and sipped from the other one before answering him. "Nelly told me," she said, holding the cup in both her hands. "She knew quite a bit about you, including the names of the last three women you dined with at the Four Feathers."

He knew the ones she meant and they'd all been women who were helping him with his enquiries. But he chose not to swallow Isabel's bait since he had no defense that didn't involve lies. "And Mistress Plunkett just let you in, no questions asked?" He tasted the wine, a malmsey.

"She asked. I told her I was your wife."

His jaw dropped. Isabel was full of surprises tonight.

"I don't think she believed me until I told her the story of how we met."

Ah, yes, the Meeting. He smiled as he recalled the beautiful girl who'd nursed him back to health after he'd fallen ill on a visit to Winchester. He'd sent a servant to the best doctor in town and the doctor had recommended one of Samuel's remedies. That remedy combined with Isabel's frequent visits to administer the treatment had cured him and after a week of her easy chatter and ready laugh, Nicholas had fallen in love. When returning home, he courted her with a stream of letters. After only a few months he'd gained the blessing of her parents but not his own. His father had only agreed to him marrying the daughter of an apothecary of little property after Nicholas reminded him (incessantly) that it was his older brother's duty to marry well, not the second son's. Finally his father had agreed, or perhaps just given up disagreeing, and they'd married the following spring.

"And that changed Mistress Plunkett's mind?" he asked.

"I told her I saw your member and had to marry you," Isabel said, eyes shining in the firelight.

He grinned. "Well I have been told it's impressive."

She made a choking sound. "I meant my father insisted on marriage!"

"But it is impressive." He put the cup to his lips and watched her over the rim. "You told me so yourself once."

She huffed. "I must have had too much to drink." She sipped her wine, draining the cup which she thumped down on the nearby table.

"And have you had too much to drink tonight?"

Isabel knew where his line of questioning was heading—straight to bed. She should walk out before that could happen, but relief at seeing him safe and the effects of the wine had made her legs unstable and she didn't want to test them yet. She would leave as soon as she felt sure she wouldn't make a fool of herself. Not a moment longer. Absolutely.

She had definitely drunk too much, but that had been to suppress the fear that had enveloped her like an icy lake. After waiting for hours at the Four Feathers, she'd decided Nick had either been injured (or worse) or gone home and tumbled into bed out of exhaustion. Not wanting to entertain thoughts about the former, she found out where he lived and convinced Mistress Plunkett to let her wait in his study when she learned he hadn't returned. The elderly landlady had agreed but only after checking that Nick's valuables were safely locked away.

Isabel had stoked the fire to life and settled herself into the grand oak chair which must be his favorite because the embroidered cushion was flat and faded from use. As time wore on, apprehension turned to sickening fear. A fear made worse by her decision not to follow him. She would have easily convinced Nelly to give her the coat he left behind at the inn and used it as a talisman, but she decided not to. Her sudden appearance in the chase would lead Nick to ask questions she couldn't answer. It was easier, safer, if she just waited.

It was the same reasoning behind her decision not to cause the hooded man to fall when he first attacked. She'd run a great risk by diverting the blade, an instinctive move that she hoped went unnoticed. Afterwards, during the longest afternoon of her life, she hadn't expected to feel such impotence when she chose not to use her powers to find Nicholas. It was as if she had suddenly lost them.

For the first time since her magic had come in, she was glad to have them, even though she could rarely use them. They were as much a part of her as her skin and life without her powers was just...unthinkable. It was a pity the rest of the world—including Nick—wouldn't see it that way.

His arrival had brought giddy relief and a lightness of heart that had resulted in her banter and the igniting of desire. His disheveled appearance may also have had something to do with the heat rising within her. His black hair, usually so ordered, stuck out at odd angles like it had been wet and then dried in a stiff breeze, his shoes were dirty, his hose ripped at the knees and his leather jerkin lay open down the front revealing the doublet beneath. When he sat, she caught a trace of his male scent, not unpleasant, and something else which was decidedly putrid. Nevertheless, his handsomeness sucked the breath from her body.

"Did you catch him?" she asked, staring at the coals because staring at him made several parts of her body throb.

"No." He sighed. "I lost him somewhere near the river. I'm sorry."

She blinked at him. "Sorry? What for? It was you he attacked, not me."

"Yes, but you must have been terrified." He leaned forward and touched her knee. The simple connection warmed her skin and she didn't want to move away.

"I suppose so. It all happened so fast, and then he was gone and you too. I didn't really have time to be frightened." Not then anyway. Fear had come only when she'd had time to think. "But as I said, it was you he wanted to harm." She shook her head which only served to make her dizzy. "Do you have any ideas why?"

He removed his hand and shrugged. The flippant gesture irritated her. It was as if this sort of thing happened every day and was nothing to be concerned about. "He was probably only a footpad or a drunkard, or perhaps a rival to your affections."

His joking about something that had left her imagining his death in a thousand awful ways made her say something she probably shouldn't have. "Or as an intelligencer, you've angered someone with your questioning. An apothecary perhaps."

His gaze flicked over her face, then he threw his head back and laughed. "Intelligencer? Me? Good Lord, Isabel, where do you get such ideas?"

"Lawrence."

His laughter subsided but a smile remained. "Ah, one of the queen's physicians. No doubt he thinks I'm investigating her poisoning."

"Attempted poisoning. And yes, he does."

"Do you?"

She blew out a breath. "I don't know. You asked so many questions in Bucklersbury Street that you must either be the poisoner or the investigator. And I know you're not a traitor."

"Thank you," he said wryly. "But you seem to have forgotten one other explanation."

"Oh?"

"That what I said is true—I was merely pricing rat poison."

"Oh." She frowned, trying to think clearly although her head felt full of mist from the wine and her rebellious emotions. "I suppose that could be possible."

"I think Lawrence Shawe is under a great deal of pressure at the moment. Consider it: he is physician to the queen and he has access to poisons through his father's shop. He must know he would be a suspect and so he sees investigators at every turn."

"He's certainly been behaving a little strange lately." She frowned at an insidious thought. "You don't think he did it, do you?"

Nick's gaze grew dark as he studied her, the creases in his brow deepening. "I hadn't given any thought as to who it might be." He drank the rest of his wine then stood and crossed to the table and the bottle. "But now that you mention it," he said, dividing the remainder of the wine between her cup and his (although pouring most into hers), "it's possible." He returned to his chair, cup in hand. "But what does concern me," he lifted his gaze to hers, "is the fact that you would also be considered a suspect because of your access to the poisons."

She waved her hand in the air and yawned. "Anyone who knows me would discount that theory immediately. I'm not a traitor."

"No, of course not. But I am concerned about what other people might think, such as an intelligencer who is..." He stopped and looked at the fire.

"Go on."

"Who is familiar with your father's case," he said softly.

"Papa?" Her body jerked, suddenly alert. A little wine spilled from her cup and she brushed it off her skirt with the back of her hand. But it seemed no matter how much she brushed, the wine wouldn't come off and the stain spread. "This has nothing to do with him."

Suddenly kneeling beside her, Nick pressed his hand over hers, stilling it. "Perhaps it doesn't," he said, quietly. "But consider the coincidence for a moment. Your father was found guilty of attempting to poison the queen and now seven years later his daughter has easy access to poisons after another attempt. Did Lawrence tell you which poisons were used? Do you stock them?"

"Yes but anyone can buy them," she said in a brittle voice. But even as she said it, she knew he was right. She must be a suspect, if not the main one. Her fingers closed around his hand and she held on tightly to the only solid object in a room suddenly spinning around her. "What shall I do, Nick?"

He brought her hand to his lips and tenderly kissed the knuckles. "Don't worry. I won't let anything happen to you. I promise."

The knot in her stomach loosened a little. Nick was a knight now, he had influential friends such as the Earl of Ashbourne and he never made promises he didn't intend to keep. The rush of relief made her lean forward and embrace him. "Thank you," she whispered.

He pulled her close. His hot breath grazed her ear and his hand stroked her leg beneath her skirts. Higher up, her inner thigh pulsed in response and she grew moist in anticipation of his next move.

"You can thank me properly in the bed chamber," he said, a smile in his voice.

She smiled back, the tension inside her easing even as another sort of tension rose deliciously within her. "Not until you do something about that awful smell." She drew away, wrinkling her nose. "When you said you chased the attacker to the river, I didn't think you meant the Fleet."

"I didn't." He sniffed his sleeve and made a face. "I stink." He rose and bowed. "Excuse me while I change into something more appealing."

She smiled as she waited in the study, thinking about Nick dressed in something more appealing, and then thinking about him dressed in nothing at all. She liked that image best.

But after a few minutes either the effects of the wine began to wear off or she came to her senses some other way because she realized the afternoon was heading in a very foolish direction. A direction she didn't want to go in. Not again. Not after their last encounter had left her heart aching more not less, and her body hungrier not sated.

She hurried across the room and snatched her coat off the hook. She had one arm in a sleeve when the door to the bedchamber behind her opened. She froze.

"Where are you going?" he asked in a thick voice.

She turned. And gasped. Nick stood before her, completely, magnificently, naked.

CHAPTER 6

The last time they'd made love Nick had kept his clothes on. There hadn't been an opportunity to compare how much his body had changed in six years. So on seeing him naked, Isabel couldn't help but stare. The glow from the fire tinted his smooth skin with light and shade, accentuating his powerful arms and legs. As if she needed her attention drawn to them. As always, the sight of his body was too compelling and she couldn't look away.

He'd always been well-formed with wide shoulders and long legs, but he'd filled out across his chest in the intervening years. Not fat, just thick with compacted muscle beneath the scattering of dark hairs.

And then there was his manhood. Now that was as magnificent as ever.

Isabel stepped towards him, her feet moving of their own accord. The room seemed to fade around her leaving only Nick, big and handsome near the doorway.

"Is this better?" he asked, hands loose at his sides.

His words roused her from her stupor. It took her a moment before she realized he was referring to her earlier comment about his odor. "I, um, can't smell you from here."

He moved closer until they were only an arm's length apart.

"Now?" Even in the poor light she could see the twinkle in his eyes.

She folded her coat over her crossed arms. "Stay where you are."

He moved forward again. "Why? Does my nakedness make you nervous?"

"Nervous?" she said, trying to lower her voice so it didn't squeak. "Don't be ridiculous. I've seen that," she nodded at his manhood, "many times. It looks a little..." she cocked her head to one side as she studied it, "different than it used to."

He frowned. "Bigger?"

"No, not bigger."

He looked down. "Smaller?" he asked, sounding concerned.

"I wouldn't like to make a guess as to what it is," she said, enjoying his discomfort a little too much perhaps.

He glanced up and his frown deepened. "You're joking, Isabel. I can tell by the flush of your cheeks that there's nothing wrong with it."

"It's the heat from the fire," she said, backing towards the door.

He shook his head, matching each of her steps with his own. "You want me, Isabel. Admit it. We'll save a lot of time if you stop stalling and just go straight to the part of the script where you shed your clothing."

"Script?" She stopped and glared at him. "Script! This is not a play, Nick. The end to this meeting hasn't been written."

"No?" He gave her a lazy smile. "Then why did you come here? You could have gone home and enquired after my well-being in the morning."

He was right and they both knew it. There was no point denying it any longer. She squared her shoulders. "Very well. I did come here to...relieve my urgings. But that has all changed. My urgings have vanished."

His smile turned wicked. "No, they haven't." He removed her coat from her arms and threw it on top of the chest next to his. Then he leaned down and brushed a light kiss across her lips. "In fact, I think your urgings are more inflamed than ever." He kissed her chin, moving down to her throat and Isabel's traitorous mind thought Thank goodness I'm not wearing a ruff to get in his way.

"But I have the perfect remedy," he murmured against her flesh. "You see, I'm very skilled at curing this type of ailment. In fact, you could call it my specialty."

She shouldn't have tipped her head back to expose more of her throat but she did. It seemed she wasn't in complete control of all her body parts. Some of them even quivered. "I am well aware," she said, breathless, "of where your skills lie. And I believe I do need some of your particular remedy after all." Forcing herself to focus, she pushed a hand against his chest until he stopped kissing her. "However it is only for tonight. Do not think this changes anything."

He looked at her through hooded lids, his breathing uneven. "You said that the last time."

She teased a curl of his dark chest hair between her thumb and finger. "Yes and nothing has changed, has it?"

"Nothing. We are still husband and wife. In every sense." His tone had gone from playful to dark, ominous.

Her fingers stopped twirling. "I meant—"

"I know what you meant." He took her hand and kissed her palm, his lips soft. "And I don't care. That is a discussion for another day. For now, I want only to see you naked." He unpinned her cuff, dropping the strip of lace onto the rushes, and pushed her sleeve up, kissing the exposed skin. When he reached the inside of her elbow he looked up. "Six years is a long time for a man not to gaze upon his wife's loveliness."

Her heart flapped like a caged bird and her head began to spin again. He still thought she was lovely? Even though the freshness of youth had faded after working as a shop assistant for six years?

She stood still as he unfastened her bodice and the extra one she wore underneath for warmth, and unpinned her partlet. He threw them to one side, she didn't care where. She helped him remove the skirts and they slithered to the floor with a rustle, bunching around her ankles. His fingers fumbled with the laces of her chemise and he cursed.

"Too many clothes," he muttered. He finally got the chemise off, exposing her breasts.

When she kicked off her boots, she stood in only her hose, having removed her hat when she arrived.

His hungry gaze grazed down her body. Her nipples tightened in response and her pulse thumped an erratic beat. Far from being embarrassed, she relished the way his attention made her feel—womanly, beautiful, hot. Very, very hot. He didn't speak, didn't move, didn't even appear to be breathing. He just looked. And then he responded in the most basic, manly way. He grew hard.

"Sit," he said, nodding at the chair near the door. She sat. He knelt in front of her and sucked a nipple into his mouth, circling the other with his thumb. She gasped as her body throbbed in response. But he stopped—too soon!—and turned his attention to her left foot, massaging it before working up to her knee. Then he drew down the hose slowly, as if it were made of the most delicate silk, his knuckles caressing her flesh. She blew out a jagged breath as he repeated the sensual task on her right leg. "Do you think you can make it to the bed this time?" he asked, a wobbly grin tugging at his mouth.

She nodded, not trusting her voice. When she stood, he scooped her up in his arms and carried her into his bedchamber. He lay her gently on the large bed, leaving her legs dangling over the side, then knelt on the floor at her feet. Slowly, interminably, he kissed his way up her leg to her thigh then...

Oh my! It seemed Nick had learned a thing or two in the last six years. A very, very good thing she thought as she floated away. The tide within her rose, filling her from head to toe. She hovered at the brink in excruciating bliss, waiting, wanting to spill over the edge but not yet, not yet. Until finally the dam burst and she bucked into him, her gasps filling her ears.

When her breathing returned to normal and her body ceased twitching, Isabel opened her eyes to see Nick stretched out alongside her, smiling like he'd just found the key to a treasure chest. He rested a hand over one breast as if it was the most natural place for it to be, and said, "Now that was interesting."

"Very." She rose up on one elbow and gently shoved him onto

his back. "Now let me return the favor." He groaned as she slid down, kissing a trail from his hard chest to his thick erection. He tasted clean and a little like the neroli he must have used in his washing water. Delicious. She reach down and under, cupping him in her palm. She massaged and concentrated on stroking his shaft with her tongue. His moans intensified when she switched from licking to sucking, growing louder and more primal.

I'm causing that reaction.

His body tensed beneath her and his fingers dug into the coverlet, scrunching it in his fists. With a loud, long grunt, he jerked once and exploded into her mouth.

She moved slowly up his shuddering body and built a tower with her fists on his chest, resting her chin on top. She watched his face change from flushed pink to its natural tan and the softened features regain some of their form. When he opened his eyes, she smiled at him.

"Also very interesting," he said to her, his voice laced with something she couldn't define.

"Very," she said, her body still humming from her own release.

He sat up abruptly, dislodging her ungracefully.

"What did you do that for?" she said not hiding her annoyance. She'd just done for him something she never thought she'd do and he treated her like a...whore.

"Where did you learn to do that?"

She shrugged, confused. Then it suddenly occurred to her— he was jealous. No, not jealous. Possessive. He was afraid she'd learned that skill on someone else. She'd actually learned it from Meg and Meg's friend Anna. Some of their conversations had been very...detailed.

But Isabel was in no mood to enlighten him. She didn't have to make him feel more secure in their relationship. They had no relationship. It had ended years ago and sometimes, like now when he was being arrogant and dull-witted, she wondered if that wasn't such a bad thing. "Perhaps I learned it the same way you learned your little trick," she said, getting up and storming out to the study and her clothes.

He followed her. "What does that mean?"

She sat down in a chair and put her hose on before she answered. "It means you just ruined a pleasant experience," she said, reaching for her underskirts.

"Ruined? Pleasant?" He stood in the center of the room, his arms crossed. "It was better than pleasant, my sweet."

"If you think so." She pulled her chemise over her head and stepped into her first underskirt. "And I'm not your sweet anything."

"Definitely not," he said, his voice flat, making her glance up at him. His face had hardened, his mouth a thin, white line. The fire had died so it was too dark to see his eyes but she'd wager they were as tumultuous as stormy seas.

She pulled up her other skirts and put on the bodices, fastening the ties, and shoved her feet into her boots.

"You can't walk back to Bucklersbury Street alone," he said. "It's dark now."

"I'll be fine." She stuffed her partlet into her skirt pocket then picked up her coat and threw it around her shoulders. Thrusting her fingers into her gloves and clamping her hat on her head, she strode for the door without looking back at him.

Somehow he reached it first, blocking her exit. He looked like a Roman gladiator, ready to do battle, except his only weapon wasn't as sharp as it had been although it still looked dangerous. She raised an eyebrow at him.

"Stay," he said gently, suddenly looking more like a puppy than a gladiator. "I'm sorry I implied...what I did."

She wondered if his hesitation meant he wasn't sorry or if he wasn't sure what he'd implied. Being a man, it could be either.

"Please move out of my way," she said.

"Stay, Isabel."

"No. It was foolish of me to come here and it was foolish to do what we just did, but it would be worse than foolish if I stayed tonight. I don't want you to get the wrong idea, Nick, and as I said earlier, it doesn't—"

"Mean anything. I know."

She swallowed but never took her eyes off his. Being firm was the only thing that would get her out of this mess.

"If you insist on going," he said, "then at least wait until I get dressed so I can escort you."

"I managed to get here without an escort."

"That is not the point." He moved away from the door slowly, as if he expected her to rush through it as soon as relinquished his position.

She decided that pressing her point would only end in another argument, and she hated arguing with Nick. It usually didn't get her anywhere because he was as stubborn as an ox. Besides, she didn't want him getting suspicious if she protested too much. She knew she was safe on the streets after dark—that awful episode with his mother had shown her what she was capable of—but he didn't. Best to allow him to think he was protecting her.

The walk back to Bucklersbury Street seemed to last forever because neither spoke a word. She couldn't be sure if his silence was due to his simmering anger or his concentration on their surroundings, listening for footpads. With his hand resting on the hilt of his sword, he looked prepared to do battle with anything that emerged from the shadows. It wasn't until they reached the shop that she felt she should say something.

"Thank you for the escort," she said at the front door.

"Any time, day or night." His voice sounded like a rumble coming from deep within his chest. She couldn't see his face in the darkness but she knew he was looking at her, could feel his entire attention focused on her.

She shifted her weight and wondered whether it was proper to kiss estranged husbands you'd just had a liaison with on the cheek, the mouth or not at all. A bitter wind blew her hair back from her face and she shivered. It was too cold to be deliberating etiquette on the front porch, even with a warm man standing so close she could smell their recent encounter on him.

"Good night, Nick."

"Isabel," he said, tugging her coat tighter beneath her chin, "I want to see you again."

"Yes," she said, almost continuing with I want to see you too. But she stopped herself in time and instead told him, "I know." And left it at that. In truth, she didn't see how she could avoid him anymore. They seemed to have started something, something out of her control like a boulder hurtling down a hill. It was exciting, thrilling and yet stupid and dangerous. That boulder could crush her but she felt completely incapable of getting out of its way.

* * *

AFTER HE LEFT Isabel at the Bucklersbury Street shop, Nicholas had spent the remainder of the night wondering who was trying to kill him because it was easier than trying to work out whether Isabel wanted to see him again or not. Her response outside the shop had been non-committal although her body's response to his touch had been a resounding yes. Towards dawn, he fell asleep without an answer to either mystery.

When he awoke, he decided to return to Bucklersbury Street since whoever wanted him dead was most likely linked with his current investigation and the apothecaries' street seemed to be at the center of it. Besides, Isabel was there, and he couldn't allow a day to pass without seeing her.

She glanced up when he opened the door, as did her customer—the woman he'd seen there the day before. A whore going by the large circles of vermilion on her cheeks and extremely low bodice. Too scrawny and tired looking to be a good one though, which probably accounted for the patched-up rags she wore and the tattered marigold wig. She sat on a stool opposite Isabel who stood behind her workbench, no open jars in front of her, no weighing scales nearby, no scoop in hand. Apparently the whore had come for conversation, not a remedy. Isabel would be good at dispensing advice with her no-nonsense practicality and a bluntness he'd found himself the target of lately.

"What are you doing here?" she said with genuine interest. The whore looked from Isabel to Nicholas, her painted eyebrows raised.

"I came to return something of yours."

Isabel frowned. "What?"

His gaze shifted to the whore then back again. "Come here and I'll show you."

She huffed. "Nick, whatever it is, you can give it to me in front of Meg."

He shrugged and pulled out her lace cuff from his pocket. He'd found it on his study floor that morning and decided it provided the perfect excuse to visit. She couldn't possibly be without one of her finest cuffs a moment longer. "Sorry it's scrunched."

Isabel colored. The whore—Meg—smiled, not even pretending she didn't know what it was or why he had it. Nick approached the workbench and handed the cuff to Isabel.

"Thank you," she said. When he didn't leave she added, "Is there something else?"

"I want to talk to you," he said.

"You've done a lot of that already."

"Not about..." he looked at Meg who watched him expectantly, "...that, about the other thing."

Meg giggled. "I was leaving anyway," she said.

Isabel reached across the bench and touched her hand. "Think about what I said, Meg."

Meg closed her fingers around Isabel's, her smile fading. "Thanks." She hopped off the stool and gave Nicholas another sweeping glance as she swished past him and out the door.

"A friend of yours?" he asked once the door swung closed.

Isabel nodded, brushing the counter top with her hand as if to clean it although it was spotless. She kept her gaze on her task. "Meg works at a whorehouse in Bankside. She often comes in for cures or sometimes just to pass the day somewhere warm. I've been helping her with a personal dilemma."

"I also have a dilemma," he said, sitting on the stool Meg had vacated.

She glanced up at him accusingly. "You said you weren't going to discuss our relationship."

They had a relationship? "I'm not going to," he said, thinking quickly. An idea began to form in his head—an idea to get her home with him where she belonged. "I wanted to ask you who you think might want to kill you," he blurted out.

81

Her eyes widened. "Kill me? I thought the attacker was after you?"

He shrugged. "Perhaps. But I don't want to assume anything until I know for sure. Isabel, your life could be in danger right now."

"Oh," she said flatly. "Right. Then I'd best be careful."

"Exactly what I was thinking. If you start packing immediately, I can arrange for your things to be picked up later."

She blinked at him. "What are you talking about, Nick? I'm not leaving."

"Yes, you are. It's too dangerous here for you—"

"Me? What about you? That man outside the Four Feathers could very well have been trying to knife you. In fact, going by the angle of the blade, I'm sure he was." Her frown deepened. "Besides, you said yourself it was probably just a footpad. If that's the case, it won't happen again and there's no need for concern."

The challenge in her voice was unmistakable. It seemed she didn't believe it was a mere footpad any more than he did. He had to be very careful. She already suspected he was a spy. He didn't want to give fuel to her theory.

"And what if it's not a footpad?" he said. "What if it's the same person trying to frame you for the poisoning?"

"Frame me?" She paled and pressed her fingers to her lips. "Do you really think that's what's happening?"

He stood and walked around the end of the workbench to take her in his arms. But he stopped himself and instead caught her elbows. "I don't know. It's a possibility. But as I said last night, in light of what happened with your father, there's too much coincidence. The poisoner could be seizing on your family's history to throw suspicion onto you."

"Me?"

He nodded.

Instead of melting into him for comfort as he hoped, she drew away, shaking a little. "Then if I'm the one he's trying to frame, why kill me?"

She had a good point, one he hadn't entirely thought through yet. "I don't know," he said. "But for now, I want you away from here. It's not safe."

"And you?" she said, thrusting her chin forward. It seemed she wasn't prepared to give up. "If this man is after you?"

"There's no reason for him to be after me," he said, wishing she would stop challenging him and start believing him. Wishing he didn't have to add lie to lie. "Anyway, I can take care of myself."

"So can—" She broke off with a shake of her head. "Nick, I'm not going anywhere. Besides, I have nowhere to go. And no, I won't move into your lodgings with you."

Damn. Time for Plan B. "I was thinking you could return to Lyle Hall. You would be far from danger there and—"

She barked out a laugh without a shred of humor in it. "I think I prefer London's dangers to the Kent ones, thank you."

"Please, just consider—"

"No!"

Whatever did she have against their Kent home? "Isabel, be reasonable, I can't keep you safe if you stay here."

"I'm not asking you to." She sighed and leaned back against the bench. "Nick, don't worry. I'll be fine. As I said, I don't think I was the target."

He didn't think so either but he couldn't be sure, and he didn't want to take the risk of being wrong. But it seemed he had to take the risk because Isabel was determined to stay. And, he was quickly learning, these days a determined Isabel couldn't be forced to do anything against her will.

Abandoning the first part of his mission, he concentrated on the second. Information. He casually wandered over to the shelf stacked with books and ran a finger along the spines. The scent of leather lingered pleasantly beneath the ever-present smell of the herbs. He counted twelve volumes in all, a considerable library for an apothecary particularly since some of the books were sizable and quite beautiful. He picked out one book, leafed through it, glanced up at Isabel to see if she was watching (she was), then returned it and pulled out the large herbal where he'd found the handwritten note.

C.J. ARCHER

"Are you interested in learning about herbs?" she asked, crossing the floor to join him.

"I'm interested in what interests you."

She rolled her eyes and he returned to the book, a little bruised at her off-handedness. He pretended to randomly look at pages then just happened to come across the poisonous concoction that had been swallowed by the queen's unfortunate lady. The piece of paper slid to the floor.

"What's this?" She picked it up. "Your courage in this life will be rewarded in the next," she read. "I wonder what that means. And who is S. de B.?"

Nicholas knew. It had taken him some time to remember where he'd seen those initials before but finally it had come to him. Simon de Beaufort, the earl of Croxley. Scholar, adventurer, supporter of the New Sciences, Catholic and a friend to traitors. And patron of Samuel Camm. Isabel's father had even dedicated one of his books to the earl. Although the Privy Council had suspected he was behind at least two traitorous plots, they had never been able to find conclusive evidence and so the earl had never been charged.

Samuel's association with Croxley weighed heavily against him. It had been Nicholas's job to discover his father-in-law's movements prior to the poisoning attempt seven years ago and he had been the one to report on the number of visits between the two men, and their nature, to his superiors. The evidence had been damning.

"I know who it is," he said, playing out the scenario he'd devised that morning. He'd decided to keep to the truth, or as close to it as possible without giving his position away. "Simon de Beaufort."

"The Earl of Croxley? But why would he leave a note in my herbal?"

"He was your father's friend, wasn't he?"

"Yes," she said, returning the paper to the open page. "But I don't know why he'd leave a note in my book."

"It's more likely the person he wrote it to left it there. Isabel, what do you know about Croxley?"

She shrugged. "That he owns a large part of Durham and he

financed some of Papa's work. He knows a lot about medicines and is interested in debunking many old theories, as was Papa."

"Do you also know the Privy Council believes he's behind one or two plots to overthrow the queen?"

She paled. "No, I did not. But how do you?"

"Ash told me."

"Why are you discussing this business with him?" Her voice rose and she wiped her hands down her skirts as if rubbing off a stain.

"He's a friend and he knows people in the Privy Council." At least that wasn't a lie. "I wanted to find out about Croxley after I saw this note the other day. He seemed the best person to ask. You can trust him, Isabel."

"The same way I can trust you?" she snapped.

He took a step back, struck by the vehemence of her accusation. "You can trust me."

"Can I? You haven't yet told me why you were always away after our marriage," she said.

"And you haven't told me why you left," he countered then regretted it as she stiffened. This wasn't how it was supposed to be. They were supposed to discuss it calmly, rationally and preferably just after making love. "I'll never let anyone hurt you, Isabel. You can rely on that."

She said nothing but her gaze dropped to the paper sitting in the open book he still held. After a long time, she shook her head. "I, I don't know what that's doing there. I've never seen it before."

"I believe you." He withdrew the paper and slipped it into his pocket then closed the book and returned it to the shelf. "What I do want to know is who might have left it there?"

She shrugged. "Anyone who comes in here has access to these books, but I've never seen anyone actually open one. Not many of our customers can read or write."

"What about Shawe, elder or younger?"

She shook her head. "Not even Fox, and he should use it to further his own education."

He looked up sharply. If she was the only one, then the note wasn't there because it had been forgotten. It was there because someone was framing her. It was confirmation of his theory but it didn't make him pleased. In fact, he felt sick. Someone had gone to a great deal of trouble to place the paper in the herbal where any competent investigator could find it.

Which meant someone also suspected he was a spy and had wanted him, expected him, to find it and come to the logical conclusion and arrest Isabel.

His chest tightened. Thank God he hadn't been reassigned after all. Another agent would have arrested her immediately.

He let out a long breath and watched the back of Isabel's enticing figure as she walked away from him to greet a customer. The only thing to be learned from this new development was that she was right. She was unlikely to have been the target of the knifeman since the villain would want her kept alive to take the blame.

Knowing that didn't ease his mind.

CHAPTER 7

$\mathcal{N}$ icholas followed the arrow's flight until it thumped into the mark sixty feet away. "Good shot," he said.

Ash lowered his bow. "A little off center," the earl said with a shrug.

He moved aside and Nicholas took his place. He nocked an arrow, raised the bow as he drew and let the arrow loose. It hit the corner of the strip of wood they were using as a target. A poor shot. Archery wasn't his strongest sport. Ash beat him every time which is probably why they often ended up at Finsbury Fields with their bows and arrows—tradition stated the loser had to buy the winner a tankard of ale and Ash was a stickler for any tradition that involved a tavern.

The other reason for their visit to Finsbury Fields was to talk in the privacy of open space. The fields, used mostly by practicing archers, offered the perfect venue. They looked like any of the other gentlemen enjoying an afternoon of sport in the crisp February air.

They each had another shot. Ash's arrow hit the middle and Nicholas's missed everything, including another archer but only by inches. Nicholas held up a hand in apology when the other man shouted obscenity-laden advice on shooting straight.

"You're distracted," Ash said, his gaze unwavering. "Usually you don't miss completely."

"Usually I haven't spent the evening chasing someone who tried to kill me. Not recently anyway."

Ash raised one brow. "Your wife tried to kill you? Good Lord, Nick, are you sure you want her back?"

"Not Isabel! The hooded man from the Four Feathers. I kept my eye on him most of the night until we left. He made his move outside. I'm lucky the blade didn't connect." Damn lucky since he'd seen it too late to dodge it entirely. And yet it hadn't even scratched him. Strange.

"Did you catch him?" Ash asked.

Nicholas shook his head.

"Did you see him?"

"No, but he must have been young and healthy to be that nimble and fast."

"True," Ash said. "Any ideas? Perhaps a friend of your wife's watching you—"

"What are you implying?"

Ash shrugged but said nothing.

"She was as surprised as me," Nicholas went on, compelled to defend her. "I'm sure she didn't know him."

"She must have been afraid," Ash said with a casual lift of one shoulder. "A little thing like that, a knifeman attacking her husband in broad daylight. She would have tumbled into your arms in terror."

Nicholas said nothing. If there was one thing he was sure of, Isabel hadn't been afraid. Shocked, yes, perhaps even afraid for him, but not truly terrified. Certainly not scared enough to stop her walking back to his lodgings on her own in the waning light.

He avoided Ash's sharp gaze because he wasn't prepared to tell his friend that he suspected Isabel was hiding something. Not until he knew what she was hiding.

"So did she?" Ash asked, raising and drawing his bow.

"What?"

Ash let the arrow loose and watched it hit the mark true. "Tumble into your arms? Or your bed?"

Despite everything, Nicholas couldn't help smiling. He brushed his fingers along the feather fletches. Isabel's skin was just as smooth. Her silky hair had poured through his fingers and her body trembled when she peaked.

And her mouth around him had been hot and wet and...

If only he hadn't made a mess of everything. It's just that he hadn't expected such...wanton behavior from her. It had taken him by surprise. She never used to be like that, so brazen and assured.

"I see," Ash said, giving Nicholas a strange look. "But you can make love to your arrow and your wife later. Just fire the damn thing and let's get out of here. I'm thirsty."

Nicholas nocked the arrow, drew and aimed for the centre of the target. He fired and the arrow flew to the right, dropping at the last moment before it hit the archer he'd barely missed earlier in the leg. The man roared in pain, clutched his leg and turning an apoplectic face on Nicholas.

"Sorry," Nicholas called out, starting towards him. "I'll fetch a doc—." He stopped when four other archers, previously dispersed over the field, suddenly moved towards him like prowling lions.

"I think you just shot someone with four very big, very angry brothers," Ash said.

"Or four hired thugs. Either way, the odds aren't too bad," Nicholas said lightly.

"You take those two and I'll take the ones on the right."

"Now let's be reasonable," Nicholas called out to the man with the arrow sticking out of his thigh in a last attempt to settle the incident without further bloodshed. "It was an accident. It's a frequent hazard here in Finsbury." The man said nothing, just clutched his leg as blood seeped through his hose. "I'll pay for any medical expenses," Nicholas continued. "And if the injury hinders you from working then I'll pay your wages until you are able to work again."

Still the men kept coming, their thick brows drawn together in earnest as they glared back at Nicholas and Ash. Then one of them stopped, raised his bow and took aim. The others followed suit.

"Run!" Ash shouted.

They ran out of the fields as arrows rained down around

them. It was a miracle they made it to the Four Feathers with only a slight graze each. They collapsed into a corner booth, puffing, sweating and laughing.

"I need a drink," Ash said, signaling Nelly.

"Has anyone ever told you you drink too much?" Nicholas asked.

"Yes."

Ash did drink too much but he'd seen things that Nicholas didn't want to know about in detail so it was understandable. Nelly brought two tankards of ale and waited while they drained them in one gulp, thumped them down on the table and ordered another.

"I need you to do something for me," Nicholas said when Nelly left.

"Anything."

"I want you to look into Samuel Camm's case."

"Don't you already know everything about it?" Ash asked, stretching out his leg and rubbing his thigh.

Nicholas shook his head. "I only became involved after the actual poisoning. And you know how Walsingham can be."

Ash smirked. "Need to know basis only. And he assumed you didn't need to know all the details before you carried out the investigation?"

"To be fair, I didn't think I needed to know."

"And now you're not so sure. Do you think your father-in-law was innocent?"

Nicholas shook his head. "No, I investigated him myself." He sighed because that wasn't entirely true. "Perhaps he could be. I don't know. But I think I'm missing a piece of the puzzle that could help me with this latest poisoning."

"So what do you want me to do?"

Nelly deposited two more tankards in front of them. "You boys look like you need this today." She pointed to the dried blood on Ash's cheek. "Nicky here has an apothecary friend who could put something on that. Mighty pretty she was. And very ladylike. She could fix you up good and proper, M'Lord. What do you think, Nicky?"

Nicholas's grip tightened around the tankard. "Thank you,

Nelly," he said, aware that he sounded annoyed and not caring. "I think your husband is calling you."

Ash chuckled as Nelly sauntered away in a swish of swaying skirts. "She's just teasing you. So, what do you want me to do?"

"Ask some questions of the people who investigated at the time. Who else was in the palace and had access and poisons knowledge? What did Samuel say when he was accused? Was there anything else that could point to another guilty party? That sort of thing."

Ash nodded. "I'll start today. In fact, I'd best leave now anyway. Another meeting with Walsingham." He drained his tankard then stood, picking up his bow and quiver. "Be careful, Nick. Someone out there wants to kill you."

Nicholas stood too. "I carry a rapier and two daggers, not forgetting this bow. I think I'll be fine if the coward doesn't run off again."

"As long as you're only required to use the bow to whack someone. You really need more archery practice, my friend."

Nicholas snorted. "What I really need is fewer distractions."

"You enjoy the distractions too much to give them up." Ash grinned.

Nicholas grinned back. "I certainly do."

* * *

NICHOLAS HEADED home to deposit the bow and arrows and change out of his sporting doublet and breeches before heading back to Bucklersbury Street for more research. Of the spying kind, although the Isabel kind was high on his agenda too. Work first, play later. He was almost within sight of the house when he heard a whoosh a moment before an arrow struck his shoulder.

"Bloody hell!" He grunted at the sharp sting, grateful his doublet stopped it from entering too deep.

He quickly scanned his surroundings but everything seemed in order. People went about their business, wrapped against the cold in cloaks of different colors and styles according to their station. Except for Nicholas himself, none carried bow and arrows. Maybe the archer wasn't on the street at all, but on an upper storey of one of the shops, preparing to shoot again.

A small crowd began to gather around him, asking questions, looking concerned, but more importantly, shielding him from any further arrows.

"Are you all right, Sir?" asked a lad.

Nicholas nodded then gritted his teeth as he pulled the arrow out of his shoulder. He felt skin tear, but not muscle and thankfully the bloodflow was minimal.

"Lucky it didn't get you in the head," said a man wearing blue and white servant's livery.

"Let me look at it," said a woman already inspecting his shoulder.

Nicholas shook his head to dislodge the strange thickness that had set in. "Did anyone see where the arrow came from?" He squinted in the general direction of its origin—a series of shops lining the western side of Bishopsgate Street, but nothing appeared out of the ordinary. He rubbed his forehead, confused. Maybe it hadn't been from that direction at all.

The throb in his shoulder drew his attention. He had to inspect it properly, stop the blood and... Home. He had to get home and lie down. The house was close. That way... No, down there.

He waved off the crowd and headed down a short street that looked familiar, stumbling once or twice over...something. It must have been further than he thought because he was breathless by the time he arrived at Mistress Plunkett's door. He shook from the cold and the pain, burning like a raging fire in his arm and his stomach. Had he been shot in the stomach too? He couldn't recall. Everything was a blur.

He thumped on the front door with his fist, surprised to see that it still clutched the arrow. He desperately needed to rest so he leaned his head against the door frame and waited, trying to master the agony pulling his insides apart. When the maidservant finally opened the door, he staggered through it.

"Sir Nicholas, is everything all right?" she asked. "If I do say so, you look ill, Sir."

"Who is it, Mary?" Mistress Plunkett seemed to have

appeared from nowhere. "Goodness, Sir Nicholas, what's happened?"

He frowned, thinking, trying to force aside the nausea and searing pain and concentrate on staying upright. "No. Shot. Arrow." He saw the stairs and headed towards them, although the damn things wouldn't be still. They kept moving, left right then left again. He managed to reach the first step with Mary's help then doubled over as pain speared through his middle. He lay down amongst the rushes on the floor and closed his eyes. There was no way he could make it up the stairs.

"Good Lord, this is from an arrow?" Mistress Plunkett pressed a hand to his forehead. "You're cold."

Very cold. And weak. All from an arrow. A single arrow. It barely even broke the skin.

Somehow he gathered enough strength to open his heavy eyes. "Poison," he whispered. "Go...Shawe's apothecary." He curled up into a tight ball as another attack of nausea wracked his body. Through the groans filling his ears, he heard Mistress Plunkett giving Mary orders.

* * *

WHEN ISABEL ARRIVED in Nicholas's room she found a mess. The bed was in disarray, the bedsheets soaked in what was probably the source of the stench that had driven Mistress Plunkett downstairs. The ewer lay on its side on the damp rushes, an overflowing basin beside it. Nicholas was nowhere to be seen. Panic momentarily seized her. Then she heard him groan.

"Nicholas?" She ran to the other side of the big bed and found him huddled on the floor, shivering.

His red eyelids cracked open slowly as if it was the most painful movement in the world, then closed again. The tension seemed to ease a little from his shoulders as he licked bloodless lips. "Poison," he whispered.

She knelt down beside him and checked his pulse. Irregular and weak. "Do you know what sort? Nicholas," she said when he didn't answer, "this is very important. Mary said you were shot with an arrow. Where is it?"

"Here," said the maidservant from the door. She held the arrow between thumb and forefinger.

Isabel retrieved it and sniffed the arrowhead. "Monkshood," she said to nobody in particular. "Mary, I need another basin."

The maidservant nodded gravely. She still puffed heavily after running all the way to Bucklersbury Street and back but the stout girl, bless her, turned immediately to fetch a basin. She didn't even appear disgusted by what she saw.

Isabel carried the leather bag she'd brought with her to Nicholas's side and pulled out a phial of emetic. When Mary returned she told the girl to fetch water and a mop to clean the room. "Get what you need then wait outside until I call you."

Mary left and Isabel put the phial to Nicholas's pale lips. "Drink this. It'll make you ill again but will get rid of the remainder of the poison."

He drank and she held him while his body purged itself of the monkshood. Afterwards, he lay his head on her lap, his body limp, his breathing still shallow, his skin cold and clammy to touch. She checked his pulse again and felt a sliver of relief as it seemed more regular. But still very weak. He wasn't out of danger yet.

"Mary," she called and the maid entered immediately. She must have been hovering outside as ordered.

Mistress Plunkett poked her head round the door, screwed up her nose and left again. As Mary went about cleaning the room with quiet efficiency, Isabel retrieved a bottle of aqua vitae from her bag and held it to Nicholas's lips. He drank and she followed it with a cup of water from the ewer Mary had refilled.

"Shouldn't he be moving about?" the maid asked from where she was stoking the fire. "I heard that's what you should do when someone is poisoned."

"Not with monkshood. He has to lie down but he needs stimulants like aqua vitae. Are you finished?"

"Aye, I'll just gather the rushes and go."

Isabel made sure Nicholas was resting comfortably on the floor but not sleeping and stood. She opened the press and pulled out a clean shirt, hose and breeches and placed them on the fresh bedsheets.

"You'll be needing another basin," Mary said, leaving the room. She returned moments later with clean cloths and a basin filled with water.

Isabel thanked her and waited until the girl left before removing Nicholas's clothes. With none of the awe and desire of the previous night, she went about the task of cleaning him. She stroked his limbs vigorously to stimulate the blood flow, easing a little when he winced, then calmly washed the wound. It was inflamed and red but not bleeding. She found a bandage in her bag and wrapped it around his shoulder.

Although aware that this was her husband, her lover, she felt somewhat removed as she carried out her work. It was as if she had split herself in two and the practical apothecary had ordered the concerned wife to wait outside. For now, his life depended on her detachment.

When she'd finished, he opened his eyes, deep orbs sunken inside the bruised sockets. "Different to last night," he said, his voice barely above a whisper.

She gave him an encouraging smile. He must be in so much pain and yet he managed to be lighthearted for her sake. "Not really," she said. "You're naked and flat on your back."

He smiled and moved his fingers so they touched hers.

"How are you feeling?" she asked.

"Like ants are crawling over my body."

"That's one of the effects of monkshood. It'll pass. Try not to scratch," she said, noticing the fingers of his other hand rubbing his leg. "Are you still giddy?"

"I don't think so."

"Are your legs and arms in pain?"

"Somewhat."

Knowing Nicholas, that meant he was in agony. At least his breathing wasn't coming in short, labored gasps anymore but he had begun to shiver again. "Do you think you can make it to the bed if I help you?"

She pulled him up and he leaned heavily on her as they progressed slowly to the bed. He slumped down on top of it with a groan. With very little assistance from her patient, she dressed him in hose and shirt but left the breeches off then tucked him under the blankets.

When his eyes began to droop she shook him awake. "No sleeping, not yet."

He looked like he was about to protest then said, "Talk to me."

"About what?"

"About the last six years." He yawned. "Everything I've missed."

"That'll send you to sleep for sure."

"Never."

So she talked about turning up on Old Man Shawe's doorstep six years ago, tired and miserable and alone, and how she had become part of his household. She spoke about Mistress Shawe's death and Master Shawe's illness and the death of Lawrence's wife the year before. She told him about Fox the lazy apprentice, about the friends she'd made, including Meg, and about the little rituals that comprised her day. She told him a lot of things, and yet nothing of great importance but he stayed awake. Occasionally she noticed his jaw tightening and she guessed he was doing his best to suppress a fresh wave of pain gripping his insides. Once, he closed his eyes and she thought he'd fallen asleep but it seemed he was trying to master the poison. He threw up again after she told him about Lawrence obtaining the role of physician to Her Majesty and thought the timing was quite apt considering the two men seemed to dislike each other.

Some time later, he closed his eyes out of sheer exhaustion and she let him sleep. It was only then that she began to relax and the true danger that Nicholas had been in penetrated her professional mask. He could have died if she hadn't been summoned straight away. And if he hadn't kept the arrow with him, she would never have known the type of poison. And if he lived alone...

Too many ifs. Too many things that could have gone wrong. Too many ways in which she could have lost him. For the first time since her powers came in, she wished she could heal more than flesh wounds. The injury from the arrow was minor and wouldn't cause him any trouble while it healed naturally, but the poison was a different matter. She wouldn't have hesitated to cure him with her magic if she could.

The thought stopped her tears instantly and she stared at Nicholas's peaceful, pale form in the bed. She might have left him in Kent years ago with no thought of returning, but in her heart, he had always been her husband and she'd felt better knowing he was alive and well elsewhere in the world, if not on his own lands then somewhere.

But in the last few perilous hours he had almost been ripped from her forever.

The tears started again and she swallowed a sob, then another then didn't bother trying to contain the rest. When her crying eased, she sat on the bed beside him because she just wanted to be close. But it wasn't close enough so she lay down next to him and he must have sensed her because he rolled into her, resting his head on her shoulder. His breathing came more even, hot on her neck, and beneath the covers his chest rose and fell regularly. He was out of danger. Safe. With her. She kissed the top of his head and closed her eyes, not wanting to think beyond the sweet moment.

CHAPTER 8

"Who would want to poison you?"

Nicholas wanted to know the answer to Isabel's question just as much as she did. He shook his head then regretted it because the action made the incessant pounding worse. The only good thing to come of it was the softening of Isabel's demeanor. Ever since he awoke that morning, she had treated him like one of her customers, clinically asking him questions about his health then plying him with medicines, but now her brow furrowed and she sat down next to him on the bed.

"How is your head?" she asked, pressing cool fingers against his temple.

"It feels like someone has driven a spike through my skull." He tried to sit up but she gently stopped him with a hand to his chest. "Lie down. You need to rest or your recovery will take longer."

He lay back as ordered. If he needed rest then he'd best take it while he could because tomorrow he would have to restart his investigation in earnest now that the stakes had risen somewhat.

"Did you see where the arrow came from?" she asked. It seemed she wasn't about to give up on her line of questioning.

"Not exactly. One of the shops I think."

"Were there any witnesses?"

"Nobody actually saw the arrow."

She placed her fingers on his wrist and checked his pulse for what seemed like the hundredth time that morning. Surely she didn't need to check it that often. "It's most odd," she muttered, frowning down at their connected hands. "Most odd."

"My pulse?"

"This attempt on your life. Monkshood is one of the deadliest poisons and smearing it on an arrow means someone intended to cause you serious harm, if not death." She shook her head. "I just don't understand why someone would want to kill you."

"Perhaps the arrow was meant for someone else and missed its target." It was a blatant attempt to deceive her but hopefully she fell for it. He suspected if Isabel thought someone wanted to kill him she would not give up until she found out why. And he certainly couldn't have her doing that. "It happens all the time. Archery is bloody difficult to master, as I keep reminding Ash."

"Mary said you had your own quiver and arrows with you but no bow. You must have dropped it." She still held his wrist but seemed no longer to be thinking about his pulse. "Were you practicing before you were poisoned? If so," she continued without waiting for an answer, "it's extremely coincidental that a poisoned arrow should strike you on the same day."

He'd been thinking the same thing when his head didn't violently object to the exercise. But he said nothing, just shrugged.

"Was Lord Ashbourne with you?" she persisted. "Perhaps he can shed some light on this subject."

"I'll send for him."

"I already did."

"You're very efficient," he said. And competent. Too competent. He hadn't wanted Ash to know of the poisoning yet. Not while the earl still considered Isabel a suspect.

She let go of his wrist finally but he caught her fingers in his. "I haven't had a chance to thank you properly for saving my life," he said.

She pulled free. "Any apothecary or doctor could have done what I did."

"But they didn't. Mary said you ran all the way here, and

from what I recall, it wasn't a pretty sight that greeted you. Not all women could have done what you did."

"Not all women have my experience," she said, standing, severing the connection between them.

"Isabel." He waited until she looked at him. "Isabel, what's wrong? I know last night was...messy, but why are you acting like we mean nothing to each other?"

"Because we do mean nothing to each other." She turned away and began packing her bag, her back and shoulders rigid.

"Where are you going?"

"Back to the shop. You don't need me anymore."

"Yes I do. What if I have a relapse?" He sat up, felt like his head would spin right off his neck, and slumped down again.

"You won't." She snapped her bag shut. "Just get plenty of rest."

What had brought about this sudden desire to leave? A few moments earlier it seemed she had been prepared to stay but her attitude changed after he'd thanked her. "But you'll need to check my pulse again," he said, hearing how pathetic that sounded and not caring.

"I'll come back later and do it." She spoke like his prim maidenly aunt who used to tell him little boys should be learning their lessons quietly in the schoolroom and not tearing around the house wearing Father's old armor and carrying a wooden sword. He'd have to do something about that. He preferred his soft, concerned Isabel better.

"Will you check my other vitals then too?" He lifted the blanket. "One in particular is suffering from lack of attention."

She looked back at him, one eyebrow raised, and thrust a hand on her hip. "This is serious, Nick."

"I am serious!"

"Didn't I tell you too much exertion could kill you until you've fully recovered?"

"At least I'll die happy." He grinned and finally the edge of her mouth quirked into a smile. He was about to ask her how long before she would return when there was a knock at the door. Before he could invite the visitor in, Ash burst into the room like a winter gale.

"What the devil happened, Merritt?" he barked, crossing the floor in three great strides. "Your landlady's maid tells me you nearly died from a poisoned arrow."

"His landlady's maid is correct," Isabel said from near the door where Ash had walked straight past her.

The earl turned and bowed. "My apologies, m'lady, I didn't see you there."

"I prefer to be called Mistress Camm these days," she said with a tip of her chin. "Or just Isabel."

He bowed again. "As you wish. I assume you were the apothecary who tended him? Is he going to be all right?"

"He'll be fine if he rests."

"So he'll be out of bed by tomorrow."

"Not tomorrow—"

Nicholas cleared his throat and they both looked at him as if they'd just remembered he was there. "I'll take it one day at a time," he said.

Isabel shook her head. "But tomorrow is too early—"

"He has work to do," Ash said and Nicholas groaned. Why couldn't Ash keep his mouth shut?

"What sort of work?" Isabel asked, looking from one to the other. "To do with the estate?"

"Yes," Nicholas said before Ash could say something foolish.

Isabel frowned. "It'll have to wait. He won't be well enough to get out of bed for a few days yet. Now, Lord Ashbourne," she placed her bag on the floor, "I'm glad our paths have crossed as I wanted to ask you if you knew who might want to kill Nick."

"Well, actually—"

Nicholas coughed again and gave Ash his best don't-ruin-this-for-me glare. Ash glanced at him, raised a brow and turned back to Isabel. "No. He's a saint. Can't think of a living soul who'd want to poison him. Or a dead one either for that matter." He ended with an unenthusiastic shrug.

Nicholas sighed and tried to disappear into the pillows.

"But you were practicing archery together just before this incident." She sounded frustrated and a little irritated. Perhaps she suspected they were hiding something from her. "It seems a rather great coincidence that Nick should be shot with a poison arrow just after you finished your practice. Do you agree?"

Ash chewed his lip, frowning. "Yes. It is a great coincidence."

Not so great for me, Nicholas thought as his stomach cramped again.

"Do you think that archer you shot by accident was getting his revenge?" Ash asked.

"You shot someone?" Isabel cried. "What were you shooting at people for?"

"He missed the target," Ash explained.

"Good Lord, Nick," Isabel said, "you need to practice more."

"Thank you," Nicholas said, rubbing his temple. "Weren't you about to leave?"

"No." She approached the bed and turned to Ash. Although a great deal shorter and slimmer than the earl, she somehow seemed just as imposing. Heaven help anyone who crossed her. Wait—he was the one who needed divine assistance when it came to Isabel. "Tell me about this man Nick shot. Could he have been angry enough to try to kill him with a poison arrow?"

Ash leaned against the bed post near Nicholas's feet. "His henchmen—"

"Henchmen! Oh Lord, this just gets worse. Why is it trouble seems to follow you about, Nick? First the knife attack outside the Four Feathers and now this. Perhaps I should lock you away for your own safety."

"And tie me up," Nicholas said with a grin.

Isabel colored and Ash coughed. "Please refrain from any titillating talk until I'm out of the room. As I was about to say, his henchmen didn't follow us to the inn so unless they had luck on their side, it's unlikely they found him again after he left."

"So it must be someone who had followed you there or had been watching the inn and waiting for you to show up." Isabel peered down at the floor and rubbed her chin. It seemed she would remain until she had figured out the puzzle. And if she figured it out, his secret would be in grave danger of being uncovered.

He gave Ash a pleading look. Ash mouthed "What?" then

when Nicholas jerked his head at Isabel, the earl's lips formed an "Oh" and he nodded.

"Ah, Mistress Camm, I need to speak to Nicholas alone."

"Alone?" she said, looking up.

"Yes, we have, ah, manly things to discuss." He winked at her and Nicholas rolled his eyes. Thank God Ash had never been allocated actual spying duties—he was a terrible liar.

"Manly things?" Isabel prompted. "If they are of a medical nature, perhaps I can help."

"Ah, no, thank you. Not medical. Just...personal."

She stood. "Then I'll wait outside."

"The discussion could take some time," Nicholas said. He needed to get her away from Ash before the earl said too much. "And you did say the shop needed you. It's not my place to say, but that apprentice of yours didn't seem capable of taking on the responsibility on his own for an entire day."

She nodded and walked to the door where she picked up her bag again. "He would be if he wasn't so idle. I think he has a problem taking orders from a woman." She waved towards Nicholas then looked at Ash, bowed awkwardly, blushed and hurriedly left.

Nicholas sighed. "Ash, can you at least try to remember that I don't want Isabel to know about my spying."

"Sorry, forgot what with all the worrying about your life being in the balance." He folded his arms and gave Nicholas a crooked smile, the one that all the ladies swooned over. It didn't work on Nicholas. In fact, he was beginning to think Ash had deliberately let a few things slip in the conversation with Isabel.

"My life was in the balance last night. It's not today. Thanks for your concern."

"I was concerned." Ash sat on the edge of the bed looking surprisingly sheepish. "I'd hate to lose you. You're the only man I know who can match me drink for drink."

Nicholas laughed. "I can't but that never appears to concern you."

"Well it's concerning me now. Do as the apothecary says and stay in bed until you're completely well."

"And who will continue my investigation?"

"I will."

"You!" Nicholas snorted. "The whole of Bucklersbury Street will know you're an agent of Walsingham's by nightfall. Not only can you not lie to save your life, but your interrogation technique is akin to being rammed up the arse by a bull."

Ash winced. "I get the feeling you think I'd make a terrible spy. Well, it may interest you to know that this terrible spy has some information for you."

Nicholas sat up and was swamped by a fresh wave of nausea for his efforts. He lay down again, closed his eyes until his stomach ceased rolling then opened them upon Ash's concerned face. "Go on."

"You should rest," Ash said.

"If this is anything to do with Isabel or her father then I want to know about it now. Tomorrow might be too late."

Ash looked like he would object again but then he leaned back against the bed post with a sigh. "Very well. The information I have concerns the original incident involving Samuel Camm. After hearing your theory about the two cases being connected, I tried to find out what exactly happened to put suspicion on Samuel six years ago."

"Seven. It's been six since Isabel left."

Ash took a deep breath and went on. "Samuel Camm had come to London at Her Majesty's specific request to discuss some of his new medical theories."

"I know that."

"But did you know that three other apothecaries had also been invited and that they were more than merely rivals to Camm. In his latest book, he debunked theories from all three. Although he didn't name the apothecaries specifically in the tome, it seems fellow members of the Grocers Company easily guessed."

Nicholas sank further into his pillow. The powerful Grocers Company was the guild to which all London apothecaries had to belong in order to set up a shop in the City. It also held much weight outside of London. Although reputable apothecaries in other centers, like Samuel in Winchester, wouldn't be members, they would certainly know some of them in a professional capacity.

"Their reputations would have suffered as a consequence," Nicholas said.

"And their businesses. Rumors spread like fire," Ash said. "It would only take one member of the Grocers Company to speculate to another colleague on the street where he could be overheard and soon enough the entire City hears that Pullman the apothecary can't really cure the French Pox with quicksilver."

Nicholas frowned. "Pullman? Was he one of the three?"

Ash nodded. "And Lawrence Shawe."

"But he's a physician not an apothecary."

"His father, also named Lawrence. He was living in Winchester at the time. Samuel Camm's home town."

Nicholas nodded. "They were friends, so Isabel told me. That's why he gave her employment here in London."

There was a long silence in which Nicholas was only vaguely aware of Ash watching him.

"I can hear your brain spinning inside your skull," Ash said after a while.

"Feels more like hammering to me." Nicholas rubbed his pounding temples. "What I don't understand is why Samuel would discredit his own friend."

Ash lifted one shoulder. "Camm might have been one of those fellows to whom friendship means nothing compared to professional notoriety." He shrugged again. "Perhaps the question you should be asking is why Shawe was so good to Camm's daughter after his so-called friend savaged his reputation."

Their gazes met and Nicholas could see the unspoken accusation in the earl's eyes. "Shawe felt guilty for something," Nicholas said, feeling like he was in a game of catch up where Ash was two paces ahead. Damn his aching head.

"And what could he possibly feel so guilty about that he takes on a young woman he hasn't seen for some years, who had never undertaken an apprenticeship—"

"Not officially," Nicholas cut in. "But she worked side by side with her father for some time before we wed."

"—and who is a fugitive from her own marriage," he

continued as if Nicholas hadn't spoken. Ash crossed his arms and looked expectant.

"You think Shawe had something to do with Samuel's arrest or perhaps the poisoning itself?" Nicholas shook his head. "Perhaps he just felt guilty for not visiting his friend in prison. Perhaps he just liked Isabel. There are too many other possibilities and you're forgetting one thing."

"What?"

"I investigated Samuel myself. He was guilty."

"Did you actually see him make the poisonous concoction that was intended for the queen?"

"No, but he certainly was involved with Croxley and others known to Walsingham."

"That doesn't make him a traitor."

Nicholas shook his head, part of him wishing it was true and Samuel was innocent of the crime. But that would mean he'd helped send his own father-in-law to his deathbed for nothing and that certainly didn't ease Nicholas's conscience. No, it couldn't be true. It simply couldn't be. "I intercepted letters between them that left no doubt that Samuel was involved." Even as he said it, doubts began to infiltrate his thoughts. The similarities between the two treasonous events were too coincidental, and the fact that Isabel was being set up for the latest poisoning...perhaps her father had been set up in just the same way.

"Who was the third of the discredited apothecaries at Whitehall?" Nicholas asked.

"A man by the name of Finch. Deceased two years ago so we can strike him from our list of suspects in this current case. And Old Man Shawe, if he is indeed house bound."

"Bed bound according to Isabel. But that doesn't mean his son can't be involved on his father's behalf."

"The question is...why? Why set up first Camm and then his daughter seven years later? Do you think Camm's book had something to do with it? Perhaps as revenge or a means of removing a thorn in the side of the apothecary most damaged by the accusations."

"Or perhaps it was merely convenient to blame Samuel,"

Nicholas said. "Perhaps he was in the wrong place at the wrong time." But he shook his head just as Ash said, "No. I don't believe in coincidence on this scale."

"Neither do I," Nicholas muttered. He rubbed his temple again, feeling like his head would explode if he continued chasing the thoughts around.

"You're tired." Ash stood. "I'll go so you can rest." But he didn't make any movement towards the door, nor did he look at Nicholas, just down at his hands.

"I think you're about to say something I won't want to hear," Nicholas said.

"Actually it's a question you won't want to hear." Ash's gaze lifted. "Do you think your wife had anything to do with your poisoning?"

Nicholas realized how exhausted he was when his anger didn't flare. His head ached, his limbs felt leaden and he couldn't think properly but he did feel a kind of sympathy for Ash. The earl had never known love the way Nicholas loved Isabel. He didn't understand what it was like to know a person so thoroughly that any question of their betrayal was utterly ludicrous. Isabel would never harm him, of that he was sure. Not physically at least.

"At some point last night," Nicholas said, his gaze locked with his friend's, "I woke up in this bed in clean clothes. I don't know how long I'd been here and I don't recall how I got here but Isabel was asleep beside me, her cheeks damp and her eyes swollen from crying. She is not trying to kill me, Ash."

The earl nodded once. "Then we best find out who is before he tries again."

* * *

"WHAT AM I TO DO?" Meg wiped a tear from her cheek, smearing her white paint and revealing pock-marked skin beneath. She sat on a stool, her elbows resting on Isabel's counter which made her shoulders stoop and her back arch like an old crone. Her yellow wig lurched to the right so that it seemed her head was lopsided. She was even more disheveled than usual.

Isabel reached across the counter and took one of her friend's hands. Meg squeezed it and gave her a watery smile. "Perhaps it's a blessing in disguise," Isabel ventured. She had arrived home exhausted, her neck aching from lying awkwardly on Nick's bed, her nose red from crying and her head spinning with questions. She had been trying to think of answers to those questions as she methodically went about her work when Meg had walked in, looking like she'd lost everything.

And, in a way, she had. Her whoremaster had left her. Or, more precisely, had told her to leave. Biggin, the shadowy figure who procured clients for Meg and many other girls Isabel had served over the years, had told her in blunt terms that nobody wanted a skinny, flat-chested whore. It seemed she was costing him more than she was making so he told her to find another whoremaster.

"A blessin'?" Meg blubbered, bursting into fresh tears. "How can it be a blessin'? I've got no money, no protection and no home."

"No home!"

Meg shook her head and her wig tipped even further to the side. It was precariously close to sliding right off. "All his girls live in his dirty stinkin' house by the river," she mumbled through her tears. "He told the others not to let me in this mornin'. Some of them said they wanted to but were too afraid of Biggin to go against him. Oh, Isabel, what will I do?"

Isabel offered her a handkerchief. "I think when you've recovered from the shock, you'll be glad to be rid of him. He sounds like a brute." Although Meg had never mentioned it, Isabel was sure Biggin beat her and the other women. They often came in for a pot of fermented comfrey leaves for their bruises, muttering the whoremaster's name to each other in frightened or angry tones. Isabel was certainly glad her friend was rid of him but she had to make sure Meg didn't return to the Bankside and find herself in an even worse situation. So she did the only thing she could think of to keep Meg out of trouble. "In the mean time, you can stay here," she said.

Meg looked up, wide-eyed. "What, in the shop?"

"In my room. You'll have to share with both myself and the maid but we'll all fit somehow."

"I don't care," Meg said, brightening. "I'll sleep on the floor. It's gotta be cleaner than Biggin's place. He's got more fleas in his beds than the rats have on their backs. Oh thank you." She leaned over the counter and hugged Isabel fiercely. "But are you sure?"

"Of course. I wouldn't offer if I didn't want to do it. It'll be fun. And Lord knows," she sighed, "I need some fun."

Meg drew back and frowned. "You've been crying. Here I am speakin' about my own silly troubles and here you are takin' care of me when all the time somethin's wrong. What is it, Izzy? Tell me."

"My...friend has been poisoned. I was at his place last night helping him recover."

Meg's jaw dropped and she placed the hand that held her handkerchief to her chest. "Him? A man? You were at a man's place all night?"

Isabel nodded and waited for Meg to digest that piece of information and move onto the more murderous part of her revelation.

"And he was poisoned you say?" Meg leaned forward conspiratorially. "How terrible. Will he live?"

"Yes." Isabel silently blessed her good fortune that she'd arrived in time to administer the emetic.

Meg blew out a breath. "That's a relief. Sooo," she said with a girlish shrug of her shoulder, "tell me who he is. No, wait, I know! That merchant I've seen in here many times. The one who wears the dark velvet gown and gold chains." When Isabel shook her head, she went on: "The apothecary from the enormous shop down the road? Or maybe the one with the two gold rings on his fingers? No? Then that customer who arrives in a coach—"

"No. None of them. His name is Nicholas Merritt." Isabel decided not to use his title. Meg might faint from excitement if she knew he was a knight. "You met him the other day in fact."

Meg took only the briefest pauses before brightening. "Yes, I remember him. Very handsome but plainly dressed." She said it as if it were a major failing.

Isabel opened her mouth to defend him then closed it, partly because she didn't want to appear too familiar with him but mostly because Meg was talking again.

"So, tell me, what's he like?"

Isabel lifted one shoulder, not sure she wanted to describe the man she loved. Her heart was raw enough after the previous night, she didn't need to think about what she had given up forever too. "He's...polite. Funny and quite mischievous really."

"No, no, I mean," Meg's voice dropped to a whisper as she leaned forward, "what's he like in bed?"

Isabel froze. How did she know they'd slept together? As if reading her mind, Meg threw her head back and laughed. "The cuff. Remember? He brought it back the other day." She winked. "I can only think of one reason why he'd have one of your best cuffs in his pocket."

Isabel tried to control her smile but couldn't. It broke out slowly and spread into a grin. "I remember."

"He means more to you than a casual lover, don't he?"

The smile vanished. Isabel picked up a pestle lying nearby and twisted it between her fingers. She felt Meg's gaze on her, persistent and patient. "I left him six years ago," she finally said, "not because I stopped loving him but because being with him had become...impossible. That was a terrible time in my life. I thought I would never feel so frightened, so lost as I did then. I was wrong. Last night was much worse. I would have given anything, even my own life, if it could have saved his." The words raked across her nerves. It hurt to voice them, to hear them, but it was the truth. She had been terrified. Watching Nick lying so still in the bed, his breathing thin, his skin as white as Meg's face paint, she knew what it was like to be on the brink of losing her soul. Because Nick owned her soul and if he had lost his battle...

It didn't bear thinking about.

Isabel put the pestle down on the counter, the clank ringing loudly through the shop. Eventually she looked up at Meg, blinking back at her through tears.

"Oh, Izzy." Meg held Isabel's hand and shook her head. "Don't cry, you're supposed to be the strong one."

Is that what everyone thought? If only they knew how vulnerable she sometimes felt, how often she wondered if she was doing the right thing, or how she wanted to hide in her room some days and not face the customers, the members of the Grocer's Company or Fox and his disobedience.

Meg shook her head. "If love hurts like that then I want nothin' to do with it. Give me a man to tumble and a roof over my head and I'm happy."

"In that order?" Isabel asked with a half-smile.

The front door opened before Meg could answer. Lawrence strode through it and up to the counter. He didn't even acknowledge Meg, not even with a scowl which was his usual greeting for the whoring customers. He slapped his gloves down on the counter and stamped his fist on top of them then said: "That Merritt fellow is a damned liar."

CHAPTER 9

"*A* liar?" Isabel tried not to appear too interested in Lawrence's proclamation for fear he suspected she had more than a passing interest in a man she claimed was merely a customer. "What has he lied about?"

"He's a knight," Lawrence said with more than a little irritation. It must be infuriating to find out a man he didn't like out-ranked him.

"A knight!" Meg's jaw dropped. "Izzy, you never said!"

Isabel squeezed Meg's hand in the hope it would keep her quiet. All she needed now was for Lawrence to find out she had also lied to him about knowing Nick. She could find herself not only unemployed but homeless as well and then where would that leave her?

"Actually he did mention it," Isabel said with a dismissive wave. She picked up the pestle and returned it to the mortar then swept the off-cuts of various herbs onto the floor where they would remain until the maid changed the rushes later in the week. "How did you find out?" she asked, dusting her hands.

"I've been making enquiries," Lawrence said.

Isabel looked up. "About Ni...Merritt?"

"Sir Nicholas Merritt," Meg corrected, sounding pleased. It wouldn't be every day she could claim to have met a knight of the realm. Being a Bankside whore, she was probably more used to drunken bear handlers, drunken wherrymen and drunken tavern patrons.

"Enquiries?" Isabel frowned. "What in God's name for?"

His gaze flicked to Meg and back again. "You know," he muttered.

Yes, she did. So he still thought Nick was working for Sir Francis Walsingham as intelligencer. She had to agree it was a likely scenario. It certainly explained why he had turned up in Bucklersbury Street and started asking a lot of questions about poison. It also accounted for the attempts on his life.

Dear lord. Her husband was a spy!

The room began to spin and she gripped the edge of the counter to steady herself.

"Are you all right?" Meg asked. "You've gone awful pale. Hasn't she Master Shawe?"

Lawrence was around the side of the counter before she even finished her sentence. "Sit down, Isabel, you look unwell. Can I get you some aqua vitae? A tonic of rosemary?"

Isabel sat on the stool but shook him off. "I'm fine. Just a headache. What else did you find out from your enquiries?"

He pouted, no doubt put out that his fussing had been brushed aside as easily as the off-cuts from her herbs. "Very little. He owns a great parcel of land in Kent, he's extremely wealthy and was knighted a few years ago but no one could really tell me what for."

"Extremely, you say?" Meg turned her barely controlled smile on Isabel.

"I'm sure extremely is an exaggeration," Isabel said.

"Why would you say that?" Lawrence frowned. "Do you know otherwise? I thought he was just a customer."

"He is. I'm merely surmising. He does dress rather plainly for someone of extreme wealth. And his lodgings are nothing out of the ordinary."

"His lodgings?" Lawrence burst out, sending spittle onto the counter top. "When did you visit the rogue's lodgings?"

He probably would have heard about her visit soon enough since Fox and Lucy the maid both knew that Isabel had been called away and hadn't returned until the morning. It was best

Lawrence heard it from her first. "Last night." She held her hand up to silence him as he began to splutter again. "He was poisoned and sent for me since I'm the only apothecary he knows."

"He could have called for a doctor."

"Yes," Isabel said evenly, "he could have. But he called for me. I administered an emetic."

"What type of poison? How was it consumed?"

"Monkshood, on an arrowhead."

"Good Lord!" Lawrence rubbed his pointed beard. "Attempted murder," he said to no one in particular. He stared right through her for a few moments then shook his head as if he couldn't believe it. "You have to keep the patient still for monkshood."

"I know."

"But not sleeping, not for some time. And he should have taken some stimulants to counteract the monkshood. Foxglove, aqua vitae..."

"Yes," Isabel said.

"She's an excellent apothecary," Meg said from where she hovered on Isabel's other side.

"Yes, of course," Lawrence said quickly. "Father taught her well."

Sometimes good men could be very stupid. Old Man Shawe had certainly taught her a great deal but Lawrence seemed to have forgotten she had been assisting her own father since she was old enough to lift a jar and most of her knowledge had been gained from him.

The shouts of a carter urging his horses through the muddy street outside and the crackle of the fire under the cauldron seemed louder in the ensuing silence. Isabel was relieved when Lawrence broke it by clearing his throat.

"Are you sure you don't want something for your headache?" he asked. "I can prescribe a new tonic I heard about on a visit to Rheims last month."

"No, thank you, I think I just need some sleep. It was an exhausting night."

"Of course." He shouted for Fox and the apprentice came

running through the rear door. "Take over from Mistress Camm. I'm ordering her to rest."

The apprentice nodded and removed the apron he wore when distilling herbs. Lawrence took Isabel by the elbow and helped her off the stool. Once she had two feet on the floor, his hand moved to her back and began rubbing in a gentle, circular motion. She was sure he meant it as an intimate gesture but she was reminded of a mother encouraging the wind from a baby and she smothered a snigger.

Lawrence's hand dropped away immediately. "Oh, and one other thing I learned from my source." A smug smile crept across his face. "Merritt is married."

"Married!" Meg cried, her eyes wide. "But—"

"He did mention something about a wife," Isabel cut in before Meg revealed too much of their last conversation.

Her acknowledgement seemed to deflate Lawrence somewhat. "Right. Good."

"Not that his marital status is of concern to me," she continued. "He is only a customer."

"I'm not so sure that's all he is. In fact, I'm convinced he is spying on us and the other apothecaries. He lied about his knighthood and I'm certain he's not telling us the truth about his visits to Bucklersbury Street. Beware, Isabel. Do not let his joviality fool you into trusting him."

"Rest assured, I am not easily fooled, Lawrence."

"I never meant that you were, I merely—"

"I understand," she said, perhaps a little too dismissively to the man who was her employer's son. She softened it with a smile. "I'll also try to find out if he really is working for the Privy Council as a spy."

Lawrence drew in an audible breath. "But that would mean visiting him again."

"Of course. I need to follow up on my patient anyway."

"Oh. Right." That seemed to appeal to his physician's senses because he nodded gravely. "Of course."

She yawned. "But not today."

Lawrence left and Isabel gave instructions to Fox before turning to Meg. She'd been reluctant to tell Lawrence that Meg would be staying in her room. Not that she expected him to demand rent. Her reluctance stemmed from the fact that he would disapprove of a whore, even a reformed one, living in his father's house. Isabel had no doubt the old man would approve, however. He was a generous, kind-hearted soul. She would speak to him before her nap and apprise him of the situation.

"Don't worry about me," Meg said, walking towards the door with a spring in her step that hadn't been there when she entered. "I've got errands to run. I'll bring my things back with me later."

After a sound sleep, Isabel awoke in the morning with a clear head and a determination to find out whether Nick worked for the Crown as a spy.

Work.

That was the word Lord Ashbourne had used when he asked about Nick's recovery. She stopped in the midst of washing her face, the water dripping from her hands into the bowl. Was the earl a spy too? It would explain how the two of them had met. It also made sense that someone of his rank was involved with such an important investigation.

After breaking her fast, Isabel walked to Mistress Plunkett's house determined to get some answers out of Nick no matter what it took. She wouldn't allow his joviality, as Lawrence called it, to sidetrack her. If he laughed off her suspicions then she would persist, if he tried to change the subject then she would steer the conversation back on course, and if he tried to woo her with sweet words and his naked body then she would turn her back and block her ears. Well, perhaps nothing so childish as that, but she was prepared to do battle to learn the truth.

She was tired of his deceit. She knew in her humors that his sudden and inquisitive reappearance in her life was somehow linked to his long absences all those years ago when they were first married. This time she would get her answers. Six years ago she had been easier to distract, but not anymore. She wouldn't fall for his charms again.

She frowned as a thought occurred to her. When had he started his career as a spy? Before their marriage? Soon after?

Yes, that must be it. It made sense. He'd changed considerably after the first few blissful months. Coupled with the absences...

A thought tugged at her consciousness but stayed just out of her reach like a teasing sibling.

She shook her head to dislodge it but that only served up a different one. How could she demand he be honest with her if she couldn't be honest with him in return?

And what if he refused to give her an answer unless she first told him why she had left? It was certainly something he would insist upon. She could only hope he wasn't thinking clearly yet after his poisoning ordeal.

Her pace slowed as she drew closer to Bishopsgate Street but she found her feet still propelled her towards Nick like they had a mind of their own. She stopped outside Mistress Plunkett's house and peered up at his third storey window with a sigh. The light tones of a woman's voice drifted down to her. The wind whipped up and whisked some of the words away but Isabel heard her say, "Darling...been killed."

Darling? She stepped back onto the street for a better look but the woman wasn't close enough to the window to be seen. Isabel craned her neck and stepped even further back but a horse ridden too fast on the slippery stones nearly knocked her over so she retreated to the side of the road.

Perhaps it was only Mistress Plunkett up there. Yes, that must be it. But 'Darling'? And the tone had been chiding, familiar, not that of a landlady to her tenant.

The maidservant let Isabel in when she knocked. "Mary, who is upstairs with Sir Nicholas?"

"Mistress Merritt," Mary said taking Isabel's cloak and gloves.

"But I—" am Mistress Merritt she stopped herself from saying. Mistress Plunkett knew Isabel was Nick's wife but she'd apparently not passed the information onto her maid. Isabel frowned, momentarily struck dumb as all sorts of wild (and illegal) scenarios filled her head. But when reason prevailed, she realized the only other Mistress Merritt she knew of was Constance. His mother.

"I see," she said bleakly. Those wild scenarios were looking more appealing.

Mary stood aside but Isabel didn't move. The same feet that couldn't wait to see Nick now didn't want to go anywhere near him. Or, more to the point, anywhere near the woman with him.

"Perhaps I'll come back later." She spun on her heel and strode to the door.

"Your cloak and gloves!" Mary called after her.

"Oh, yes, of course." She turned back to take them but froze when a black shadow emerged at the top of the stairs. Isabel handed her cloak and gloves back to Mary. Fleeing now would only look cowardly and that was not how she wanted to appear in front of Constance Merritt.

Her mother-in-law, dressed in a widow's black velvet gown and severe black hood in the Spanish style covering her hair, descended the stairs as if they were her own at Lyle Hall and she were the queen herself.

Mary drew in a gasp and bowed as if before royalty. Isabel couldn't blame the girl. A tall and sturdily constructed woman, Constance was an imposing vision in her widow's clothes. Isabel had often felt the same revered dread when the Merritt family matriarch had entered the room, but she was surprised to find that she no longer feared her. Why should she? There was nothing else Constance could do to Isabel now. She'd already done her worst.

Isabel waited at the bottom of the stairs until Constance reached her. But Constance stopped on the last step so she remained towering over Isabel. Her eyes, blue like her son's and yet lacking their warmth and humor, flicked over her daughter-in-law.

"Well," she said in that odd way she had of speaking without moving her jaw, "it seems you have broken your agreement."

The public acknowledgement of not only their prior arrangement but their prior knowledge of each other surprised Isabel. She had expected Constance to pretend to be meeting a stranger, which is exactly what Isabel herself had decided to do. It would serve both of their interests to play the game—Isabel wanted to stay out of Nick's life and Constance wanted to keep her out of it. But then, Mary was the only witness and to Constance, a maidservant wasn't the public. She was nobody.

Isabel could sense Mary's sudden interest in the conversation by her stillness. "Not intentionally," Isabel said. "Nick walked into my shop—"

"Your shop!" Constance's sharp eyebrows forked. "I do believe Master Shawe isn't dead yet."

"No, that's not what I meant, I—"

"Nor is his son," Constance added before Isabel had finished, "who will inherit the business. Not you."

"Lawrence is a physician not an—"

"Lawrence is it?" Constance peered down her beaked nose at Isabel. "Rather impertinent to address a man of his standing by his first name, don't you think?"

"I find it easily differentiates between the father and son," Isabel said, her own jaw tightening as she tried to keep her temper in check. "And Lawrence doesn't seem to mind."

"I'm sure he doesn't," Constance said under her breath.

"If you're implying—"

"Oh dear, now this is rather awkward," said Mistress Plunkett emerging from her parlor like a rabbit from its hole. Her gaze darted from Constance to Isabel and back again, probably wondering how to handle the odd situation of mother-in-law seeing daughter-in-law after six years estrangement. "Mistress Merritt the elder," she said to Isabel, "arrived this morning and will be staying in my guest rooms until Sir Nicholas is recovered." She cleared her throat. "Isn't that lovely?"

The warmth of the fire drifted out of the parlor and swelled around Isabel, but it wasn't enough to melt the ice that had settled into her bones at the first sight of Constance. "Lovely," she echoed.

"And, she didn't even know of Sir Nicholas's predicament until her arrival, did you Mistress Merritt? What a shock for you, poor thing." Mistress Plunkett clasped her hands, prayer-like, and faced Isabel. "She'd already decided to come to London to visit him, but to be greeted by this calamity...what a trial." She shook her head. "And, ah, Isabel here," she said to Constance, "cured your son."

"He's not completely cured yet," Constance said.

"Which is why I've stopped by this morning," Isabel said through a forced smile. "To check on his recovery." She moved towards the stairs but Constance blocked her way.

"I've sent for a doctor," she said. "He'll ensure Nicholas receives the correct cure."

"He has received—"

"The doctor will also monitor my son's recovery. So you see you're no longer required here. Good day." Constance remained an impenetrable wall on the stairs, looking remarkably like a witch from the old verses in her black widow's clothes and fearsome expression.

The irony made Isabel smirk despite her seething anger and that clearly rankled Constance even more. Her back stiffened, her forehead grew heavier and she looked like one of the angry bears in the baiting ring ready to lunge. Isabel's smile broadened. It wasn't intentional, it just seemed to happen.

"Good day," she said, taking her cloak and gloves from Mary again and heading for the front door. Constance followed a nervous looking Mistress Plunkett to the parlor but instead of entering, she stopped and pretended to admire a small tapestry hanging on the wall. It seemed the old crow wanted to make sure her daughter-in-law left.

Mary, having followed Isabel, looked from one to the other with a confused frown.

"Never mind, Mary," Isabel said quietly so Constance couldn't hear. "It's a long and complicated story. Can you tell Sir Nicholas that—" What? That she had been turned away by his own mother? That would only lead to questions she didn't want to answer. "Nothing. Pretend I was never here."

On the walk back to the shop, Isabel tried to suppress the unease rising within her. But by the time she reached Bucklersbury the unease had turned to dread. In Constance's eyes, Isabel had broken her promise. She was back in Nick's life after walking out of it at his mother's urging. No, not urging, insistence. Constance had made Isabel promise to never see him again, and clearly that was no longer the case. It didn't matter that Fortune had played a major hand in their reunion.

Constance would never see it that way. She wouldn't want to. And Isabel was in no doubt that her mother-in-law would exact payment for the broken promise in the most terrible way she knew how.

She would tell Nick why Isabel left.

She would tell him about the witchcraft and the uncontrollable powers that had nearly killed his mother six years ago after the two women argued. She would remind him that Isabel would taint his reputation and worse, her witch blood would infect the family line. Their daughters would be witches in the eyes of the law and God. Constance would ensure Nick hated and feared his wife and then she would renew her endeavor to have him abandon her.

Isabel expected nothing less.

She felt sick to her core. She stopped and rested against a post outside St Mary Woolchurch to catch her breath because it seemed to have suddenly left her. Her vision blurred as tears welled and she gripped the post to steady herself. Damn her ill luck. No, damn interfering mothers-in-law.

She didn't expect Nick to stand up for her against the old crow. He was a clever man. He knew the way of the world—that a man's duty was to his family name and lands first—and he would see that his mother was right. Being married to a witch would only bring the wrath of the queen's representatives down on himself. If he insisted Isabel remain his wife then he could lose everything—his lands, his knighthood and his position at court.

And he wouldn't be the only one to suffer. His younger sister would not be able to secure a good marriage, his servants and tenants would lose their generous master and possibly even their employment and farms. A lot of lives and livelihoods depended on Nick.

He was not a man that let people down.

Isabel forced herself to continue on to the shop. The cold wind bit into her skin, numbing her face but unfortunately not her mind. She couldn't stop the terrible, insidious thoughts about her bleak future. Bleak only if she allowed Constance to ruin it. In the end she came to a conclusion—there was only one way to circumvent the ruination of both her life and Nick's.

Flee.

The idea pecked at her as she opened the door. She greeted Fox and his customer, a woman whose name escaped her, as if the day was like any other. She told Fox to keep serving while she checked their supplies in the storeroom.

But instead of checking the stock, she sat on a barrel and thought through what she needed to do for her flight from London. She would need to pack and organize someone to take care of Old Man Shawe then tell Lawrence and Fox she would not be returning. What reason would she give? Something...she would think of something.

Meg would worry, so she would need to be told too. Perhaps her friend would come with her now she was also at a loose end. They could go...

Where? The question struck Isabel like a blunt axe. She had nowhere to go. She had no family, no money, no friends outside of London. She was all alone, even worse off than the first time she left Nick. Back then she had the name of someone who might help, Shawe, and a place, Bucklersbury Street in London.

But it was all different now. She doubted anyone in her hometown of Winchester would remember her, let alone care. Her parents were gone, their friends were old and unlikely to help a girl who had left her husband.

She had seen what happened to women like her, women with no one to take them in. They became whores or beggars or worked as washerwomen for barely enough money to feed themselves. They worked until their muscles screamed in agony and their fingers were nothing but bloody stubs. They suffered the insults of the respectable married women and the lurid advances of the men. No one wanted to help them, no one cared if they went without food or shelter or if their clothes were riddled with fleas and their bodies riddled with disease. Eventually, through the constant grind to stay alive, they lost the will to live. If they were lucky and someone knew their name, they were buried in a marked grave on consecrated ground. But that was rare for a woman with no husband, no family, no friends.

Most simply faded into the mists, not a thought spared for them, not a memory wasted.

The horror of Isabel's future stretched before her.

Damn Constance! The heartless, conniving, ruthless crow! Isabel swiped at a tear then jumped off the barrel and kicked a jar. It slammed against another earthen jar, smashing them both into the wall with a loud crash. She'd forgotten how destructive her temper could be. It was the reason she hadn't lost it since that day six years ago. That awful, cursed day when everything had gone wrong and her life had changed forever.

The jars' contents scattered amongst the pottery shards, the scents rising above the others in the small room. Isabel bent to clean up the mess. She picked up the dried leaves but they disintegrated in her hands, making an even bigger mess on the floor. She stared at the untidy room, willing it to be clean but it seemed her powers, her damned powers that had got her into so much trouble in the first place, didn't extend to neatness.

Suddenly the mess seemed insurmountable, like a huge mountain she had to climb. She knelt amongst the herbs and broken jars and burst into tears.

CHAPTER 10

he physician's hands were cold and he smelled faintly of vinegar. Isabel's hands were never cold and she always smelled delicious.

It wasn't Dr. Kendall's fault that Nicholas didn't listen to a word he said—he was probably an excellent doctor—it was more that Nicholas couldn't get his mind off Isabel. She should have returned to check on him that morning but according to his mother, Isabel had sent word that she would not. It had left him with a sense of hollowness that he couldn't banish.

The arrival of his mother had been the other surprise for the morning. It seemed she had left their estate in Kent the moment she received his message to send Isabel's belongings. He was pleased to see her—perhaps she could convince Isabel to tell him why she had left. And also to return.

But he was beginning to have doubts that his mother would co-operate. She didn't seem all that eager to visit Isabel, even after he told her she had saved his life.

"You're lying in bed looking paler than a ghost," she had said in her typically stoic way. "She has not cured you. I'll send for a physician."

And she had. But Dr. Kendall had said nothing Nicholas didn't already know from Isabel herself. In fact, the physician even asked Mary to fetch a tonic from Shawe the apothecary until Nicholas showed him the bottle Isabel had left.

"It seems there is nothing more I can do for your son, Mistress Merritt," the doctor said, packing his instruments into his bag. His mother paid him and he bid them both good day with a nod.

"See," Nicholas couldn't resist saying when the doctor had left, "I told you she was a very capable apothecary."

"She's not an apothecary," she said from the foot of his bed.

"She's as good, if not better, than most."

"And yet she is not an apothecary. She is a shop girl."

It seemed his mother would never accept the fact that Isabel had made a life for herself here in London. A life that didn't involve her son, a life that didn't need him.

The thought caught him off guard. He felt dizzy, nauseous, as if the effects of the poison hadn't entirely worn off. But it wasn't the poison that made his heart clench, it was the realization that Isabel had moved on. Over the last few days he had been hoping she would tell him why she had left so he could fix it and get her back, when all along he hadn't considered that she didn't want it fixed.

That she didn't want to come back.

"What is it?" his mother asked, sitting on the edge of the bed, leaning over him with a deeply furrowed brow. "Are you going to be sick? Shall I call Dr. Kendall back?"

He waved her away. "No. Just...send for Isabel."

The black velvet of her gown shushed ever so softly as she stiffened. "The doctor—"

"Forget about the doctor! I need to see Isabel." He rubbed a hand through his hair in an attempt to calm his frayed temper. "She should have been here this morning. It's not like her to break a promise."

"Do I need to remind you that she broke a very big one?" She flicked dirt or lint or perhaps nothing at all off the bedcovers.

"That's different." But his denial sounded as hollow as he felt.

His mother stopped her fussing and placed her hand over his. "She's changed hasn't she? Hasn't she, Nicholas?" she urged when he didn't answer.

He shrugged. "She's still the same underneath. Still kind, considerate—"

"Kind! Considerate!" She snorted. "You think a woman who leaves her husband is kind and considerate?"

He looked down at their hands. "I'm sure she had a good reason," he added quickly.

"A good reason? What reason could be good enough to humiliate you in front of everyone? Not just your family and friends, but also your servants and tenants! What she did to you was an outrage, an abomination against God."

"Mother," he said on a sigh, "we've been through this." Many, many times over the years. Whenever he spoke to her about renewing his search for Isabel, his mother had urged him to abandon it for good. He supposed that as a mother she was angered on his behalf and that she felt hurt to see her son so distraught. It explained why she couldn't forgive Isabel, and why she didn't want Isabel back in their lives—she must be afraid she would hurt him again. It was a valid reaction under the circumstances.

"Perhaps you can help," he said, sitting up. "Isabel might open up to you about her reasons for leaving. Then you could tell me and I could fix it."

"I doubt she'd speak to me," she said, her voice low and ominous. "Besides, I won't attempt to speak to that wretched girl."

"Mother—!"

"And nor should you, Nicholas. As I told you from the start, you're best to be rid of the scheming little whore."

His head jerked to the side as if she'd slapped him. It took him a moment for his wits to gather and his body to react, but when they did, he went cold, like he'd fallen into a frozen lake. But instead of being numbed by the ice, he felt invigorated for the first time since the poisoning. He gripped his mother's arms and shook her until she looked him in the eye. "That's enough!" He barely recognized the harsh, raw voice as his own. "You will never call Isabel that to my face again. Now get out."

When he let go, she rubbed her arm then let her hand drop to her side. He turned away, too disgusted to look at her.

"Listen to me," she said. When he didn't look at her, she caught the side of his face, forcing him to turn his head. "I am your mother. I only want what is best for you. I know what is best for you." Her eyes glistened with unshed tears, catching him off guard. His mother never cried. Not even when Father had died. "Seek an annulment."

He moved away so that her hands were left holding nothing but air in a supplicating gesture. "No," he said.

"You don't understand. You're not seeing things as clearly as I am. She will only undermine everything you have achieved since she left. Your knighthood, the expansion of your landhold-ings, your rising position at court—it will all be ruined if you do not cut yourself free from her."

He frowned, shaking his head, partly because he didn't know this woman anymore and partly because he was honestly confused by her remark. "Why would she do that?"

"Because she humiliated you once, she will do it again. If you do convince her to return with you, how can you be sure she will stay this time?"

"I..." He didn't know. Damn it, another point he hadn't considered because he'd been too preoccupied with getting Isabel back. "If I can fix what is wrong, then she will stay."

His mother shook her head. "Don't you see? She likes it here. She likes being an apothecary's assistant. She likes to associate with the filth of London's streets."

"Filth? Mother, what are you talking about?"

"Her customers, her friends, are whores, Nicholas."

"How do you know?" he asked, already knowing the answer anyway. How could he not—he was his mother's son after all.

"When I received your letter, I learned what I could about her life here. It was the least I could do to protect you from yourself."

"Myself?"

"Yes." She set her jaw as if ready for a battle of words and wills. "I knew you would try to woo her again once you found her. I sensed it from your letter. But I also knew that would be the worst thing for you to do. Nicholas, listen to me." She clutched his hands and brought them to her lips. "Listen to my reason. I am your mother. I would never do anything to harm you. But she—"

He pulled his hands away. "She is the only woman who could make me happy. Even if Isabel doesn't come back to me, I won't get an annulment because I don't wish to be married to anyone else."

She sat as stiff as a fence post, blinking back at him as if he had said something so incredible she couldn't possibly comprehend it. "But your future and the future of the Merritt family depends on you begetting legitimate children! You must remarry. You must find a woman who will have you. There are many suitable—"

"Don't." The word rumbled from deep within him, bubbling to the surface along with uncontrollable vibrations that racked his body.

"You're shaking," she said, reaching for him.

"Leave." He turned his face away so he didn't see the righteous indignation he knew would be imprinted there.

A moment later the door closed softly behind her swishing skirts and he closed his eyes. His ragged breathing and the wild thumping of his heart filled his ears, drowning out the crackle of the fire. He lay against the pillows and slowly became aware of the smell of the burning wood and clean rushes, the shouts of shopkeepers and children playing outside, the cracks of the carter's whips as they drove their drays along Bishopsgate Street. Finally his anger dissolved, replaced by a renewed determination to get better so he could speak to Isabel. The issue of her departure was going to be resolved once and for all.

But that could be too long. He needed to see her immediately.

He called for Mary and the maidservant came running. "I want a message sent to Isabel at Shawe's apothecary at once. Tell her I need to talk to her. Urgently," he added.

Mary bobbed. "Very well." She began to close the door but stopped. "It's a pity she didn't come up when she was here before. Could've saved herself another walk."

"What?" Nicholas sprang out of bed but regretted the swift movement when dizziness swamped him. He gripped the bedpost to steady himself. "When was she here? Why didn't you show her up?"

Mary looked alarmed and he apologized for his vehemence. "Mistress Merritt, er Camm, came by this morning," she said, lowering her eyes, "but left when Mistress Merritt, your mother, told her she'd sent for Dr. Kendall."

"Mother?" Nicholas shook his head, unable to believe what he was hearing. "Mother saw Isabel? Today?"

Mary blinked. "Yes. Downstairs. Mistress Plunkett was there too if you don't believe me."

"I believe you. Thank you, Mary."

She nodded and lowered her eyes again to his legs.

He looked down and saw he wasn't wearing any hose, just his shirt which stopped above the knee. "And Mary?"

"Mmmm? I mean, yes, Sir Nicholas?" She looked up again and met his gaze, her cheeks aflame.

"Please send my message to Isabel immediately."

"Yes, Sir." She left and closed the door behind her.

Nicholas sat on the bed, feeling as though he'd run the entire length of London. It was as if he couldn't get enough air into his body. He wondered if it was a lingering symptom of the poisoning or the shocking news of his own mother's lies.

Damn it, Mother, you're not helping.

There was no point calling for her. She had already made it clear what she thought of Isabel. Her lying to him about Isabel's visit reinforced her view. Her plea to his sense of duty hammered it home.

Well, to Hell with his duty. He'd fulfilled his obligations as best he could. He'd built on his father's fortune and extended the family's influence into the deepest inner sanctums at court. He'd done his duty to his family name because he'd had nothing else to do in the last six years. Now it was time to do his duty to his wife.

He lay down on the bed with a loud sigh and closed his eyes. How much damage had his mother's antics done to his fresh relationship with Isabel? And was he too late to mend it or had the single, weak thread that he'd been trying to strengthen these last few days been severed forever?

* * *

WHEN THE BITTER cold wind blew into the shop as the door opened, the hairs on the back of Isabel's neck rose in response. She looked up and wished she'd stayed out back with only the jars of herbs and her thoughts for companions. They would have been better company than the woman who'd entered the shop.

"Constance," she said. "I assume this isn't a social call."

Constance didn't answer immediately. Instead she looked around, her sharp, all-seeing gaze taking in the counter, the jars, the books and finally Isabel. She wrinkled her nose, but whether at the smell the shop always emanated (a delicious blend of the herbs cut, boiled or distilled that day) or at her daughter-in-law's presence, Isabel couldn't tell. Constance drew herself up to her formidable height and held her head high. A challenging stance, ready for battle. Well, Isabel was ready too. She'd had her cry, vented her frustrations at this new setback, and now she had to face her demons—demon—head on.

But the last thing she would do, the very last thing she would ever tell this woman, was that she had won and Isabel was going to leave Nick. Again. It may be the truth but she couldn't abide seeing the triumph in Constance's eyes when she told her. So, she simply would not tell her.

"I wanted to ensure you weren't going to do something foolish," Constance said.

"Foolish?" Isabel cocked her head to the side. "You mean visit Nick again?"

"I mean stay in London." She wandered idly to the bookshelves and inspected the tomes without picking them up. "You understood me earlier, did you not? If you see my son again I will report your...peculiarity to the authorities. I'm sure the news will intrigue them."

Isabel shivered as a chill seeped into her bones. Partly to stall for time to collect herself and partly to warm up, she walked slowly to the fire. She stretched out her hands to the flames then turned around to feel the heat on her back. When she felt more composed, her temper under control, her gaze slowly rose to look at Constance standing on the other side of the room, one knife-sharp brow raised as she waited.

"I understood you perfectly," Isabel said, trying hard to keep her voice steady.

"Good. You see, now that he knows where to find you, it's not possible for you to remain here and keep your part of our agreement."

"I said," Isabel said through a tight jaw, "I understand. Now, unless there is anything else, you may go."

Constance prowled around the shop as if she hadn't heard her, looking more like a crow than ever with a stern hood covering most of her gray streaked hair and her hard eyes taking in everything over a beakish nose. "Your marriage will be annulled," she finally said.

"I see." Isabel expected as much but hearing it spoken by this grim-faced woman made her believe it more. She'd lived six years beneath the specter of an annulment—thinking Nick had got one—but it had never seemed as real as it did now. "Then you will have what you want. I will be out of Nick's life. However, if you want my advice, you should treat his next wife more like one of the family if you want her to dutifully bear his heirs then fade into the background like an old piece of furniture."

Constance's lips flattened, hardening her jaw line. "Your kind could never have belonged to our family. My son made a mistake marrying you."

"My kind?" Isabel's fists clenched at her sides. She must control her anger or the consequences could be fatal. She almost didn't care—and that scared her. "Are you talking about my...female inheritance or my family's lack of fortune and status?"

"I will not be drawn into the particulars," Constance said. "But you are a scheming, greedy girl who will do anything to further herself."

The accusation was so far off the truth Isabel almost laughed. She crossed her arms over her chest and fixed Constance with a level, sure gaze. "I fell in love with your son," she said, "and he fell in love with me. And that bothers you more than anything, doesn't it? You can't abide having him love someone else. You would rather see him unhappy than see him with me."

"Love?" Constance snorted. "This has nothing to do with such a frivolous, common notion. But I do wonder how you can speak of love for Nicholas after what you did to tear his beloved family apart."

Isabel frowned, slowly dropping her hands to her sides. "What are you talking about?"

Constance scoffed. "Do not play the innocent with me, girl. You know very well what you did."

"Uh, no, I don't. Please remind me."

"You used your powers against my husband and my son, my oldest son, so that Nicholas would inherit everything, therefore making you lady of Lyle Hall with all the Merritt wealth at your fingertips."

Isabel's insides plunged. Good Lord, Constance thought she had killed them!

Perhaps she shouldn't have been so shocked at the accusation —part of her had always thought her mother-in-law suspected her of being involved in their deaths. Even so, hearing it so baldly put made Isabel want to retch. "But I was nowhere near them at the time of their accidents."

Constance shrugged. "Your powers must work from afar."

"No, they don't."

"I don't believe you."

"I'm sure you don't." Isabel had often thought her mother-in-law's fear of her powers lay at the heart of the matter, particularly her fear that Isabel had murdered the elder two Merritt men. In a way, bringing the accusations into the open after so many years of speculating was quite liberating. At least Isabel could defend herself properly against such ridiculous claims now she knew for sure what they were.

"And another thing," Isabel went on, "if I was after Nick for his money, then why did I not lavish riches on myself when he inherited? If you even bothered to notice, you would have seen that I wore simple clothing and that I don't like elaborate jewelry. I didn't even like being called mistress of the house. That title firmly belonged to you."

"And still does, despite your efforts."

Isabel sighed. There were just some battles that would never be won, some minds that could never be changed, no matter how much logic was employed. It was a waste of breath to try. "Believe what you will, but I did not murder your husband or son. I'm a healer, I abhor violence of any kind."

"Liar! You nearly killed me!"

Isabel pursed her lips, feeling her patience unraveling thread by thread. "That was an accident. My powers were new and I had not yet learned to control them."

"And what of Nicholas's current illness? What do you have to say about that?"

Isabel gasped and stared open-mouthed at Constance. "My God, do you honestly think I tried to poison him?"

"It is a coincidence that you see him again after six years and he suddenly falls terribly ill."

"But I healed him!"

"So you say."

Isabel shook her head, unable to believe what she was hearing. To think that she would have put anyone through what Nick had gone through—the piercing pains, the dizziness and violent retching. Didn't Constance see that her son would have died if not for her? Didn't she know what a horrible, cruel death that would have been? "Is that the sort of person you think I am? That I would do that to the man I love?"

Constance snorted. "Of course you would if it meant inheriting the portion due you as his widow. You've already proved what you are capable of doing."

Isabel continued to shake her head. To battle onwards in the face of such willful misunderstanding and ignorance was a waste of effort. She would never change the old crow's opinion on the subject no matter how much she argued with her, no matter how much evidence she presented to the contrary.

"Believe what you will," Isabel said, suddenly feeling too tired to have a conversation with anyone let alone with her crow-in-law. "But I have nothing on my conscience."

"Except that you are a witch."

Except that. Always that. Isabel dropped her gaze and drew

in several deep breaths. After a few moments, the calming scents inside the shop eased her temper and she raised her gaze again. "I think you should leave now." She was surprised at how gently the words came out, despite the turmoil churning within her.

"Do I have your word that you will leave London?"

Isabel strode past Constance to the front door and opened it. The wind wrestled with her skirts and lifted the rushes nearest the entrance. A few sharp needles of rain splashed on her cheek and the hand that held the door open. "I can no longer give you my word."

An elderly woman, hunched over a walking stick, her cloak covering a stooped frame, thanked her for opening the door as she bustled as fast as her crippled body would take her into the warm shop. She bypassed Constance and made straight for the fire where she stretched her gloved fingers towards the coals.

"Well," Constance said, surprise softening her features and her tone. "Then you leave me no choice. I will tell my son everything." She swept past Isabel but stopped in the doorway and looked back, perhaps waiting for her daughter-in-law to change her mind.

Isabel held her gaze, not even blinking. "Then go ahead and tell him." She closed the door in her face and turned to the customer.

CHAPTER 11

*I*f pacing his bedchamber didn't make his head feel like it was spinning out of control, Nicholas would have worn a path through the rushes. Instead he had to sit up in bed, drumming his fingers against his knee as he willed the door to open. If Mary didn't bring a message from Isabel soon—or even better, bring Isabel herself—then he would just have to ignore the nausea and go to Buckerlsbury Street himself.

When the door finally opened he stopped drumming. "Well, it's about time," he said, already half out of bed.

"Time for what, Son?"

Nicholas lay back against the pillows with a heavy sigh at the sight of his mother. He rubbed his temples as another headache brewed and his frustration rose. "What do you want? Another swipe at Isabel?"

She didn't answer immediately but hesitated at the side of his bed, watching him, her eyes unusually soft and her face slack with weariness. For her to be anything other than sharp and alert meant something must be wrong.

"What is it, Mother? What has happened?"

She opened her mouth but shut it again and exhaled a long breath through her nose. "Nicholas, there is something I must tell you. And it's not going to be easy for you to hear."

"It's Isabel, isn't it?" Panic made his heart race and his voice shake. "I sent her a message this morning and I've heard nothing since. Is she all right? What's happened to her?"

She held her hand up and he obeyed with silence but very little patience. "She is not ill or anything of that sort." She sounded irritated, as if Isabel's wellbeing shouldn't have been his first thought. "Your message never reached her."

"What? Why not? I gave Mary precise instructions—" He stopped at the subtle lowering of his mother's gaze. Experienced in the ways of liars, he guessed what must have transpired earlier. "You intercepted Mary, didn't you? Isabel never received my message because Mary never sent it." Not willing to condemn his mother if she was innocent, he tried to keep the accusation out of his tone but it wasn't easy. He knew her answer before she gave it. Knew deep in his soul that his mother had betrayed him.

"I told the maidservant I would take the message to Mistress Camm."

"Her name is Isabel to you, Mother. She is your daughter-in-law and always will be so call her by her given name."

A muscle in her cheek jumped. "Do not judge me until you know everything. I admit I intercepted the message, but I had good reason. Your wife is a witch."

He frowned, studying her closely for any sign that she had gone insane and should be carted off to Bedlam. But apart from her statement, she seemed perfectly rational. Not even an eye twitch. So he did the first thing that came into his head. He burst out laughing.

"Isabel? A witch? Good Lord, Mother, that is taking your prejudice against her a little too far. She is no more a witch than you or I. Although you do seem to dress the part these days," he added, still chuckling.

She smoothed down her skirts and lifted her nose even further in the air. "Do not insult me."

"I'm sorry," he said, suddenly turning serious, "but after all the insults you have laid on my wife, you should expect some in return. So tell me, what has Isabel being a witch got to do with you intercepting my message?"

Her fingers stilled and flattened against her skirts. "I needed to speak to her before she returned here. You see, she broke our agreement. An agreement we struck six years ago when she nearly killed me with her witchcraft."

"Nearly killed you? With her witchcraft?" Six years ago. When everything changed and his world fell apart. Six years... Anger surged, propelling him forward. He grabbed her by the shoulders, his fingers digging into the padded sleeves. "Mother, what are you talking about?"

Her eyes widened in alarm and he let go. "Her mother was a witch too," she said, as if that were a reasonable defense.

"Go on," he whispered, hardly breathing.

"Isabel and I were arguing one day and—."

"What about?"

She shrugged. "I can't recall and it doesn't matter now. The point is, she lost her temper and then I felt someone shove me very hard in the chest. I tumbled backwards into the wall. Isabel hadn't even touched me."

From his limited knowledge of witchcraft, it certainly sounded like something a witch could do. "How do you know it was her?"

"She admitted it. She apologized and told me she might have caused it to happen."

"Might have?" His own temper rose as the blood pumped loudly between his ears. "Did she or didn't she use her powers?"

Again she shrugged. "She says her powers were new and as such uncontrollable."

"There, you see? It wasn't intentional."

"She is a witch, Nicholas! That fact alone is the issue. Imagine what would have happened if she hadn't been discovered until months or even years later! Imagine if someone other than me had been the focus of her temper that day. Good Lord, everything would have come undone. Everything."

He shook his head, not quite comprehending what she was saying and still not believing what he was hearing. Isabel a witch? Why had she never told him? "Everything? Like what?"

She threw her hands up, more spirited than he had seen her in a long time. "Our family would have become outcasts, our name forever sullied and tainted by the disease of witchcraft. No one would want to know us or conduct business with us. Your sister would never have married Lord Bute, you would never have become friends with Lord Ashbourne. And worse—all the Merritts born of Isabel's womb, and their children, and their children, would have witch blood in them. Unholy abominations for eternity."

"You've really thought this through, haven't you?" He huffed out a laugh although he'd lost his sense of humor some time ago.

She blinked at him. "You don't seem concerned by what I've told you."

He shrugged. "She is still just Isabel to me."

She leaned forward and placed a hand on his arm. "Son. My dearest boy." She spoke softly, earnestly. "You have been duped by a wicked woman who only married you for your money."

He scoffed. "Don't be ridiculous." That accusation was even more far fetched than the last one. It didn't even need a vehement denial because he knew his mother couldn't honestly believe it herself. There was absolutely no indication that Isabel had married him for money. At the time of their wedding he was still only the second son and not entitled to anything except a small annuity.

He moved away, leaving her fingers caressing nothing but air. Her lips pinched into a thin line. "I didn't want to tell you this, but now I must. She used her witchcraft to kill your father and brother so that you would inherit and now she has tried to kill you too—"

"Enough!" He threw back the covers and got out of bed. Dizziness flooded him and he leaned against the bedpost to steady himself. "You have said enough, Mother." Despite his hard breathing, he sounded almost normal. "Isabel had nothing to do with the accidents because she was with me when they happened."

"She doesn't need to be present to use her powers."

He couldn't be sure about that, but he could be sure about Isabel. She was innocent. "And she certainly wouldn't poison me. I know it."

"How? How could you possibly be sure she didn't hire someone—"

"Because I know it in here." He grabbed his shirt over his heart and tugged on the sweat-soaked linen, almost ripping it from his body in his anger.

"Don't be so dramatic, Nicholas," she said with a wave of her hand. "You can't possibly know—"

"I do," he said. "But there is just one more thing I want you to tell me before you leave this house, this city, forever."

She swallowed, her skin paling as she must have realized he meant what he said.

"Tell me what happened after the incident," he said. "What did you say to Isabel to make her leave Lyle Hall without a word of goodbye?" This was at the heart of everything that had torn him apart over the last six years. He ached to know and held his breath as she considered her answer. "Well?" he prompted, leaning heavily into the bedpost in an attempt to hold himself up.

"Does it matter now?" she snapped.

"It matters. It matters very much."

She stood, her back straight, her head tilted in defiance. "I told her I would tell you and the authorities what she was unless she left Lyle Hall for good."

So Isabel had left without seeking his opinion or his confidence. She had believed he didn't love her enough to accept her as a witch. Disappointment momentarily displaced his anger until he remembered how young she had been, not only in age but experience of the world. She would have been frightened and alone, so very much alone because he had been away on a mission.

He had not been there for her.

Unable to stand any longer he sat on the bed and rested his elbows on his knees. He lowered his head, too heavy to keep up, and pushed his fingers through his hair. Damn it, he was her husband and he'd failed her. Failed her terribly. He deserved every second of the misery he'd endured over the last six years. How could he ever expect her forgiveness? How could he ever make it right?

He looked up. His mother's hand hovered only a few inches

away but it quickly dropped to her side and she turned her face away, but not before he saw the tears in her eyes.

He didn't have it in his heart to forgive her. Not yet.

"No doubt your agreement with Isabel was that she could not tell anyone where she was going, least of all me, and that she could not contact me ever again. Am I right?"

She nodded but still didn't turn to look at him.

Anger bubbled to the surface again, more controlled but no less forceful. "You didn't even give her any money," he said bitterly.

"I did!" She spun round, her eyes blazing not with tears but with hurt nevertheless. "Do you think me as cruel as that? I offered money and I told her she could keep her own jewels but when I went through her rooms the next day, her things were all still there." She licked her top lip. "I thought..."

"What?"

"I thought she wouldn't be needing them. That she had taken her own life."

A fresh wave of nausea gripped him and he pressed a hand to his stomach and closed his eyes to wait it out. Isabel would never have chosen that option. The nausea vanished and he reopened his eyes to look at the woman who had caused him so much pain.

"And all this so I would annul the marriage," he said, incredulous.

"I would never have urged that upon you if your wife had been normal instead of...what she is."

"I bet it has eaten you up inside that I have refused to do it these last six years," he went on as if she'd said nothing. "Just as I refuse now."

"Nicholas," she said in a soothing voice as she knelt before him, "what I have done I did for you."

He stood and pushed past her, not bothering to address any of her drivel. Let her spout about honor and duty for as long as she wanted. He was done with that now. He only wanted to see Isabel. To hold her and tell her he loved her even if she had horns and a tail. Oh God, he had been a fool. A stupid fool and he was going to make it all up to her. Starting with slow, meaningful love-making. Then he would take her away from all this. Perhaps a few months by the sea then they would find a new home, just themselves. His mother and sister could keep Lyle Hall. He didn't want it with them in it.

"In time you will see that I only want what is best for you," she was saying from somewhere behind him as he changed his shirt. "You must understand—"

"Mother," he said, pulling the shirt over his head, "I no longer wish to see you."

She gasped. "But—"

"I don't care if you stay here in London, return to Lyle Hall or whatever. Just leave this house and don't come near either myself or Isabel again. I will contact you if I ever want anything from you. Do you understand?"

"But..." Her protest died. She tilted her head. Her jaw was set hard and her glare was even harder as she watched him pull on his doublet and jerkin. She stood like a burnt and blackened tree stump in a fire-ravished forest, bleak and alone but defiant to the end.

* * *

ISABEL COULDN'T KEEP the new lightness out of her heart. She served customers with a smile, chatted freely with them about current events and even did some of Fox's chores for him when he failed to do them properly the first time. Earlier that day she couldn't do anything without bursting into tears or cursing Constance, God and everyone else who'd had a hand in her fate.

It wasn't that Isabel felt happy now. How could she knowing Nick was about to learn she was a witch? He might know already. He might at that moment think her an evil shrew and be thanking his good fortune that he was rid of her. The authorities might also have been alerted already. That thought alone dampened her spirits somewhat. But, all things considered, she felt a sense of freedom she hadn't felt in some time.

Freedom came with the truth. She had nothing to hide from Nick anymore. He knew her very worst, darkest secret.

Freedom, and a newfound sense of her own strength, also

came with her defiance of Constance. Isabel would not leave London. She would not leave her home, her friends or work because Constance wanted it. No, she had been driven away by her once, she would not be again. She would stay and fight and face the consequences.

The only real consequence that mattered now was that Nick would rush through an annulment. His smooth words and tender caresses would be forgotten as he no doubt couldn't wait to cut ties with her. Her heart lurched, tightened.

She would never see him again except perhaps as part of his investigation, if indeed he was a spy. Somehow that seemed not to matter anymore. She was innocent but if he now believed her guilty then she would find some way of fighting the charges. And if she failed in that, then so be it. She could face death because she had nothing to feel ashamed of in her life. She had always done what she thought to be right. Besides, she had not chosen to be a witch—surely that counted for something in the Afterlife.

It seemed fitting that she was thinking of Hell when the door opened and Nick stumbled in looking like he'd just risen from there. Startled, Isabel quickly turned to her customer and tried to recall whether comfrey should be mixed with marigold or mallow to make up a poultice for cuts.

"Isabel," Nick said, wiping the back of his hand across his top lip, "I must speak with you."

"Wait your turn," the customer snapped, her heavily made-up eyes raking over him. "I'd ask him to leave if I was you, Mistress Camm, he's dripping sweat all over your nice clean rushes."

"Uh, perhaps you should take a seat," Isabel said to Nick. She indicated the stool but he shook his head and opened his mouth to speak. "I'll be finished here in a moment," she added before he could say anything. If he was going to arrest her then he could wait.

The customer accepted her wrapped packages, paid and pulled on her gloves, all the while keeping her fierce gaze firmly on Nick. "Good day," she said politely to Isabel before turning back to him. "Now you may speak." She left, muttering about rude gentlemen and what the world was coming to.

"You have some scary customers," Nick said, watching the woman go. His breathing had calmed and the color had returned to his cheeks but he still looked like a man who'd left his sickbed too soon.

"She's a whore whose specialty is discipline, so Meg tells me. I think it's the scariness that her customers like." He smiled and she swallowed because he looked so beautiful when he was happy. And he was happy. He still looked like he needed more sleep but the new freedom in her heart was reflected in his face.

He approached the counter but instead of stopping on the other side like a customer, he rounded the end and came up to her. "Isabel," he murmured, catching her hands and bringing them to his lips. He kissed her knuckles lightly, his eyes closed, his lips lingering as if savoring the taste of her.

Isabel's insides melted, the tightness around her heart loosened and she blinked back tears. She must not cry. Crying was stupid, childish, and... She tried to wipe her tears away with her shoulder because he still held her hands, and bit her lip because it was the only way to stop it quivering.

Nick opened his eyes and let go of her hands so he could hold her cheeks instead. His thumbs traced the tracks of her tears but the gentle caress only produced more despite her struggle for control.

"Isabel, I'm so sorry," he whispered.

She frowned, shook her head. "What for?"

"Everything. My mother, not knowing, not telling you I'd love you no matter what."

Her breath fled in a loud gasp. "You love me?" It came out weak, shaky—exactly how her knees felt. Her heart on the other hand hammered against her ribcage, bursting to get out.

"Of course." He spoke as if it were never in doubt. "Isabel," he muttered, a smile tweaking the corners of his lips, "you really didn't know?"

She shrugged one shoulder. "I...wasn't quite sure."

"But," he frowned and looked uncertain, "I often told you I loved you."

"All the time," she agreed. "I just never believed it." Because he was never around, he never told her where he was going or what he was doing, and he was an incorrigible flirt with every woman in Kent and beyond. How could she have ever been sure? Especially now when he knew what she was.

"Do you believe it now?"

She nodded, smiling. Yes, she knew. He wouldn't have come to her knowing she was a witch if he didn't truly love her. "Actions speak louder than words," she told him.

His frown deepened. "What does that mean?"

"It means kiss me, Husband."

He grinned. "Your wish is my command, Wife."

Still holding her face, he gently pulled her to him. Their lips touched in kiss after brief kiss. Tasting, testing, teasing. Heat brushed Isabel's skin and coiled round her insides, pooling between her legs. She could stand it no longer. She locked him into a hard, long, fierce kiss, unable to get enough of him, wanting to sink into his warmth and strength, wanting to be devoured by him.

She pressed her body against his and was left in no doubt about his desire for her. His hands dropped from her face to her hips and pulled her in, pinning her to his erection. She reached up and ran her fingers through his hair, dislodging his hat, then caressed down his neck, shoulders and back. His muscles twitched at her touch, flexing with every movement of his body like a finely tuned lute.

A tiny shudder vibrated through him and he held her closer, as if afraid she would slip away. "Isabel," he murmured against her lips. "Let's go upstairs to your room."

"Can't," she said, pulling away, trying to gather her wits. "The shop..."

"There aren't any customers now." He kissed her hard again and she responded by returning it with equal urgency. "Come," he said, tugging her towards the back door, "before I explode. You wouldn't want your customers witnessing that, would you?" His look was all boyish innocence but his tone was that of a man with carnal pleasures on his mind and very little else.

"Most of my customers won't be shocked," she shot back, resisting him. "Nick, no, not yet. Later. I promise."

He groaned. "You're cruel." He kissed her again and she almost pushed him towards the door and up the stairs.

"No more," she said, putting her hands on his chest and trying to ignore the throb of need pulsing through her, "or I'll give in."

"That's the general idea." She held him at arm's length and he smiled at her. "You're beautiful when you're determined."

"And you're just beautiful," she said, unable to stop smiling back.

He crossed his arms and puffed out his chest. "Don't you mean handsome in a rugged and strong way?"

"No, I mean beautiful." She stood on her toes to kiss his pouting lips. "But don't worry, I'd love you no matter what you looked like."

He stared at her, unblinking, his lips slightly parted. "You love me?"

"Yes! I've always loved you. I only left because I..." She swallowed, suddenly wanting to put the past six years behind her and start afresh with him somehow. "I couldn't bear to see you despise me for being a witch."

His fingers brushed the hair at her temple. "Never."

"Well," she cleared her throat as those stupid tears threatened to return, "I didn't know that then."

"Now you do. No matter what. Understand?"

She nodded and gave him a watery smile of reassurance. But she didn't feel completely reassured herself. There was so much yet to consider. Where would they live? She didn't want to go back to Kent, or anywhere near his mother. Indeed, the more she thought about it, the more she wanted to stay working at Shawe's. But what self-respecting knight would allow his wife to do that?

Then there was the question of where he always disappeared to, and whether he was a spy, and if so, was he spying on her even as he burned her with his kisses? She moved away, just a little, and turned to her workbench.

"Nick, we need to talk."

He groaned. "You really are cruel." She said nothing and he must have sensed her unease because he moved up behind her and touched her arm. "What do you want to talk about?" He asked it quietly, reticently, and she glanced up at him to gauge his mood. The boyishness had completely vanished, replaced by hard planes and hooded eyes.

The front door opened and a customer entered. Isabel moved away to greet him and Nicholas breathed a sigh of relief. Talking was the last thing he wanted to do with Isabel because he knew what she wanted to talk about—his absences. If only he could get through these next few days without discussing his spying. All he needed to do was find the traitor, tell Ash he was quitting Walsingham's network then shower Isabel with love and constant devotion until she forgot the subject altogether.

That would happen about the same time man would fly.

He sighed as he watched her, his body aching with need, his fingers still tingling from touching her. She was amazing. The way her soft lips lifted in a smile just for him, brightening her face and making her eyes sparkle with life. She had flushed a pretty rose when he suggested they go upstairs, and he wished he could capture that color forever.

In many ways, she was so unlike the young girl he'd married. She moved around the shop with confident grace, her head high, her smile genuine and free. She chatted to the customer easily, with none of the shyness she'd possessed in her youth. Six years ago, he never thought it possible to love her more but looking at her now, he had to admit he did. He loved her so much his heart ached every moment he wasn't with her.

So he had to be with her. Always. He was serious about ending his spying days. No more missions that sent him away for months. He'd tell Ash the first opportunity he got. But he already knew Ash would insist Nicholas finish the current job. At least it kept him near Isabel.

The customer left and she turned back to Nicholas. He had never seen her eyes so bright, so full of happiness. All for him. He'd put that smile on her face. She loved him. She really did.

He hardened again and he silently cursed his errant body part. "Are you sure we can't go upstairs now?" he asked hopefully.

She grinned and stretched her arms around his waist. Her

breasts crushed against him and he couldn't keep his eyes off the flesh swelling beneath her thin partlet. He wanted to rip the strip of lace off and bury his mouth there, smell her delicious scent and lick the soft, pink flesh until her nipples peaked. God, he wanted to feel her naked so badly.

"As much as I want to, I can't," she said, oblivious to his agony. "Fox is on an errand so there's no one to look after the shop."

"What about when he gets back?"

"No!" She chuckled. "He'll know what's going on. And as much as I want to, I need to maintain some sort of respect with my apprentice. He's wayward enough as it is."

"Want me to beat him up for you?"

She mustn't have realized he was serious because she laughed. "That's very generous of you but not yet. Anyway," she said, stepping back and examining him, taking her luscious breasts with her, "you're not well enough to be beating people up or making love."

"I don't plan on doing it at the same time." He reached for her because he needed to feel her curves again and wanted to see the mounds of her breasts rising and falling with her breathing. "As to the making love part, you'll be gentle with me."

Her eyelids lowered and she stood on her toes to kiss him. "Don't be so sure," she muttered against his lips then plunged her tongue inside his mouth.

She tasted delicious and desire arrowed into his loins. He groaned and she withdrew so he groaned again. He reached for her, wanting her touch and her kiss to go on forever, but she shook her head.

"We need to talk," she said, suddenly efficient. How could she switch off like that? He was still dazed and hard. So much for his distracting techniques. Somehow he'd ended up being the one to forget his plan. He wondered if that had been her plan.

"When you found that note in my herbal from Lord Croxley, you wondered if the latest plot against the queen was in some way linked to my father's situation." She leaned back against the counter and studied a spot on the wall past his shoulder. Why didn't she look at him?

"Yes," he said, wishing he knew where she was leading the conversation so he could head her off. He shrugged. "It was merely a suggestion since the traitor is attempting to embroil you in his scheme. However," he added, glad to be able to discuss Ash's findings without bringing the subject up himself, "I recently discussed my suspicions with Ash."

"Lord Ashbourne?" She paled. "Oh, Nick, why?"

"He's my friend and I trust him." He gripped her shoulders and dipped his head to look in her eyes. She drew her gaze up to his and his heart warmed at the defiance in it. She wasn't going to stand by and watch as the traitor implicated her any more than he was prepared to let it happen.

Perhaps that's why she'd brought up the topic in the first place—two heads were better than one—and it had nothing to do with her suspecting he was a spy.

Wrong, wrong, wrong. She was far too clever not to suspect him.

"And what did Lord Ashbourne have to say?" she asked, crossing her arms.

"He spoke to his friends in the Privy Council for me." He drew in a breath and let it out slowly. "It seems there was a little more to your father's case than you may have been led to believe."

Her hands dropped to her sides. "More? How much more?"

"Before I tell you that, you should know that Ash assured me the man undertaking a crucial part of the investigation wasn't given all of the information I'm about to tell you."

She waved her hand in dismissal. "I don't care what the investigator was privy to, I just want to know what Ash found out. Was Father innocent?" She held out her hands, palms up, then as she waited for his answer, she brought her thumb to her mouth and chewed the nail. "He was, wasn't he?" She threw her hands up. "I knew it."

"Isabel, slow down." He took her hands to still them and rubbed his thumbs along her knuckles. "It's unlikely he was innocent." She tried to pull her hands away but he held them firmly. "But there is more to the case than I—that is, that anyone —at first thought."

148

He told her about the conference between her father and the three men whose signature cures he had debunked in his last book. "One was named Finch, he's now deceased, another was Pullman—"

"Pullman!" Her eyes widened. "It must be him! He's a scoundrel, a cheat—"

"And Lawrence Shawe," he said above her fuming.

"Lawrence?" She frowned then must have realized he meant Lawrence Senior because she gripped the bench to steady herself. Nicholas pulled the stool over and guided her to sit down. "He was there? Are you sure?"

He nodded. "Quite sure. He never mentioned it?"

She shook her head, staring straight ahead. "He never told me he was involved. Not once." She shook her head again. "Why would he not say anything? Even just to acknowledge it, or..." Her frown deepened and he could almost see her reaching for a thought, grasping it, studying it from various angles. She turned to him slowly, deliberately, her face distorted with tumultuous emotions all vying for release.

"He did it, didn't he? He tried to poison the queen then set Father up to take the blame. Then he felt so guilty afterwards that he took me in. It must be true or, or...why do all this for me? For the daughter of the man who nearly ruined him?" Her bottom lip wobbled. She shook her head over and over as tears began to pool. Nicholas ached for her. He wanted to tell her she was wrong, that her father must have been guilty because he had investigated Samuel himself, but he couldn't. He felt paralyzed. All he could do was take her in his arms and comfort her, but even that felt wrong, somehow sullied because of his lie.

Isabel didn't cry. Instead, she drew away from him and jumped off the stool. She faced him, her eyes flashing, her cheeks flushed with anger. "And that means he's setting me up too." She pushed past him and stalked off towards the back door. "I'll kill him."

CHAPTER 12

"*W*ait!" Nick caught Isabel's arm.

She spun round to confront him. She had every right to find the truth from a man who had been there. A man who possibly, almost certainly, implicated her father. It must have been Old Man Shawe. If not, then why help her at all? It had been something she had wondered about for years. Shawe must have guessed that she had run away from her marriage, so why risk her husband's wrath if he found her? Why get involved at all for a woman who was the daughter of a traitor?

Because he felt guilty for his involvement in her father's demise. Perhaps he assumed he could atone for his sins by helping her.

"Nick, don't." She snatched her arm away. "This has nothing to do with you."

"Nothing to do with me?" His voice sounded low, guttural, like the words were forced out with great effort through a tight throat. It stopped her cold. "Nothing to do with me?" he repeated. "Did I not make myself clear to you just now?"

She shook her head, not as a negative answer but because she didn't understand why he was so angry at her. What had she done wrong? What had she said?

"I am your husband," he said. "This has everything to do with me." He took her face between his hands, forcing her to look into his deep blue eyes. "Don't disregard me, Isabel."

She understood. She had shut him out of her life. Exactly what he had done with her after their marriage.

She reached up to his hand, warm and calloused against her cheek, and drew it gently away. "We'll speak to him together," she said.

One corner of his mouth lifted. "Good answer. But first, you seem to have forgotten one thing."

"What?"

"Shawe Senior is bedridden. Whatever happened in the past, he couldn't be implicating you now. He couldn't possibly have put the poison in the sweetmeats, or tried to stab me or poison me."

"Not personally, no. Good Lord, Nick, I thought you of all people must have considered the fact that he hired someone else to do those things."

His expression darkened. "Me of all people? What does that mean?"

Interesting that he had latched onto that part of her speech. They would have to discuss his work later. "Let's go."

They walked hand in hand up the stairs and entered Old Man Shawe's room the same way when he answered Isabel's knock. His quick, darting gaze took in their linked hands then lifted to study first Nick's face then Isabel's. If he saw the simmering anger in her glare he gave no indication. But he would have seen it. He was an astute man, and although his eyesight was failing, his other, sharper senses would certainly have perceived something was wrong.

"I was wondering when you would come for her," he said before either of them could speak.

"Excuse me?" Nick glanced at Isabel. She shrugged.

"You're Sir Nicholas Merritt, aren't you? Isabel's husband? You took your time getting here."

"I've been busy," Nick said, lamely.

"The important thing is that you got here and Isabel didn't turn you away. Or kill you." He chuckled which for him was as good as a laugh. Ever since his teeth had started falling out he had become self-conscious of his smile, something which Isabel had tried to persuade him didn't matter. As with everything to do with his health, he had dismissed her with a joke.

"She did try to turn me away but I'm stubborn," Nick said. The twinkle in his eye had returned, and not from anger, she realized. It seemed Old Man Shawe had already won him over. One charmer to another.

Well, she was resistant to charmers. They had to work harder to gain her trust than the average, plain-speaking man, not the other way around. "How did you know he was my husband?"

"Because my son told me there was a Merritt paying you a lot of attention. It seems he doesn't recall your married name. Perhaps he doesn't even recall that you are married." He tapped his forehead with a crooked finger. "My body might be useless but my mind isn't. The coincidence of the sudden reappearance of your husband and your presentation of this man in this manner are too great." His face slackened as his smile vanished. "But none of this explains why you are angry, Iza." He patted the bed beside him. "Come here so I can see you better."

She glanced at Nick but he only shrugged and let go of her hand. She approached the bed cautiously. The man in it might be a traitor, might have set up her father and now her.

She had sat on his bed every day since he'd been confined to it and chatted to him freely about what interested them—the shop, the customers, medicine, current events—and yet now she felt uncomfortable. There was so much about him she didn't know. All those friendly conversations could have been an act.

She perched awkwardly on the edge and looked down at him. When she had first arrived in London, he had been a large man, in girth and height, but illness had gnawed at him so that his body barely made a bump beneath the covers. She was reminded of a snake's skin she had seen in a jar in Pullman's shop once. Thin, colorless and empty.

"Now, Child, tell me what has brought a frown to that pretty face of yours. And what has it to do with me?"

She lifted her gaze to his. He looked directly back at her. Unnerved, she drew in a breath. "I believe you were at Whitehall seven years ago when Father...when he was accused of attempting to poison the queen."

He expelled a long breath that seemed to deflate the frail body even more. "Ah, so you have found out. Well," his hand searched out hers, found it and patted, "it was bound to happen sooner or later. I'm just glad I can defend myself while I'm still alive."

"Do you deny it?"

"No, of course not. I was there. I lodged in the rooms next to your father." He chuckled. "Lord, we thought we were in Paradise. Everything so grand, so beautiful. Iza, I hope you see Whitehall before you die. Perhaps Lawrence could take you. There are so many rooms! If we didn't have escorts, your father and I would have wandered the halls looking for our bedchambers all night. Everything was so opulent! Enormous tapestries of gold and silk on every wall, finely worked and inlaid furniture, silver plate, the library...and the people! You couldn't move for people sometimes—courtiers and servants running here and there. Ah, Iza." His face seemed to tighten, become younger, and his eyes shone as if he was actually seeing the palace again. "Her Majesty is exquisite. Her skin so pale and clear, her hair like gold, her eyes clever and quick. She sees everything. So when they arrested your father..." he lifted one shoulder, "...I assumed they were right. I just assumed he had done it. Like everyone else, I thought he was guilty because that's what we were told."

Isabel went still. He could be lying to her. He could be throwing her off the scent the way a conjurer uses clever showmanship to distract from his sleight of hand.

But in her heart she knew he wasn't. Suddenly, the trepidation she had felt moments before fell away and she was once again with the man who had helped her when she had been at her most desperate and vulnerable. The man she had cared for since his wife's death, the man who had treated her more like a daughter than her own father. There wasn't a mean bone in his body. He was no trickster out to trap her in an elaborate game.

She sighed heavily and closed her fingers around his boney hand. She squeezed as hard as she dared. "Go on."

He squeezed back with surprising strength. "Oh, Iza, you have every right to distrust me, to hate me."

"No, I—"

"I shouldn't have simply accepted the verdict. Of course I knew he wouldn't do something like that and yet I did nothing to defend his honor. I stood by..." He sank further into the pillows.

"You couldn't have known for sure." She pulled the bedcovers up to his chin, folding and refolding the edge over. Aware that she was fussing, she stopped, sat back and said what was on her mind. "Is that why you took me in? Because you felt guilty for not doing anything at the time of his arrest?"

Shawe's eyes closed and for a moment he looked like he'd fallen asleep. "Partly." His eyes opened and they were sharper than before, less cloudy. "Oh, I felt guilt all right, but even more so because of my treatment of him during our stay at Whitehall."

"Why?" Nick asked from behind them. "By all accounts, Samuel had exposed some of your cures in his latest book. Cures that had given you a solid reputation over the years and a stream of customers. If anything, you had a right to hate him."

Shawe's gaze darted to Nick. He squinted and humphed. "He's clever that husband of yours. And well connected, I hear. A formidable combination in a young man. You are correct, Sir Nicholas, he did prove that some of my more popular cures didn't work. And he did it ruthlessly, I might add, belaboring the point in his book and his lectures. That's why we had a falling out before we met at Whitehall for the conference, as Her Majesty called it. He had told me what he was going to do, out of courtesy to an old friend, he said. Well, you can guess my reaction. We were no longer friends from that moment."

"I don't understand," Isabel said, confused as to where her loyalties should lie. "Why did you feel guilty when Father ruined your life? He should have felt some form of guilt, not you." Had her father felt any guilt for what he'd done and how he'd done it? Should he? She felt torn. Her father had done the world a service by providing certain proof that some popular cures did nothing, but at what cost? His colleagues despised him, their reputations suffered and friendships were destroyed overnight. Had it been worth it?

"Because I treated him so poorly at Whitehall. I accused him of being a traitor to his profession, to his friends and my family." He nodded slowly, as if his head weighed heavily on his shoulders. "What an appalling choice of words that turned out to be. But it only gets worse, Iza. Much worse. My guilt has only increased since his death because I realized, eventually, that he was right. I've become a better apothecary for being exposed by him. I learned my lesson. It was a difficult one to swallow at first, but I have certainly tried to do my best as an apothecary since. I believe I owed it to him to at least try and live up to his high standards and dispense only medicines that are proven cures."

"And you have," Nick said. "I've asked around, and believe me, Shawe's has the best reputation in all of London."

Isabel's heart warmed to hear him say it. "And did you also believe you owed it to my father to take me in that day I showed up here?"

Shawe nodded, smiling. "Yes. But I also needed an apprentice and I knew you had studied with the best. It has all worked out, hasn't it, Iza?"

She smiled at him. How could she ever have thought he would deliberately implicate her, or her father? "It certainly has." She held his hand and felt her tension easing.

"Master Shawe," Nick said, kneeling beside her, "is there anything about that time at Whitehall that you thought was unusual?"

"The queen was poisoned and my colleague was arrested as a traitor," he said. "Is that unusual enough for you?"

Isabel raised an eyebrow at Nick. "You did ask."

"Let me rephrase that," he said with a wry smile. "There's a possibility that Samuel was innocent and someone else planted the poisons in his room that night. Do you—"

"Innocent!" Shawe raised himself up and stared unblinking at Nick. "Are you sure? Dear Lord, poor Samuel. Poor Elizabeth."

"The queen?" Nick said.

"My mother," Isabel said. After her father died in prison, her mother died only a few months later, lost and broken without her husband. She had devoted her life to being an adoring, dutiful wife. Even though their relationship had suffered after her powers came in, she had still tried to please him, perhaps even more so. When he was gone, she had nothing to live for. She had simply ceased to participate in life and so it had ended as abruptly as her husband's.

"Ah, yes." Nick touched her shoulder and she leaned into him, glad for his strength and solidness.

"So you want to know if I noticed anything that might indicate he was set up by the real traitor?" Shawe said.

Nick nodded. "But as I said, it's only a possibility that Samuel was innocent."

Did he still not believe it? Strange, considering he had been the one to suggest it.

"It's just a theory that we're working on," he continued. "You see it looks like Isabel is also—"

She squeezed his hand hard and he stopped mid-sentence. The last thing she wanted to do was upset Old Man Shawe even more by telling him she was possibly being framed in a more recent plot.

"Isabel is also what?" Shawe asked.

Nick cleared his throat. "Isabel is also very keen to see his name cleared. As am I," he added quickly with a glance at her. "So if you can think of anything that might support the theory, it would be greatly appreciated."

Shawe shook his head. "I can't. The first I knew of it was when he was escorted away by the guards. Then his room was searched. I didn't know until the following morning that they'd found poisons there."

"And what of Pullman?" Isabel asked. "Did he see Father being arrested?"

"Yes, and the other fellow, Finch. We all had rooms near each other."

"Tell us about Pullman and Finch," Nick said, still on his haunches at the side of the bed. "How did they react to Samuel's claims?"

"The same as me," Shawe said. "Badly. Pullman in particular made all sorts of threats against him. Told him he was a country simpleton who should return to the backwater he crawled out of. That sort of thing. Quite nasty it got one evening. If it wasn't for the presence of the queen's physicians and other scholars, it could have ended in blows."

"Do you know who the other scholars were?" Nick asked.

Shawe named a few well-known academics but dismissed them as having any interest in framing her father. "They were innocent bystanders to the conference really. None came under fire from Samuel."

"Then we must focus our attention on Pullman and this man Finch," Nick said.

"But he's dead," Isabel said.

"That might be worth verifying. I've known men to falsify their own deaths to run from the law or responsibility."

She stared at him. He knew men like that? Had he come into contact with them through his spying?

And why hadn't she thought of falsifying her own death? In many ways it might have been less cruel for Nick to think her dead by some unfortunate accident instead of having left him without explanation.

She dismissed the idea with a shake of her head. That was all in the past. She would not dwell on their separation again.

"What did Finch look like?" Nick asked Shawe.

"Middling height, neither large nor small, brown hair and eyes." Shawe shrugged. "Nice enough fellow with a good reputation I believe. At the time, at least. I assume that suffered in the same way mine and Pullman's did after Samuel's book was printed."

"You don't know?" Isabel asked.

"He wasn't from London. Nor was I at that time, but I'd not heard of him before and I've not heard of him since. His death is news to me."

"Where was he from?" Nick asked.

Shawe frowned as he thought. After a moment of silence, he shook his head. "I can't recall. Let me think on it, it may come back to me. However I do recall something that may interest you. There was some talk of Rheims."

"Rheims?" Isabel and Nick said together.

"What of it?" Nick asked at the same time Isabel said, "Why is Rheims important?"

"The French city and its Catholic Seminary in particular are known for recruiting English Catholics and other dissenters in schemes against our queen," Nick said. "A great many plots have been orchestrated from there in recent times."

"And how do you know this?" she asked him.

"It's reasonably well known," Shawe answered as Nick's mouth opened and shut like a puppet's without saying anything.

But where had she recently heard Rheims mentioned?

"Had someone been there before the Whitehall conference?" Nick asked Shawe.

"Both Pullman and Finch had made visits," Old Man Shawe said. "Both claimed it was for professional reasons. Apparently there is a well-known doctor there with highly regarded medicines."

Oh. When both men looked at her, Isabel realized she'd said it out loud. She pressed a hand to her lips.

"What is it?" Nick asked, touching her knee.

She shook her head, not wanting Shawe to hear that his son had also mentioned being in Rheims recently. The implications of that made her feel sick. She was grateful when the door opened, drawing the attention away from her.

But then she saw who entered and she felt worse.

Lawrence stood in the doorway, his jaw slack with surprise. He glanced at his father, Isabel and finally Nick. His mouth shut with an audible clicking of teeth and his glare turned hard. "Cozy," he said.

Nick's hand pressed firmly against Isabel's knee but he otherwise made no movement. Lawrence straightened, jerking his chin up which made the elegant feathers in his hat quiver.

"I think there's something you should know," Nick said, standing, his hand resting on Isabel's shoulder. At the sharp rise of Lawrence's brows, Nick turned to her. "Perhaps this will be best coming from you."

She didn't think it would be better coming from anyone, but he was right. She should be the one to tell Lawrence of her marital status since it was her deception. "Nick and I are married," she said bluntly. She always found the direct, honest approach worked best in awkward situations.

Lawrence blanched, began to laugh in a slightly maniacal way then stopped when he noticed no one laughed with him. "That was a fast courtship. You only just met her."

"You don't understand," she said.

Before she could continue, he went on: "And you married him even knowing about his...," Lawrence glanced at Nick's nether regions, "...malfunction? Well, if that's what you're looking for in a man then it's no wonder you and I weren't suited."

"It functions perfectly well," Nick growled. "Tell him Isabel."

"Lawrence, please," she said, "there's been a misunderstanding."

Nick puffed out his chest. "There certainly has."

Isabel rolled her eyes. Why didn't they just beat each other up and get it over with? "I mean," she said with a silencing glare at Nick, "that we have been married for some time."

"Eight years this May."

"But..." Lawrence frowned, "...you've been living here for some time and I've never seen this fellow until the other day."

"Nick and I were estranged for a while," she said. "We're together again now." That's all he needed to know. All she would ever say to anyone on the matter.

"But..." Lawrence shook his head and Isabel knew what he must be thinking, all the questions he must be wanting answers to. But the only question he did ask was directed at his father. "Did you know?"

"I knew she was married, yes," Lawrence Shawe Senior said. "I also knew Camm was her maiden name and Merritt her married name. I didn't know why they were estranged or that her husband had reappeared. But he has, and now we must deal with the consequences."

The response had been directed to his son, but it resonated with Isabel too. The consequences. For Lawrence, it meant that she wasn't a potential wife or lover. Not that he had ever proposed but she suspected he harbored feelings for her and some sort of plan in that direction had lately begun to occupy his mind.

But there were other consequences which she didn't think Lawrence had yet considered, although his father had. Just as she had.

"But he is a knight of the realm," the younger Shawe said. "And she is..."

"Yes," Nick prompted with a menacing undertone.

"Your assistant," he said to his father while looking straight at Isabel.

For a long time they stared at each other and Isabel felt like they were inside a dark cave, just the two of them with nothing but blackness surrounding them. She saw his emotions imprinted on his face—disbelief, a sense of betrayal and finally loss—and she felt terrible that she had put them there.

Nick's arm banded around her waist, releasing her from the strange spell.

"When will you leave?" Lawrence asked with a barely disguised sneer.

Hearing the question out loud caught her off guard. She hadn't had a chance to think through the details yet. Her reunion with Nick was still so new that she had only had time to bask in it. What happened beyond the day, the hour, had not occurred to her.

"I don't know," she said quietly.

"As soon as she's packed," Nick said.

She turned to him, irritation flaring without warning. "There is still much to be done first," she told him.

"Of course," Nick said. He smiled down at her but it was weak and uncertain, not full of his usual confidence. "Whenever you're ready."

She leaned down to the man in the bed and squeezed his hand. "I'll return later with your supper."

"Let Lucy do it," he said. "You have a lot of other things to do right now." He brightened. "Or perhaps your friend—Meg, was it? Yes, send her. I would like to meet my new tenant."

She laughed and squeezed his hand again as Lawrence sput-
tered. "You allowed that whore to stay here, Father? But
she's a—"

"Whore?" Old Man Shawe said. "I know. But not a very good
one, Isabel tells me. Perhaps she'd make a better apothecary's
assistant."

"Father, I most strenuously object!"

Isabel and Nick slipped out of the chamber and closed the
door on Shawe Senior's attempts to gently rile his son.

"That went well," Nick said brightly. They had reached the
bottom of the stairs and he spun round, picked her up and
kissed her mid-air.

The familiar burn of desire spread through her, warmed her.

Then all of a sudden he stopped kissing, dropping her unceremoniously to the floor. She steadied herself then caught him as
he swayed.

"Sit down," she said, directing him to the lower step.

He sat and put his head between his knees as ordered. "I
suppose you're going to tell me I'm not well enough to be out of
bed yet," he said, voice muffled.

"No, I'm going to tell you to stop talking and breathe deeply."
He did as he was told. "Good. Now I'm going to tell you that
you should be in bed. I'll have a pallet prepared for you in Fox's
room."

He groaned. "I can walk home."

"No, you can't. Your body is still weak. You'll stay here
tonight."

He lifted his head. "I must return home."

"Why? Because your mother will worry?" she said with mock
sweetness.

"No, because I need to see Ash. There's a lot I need to tell
him."

"Why?" she challenged. Because Lord Ashbourne was his
spying partner and he needed to discuss Old Man Shawe's
conversation with him? Say it. Admit it.

But he didn't. Instead he lowered his head again and
groaned. She took that as assent that he would be staying in
Fox's room for the night.

* * *

THERE'S nothing like a reunion with a loved one to make a man forget he'd been poisoned. If only Nicholas had been sleeping with his loved one then perhaps he wouldn't be leaving in the middle of the night when he should be resting. He paused in the act of slipping on his boots. Why wasn't he sleeping with his loved one? They were married, after all.

Fox's loud snore erupted from the bed which the apprentice shared with another male servant of the household. With noise like that it was no wonder Nicholas had woken up with a start. At least the few hours rest he did get seemed to have helped his recovery. He felt refreshed and ready for the walk to Ash's house. His friend wouldn't mind the late night visit. He was used to it, even expected it during an investigation since it was safer for his agents to check in under the cloak of darkness.

Nicholas grabbed his coat, hat and gloves and stepped out of the room. He paused outside Isabel's door but decided not to enter. Not only would that invite unwanted questions and suspicions, but he hated waking her. Besides, he would be back before sunrise so she wouldn't even know he'd left. He moved on, down the stairs, through the silent shop to the street.

Outside, the cold air pricked his ears, nose and cheeks but he was thankful there was no wind to spear into his bones. The city was quiet, the curfew bells having sent all law abiding citizens to their warm beds. The London winter had probably sent any non-law abiding citizens to their beds too, or someone else's. Only a desperate man would be out on a February night.

Somewhere past the row of shops on the northern side of Bucklersbury, the Watch shouted that all was well. Nicholas waited to see where the next call came from before heading off in the opposite direction. Explaining his reasons for being out and about at that time of night would be no more than a nuisance for a man of his rank but it was a nuisance he could do without.

He passed the four- and five-storey shops lining Cheapside, the peaks of their pitched roofs disappearing into the night sky above. He turned left into Paternoster Row and passed the great hulking form of St Paul's Cathedral, eerily quiet without the crowds. Instead of going towards Ludgate which was closed at night along with London's other gates, he headed south towards the river. Used to going silently about his business, his footsteps barely made a sound.

So when he heard the faint clack clack of boots on stone behind him, he froze.

Someone was following him.

He sank into the shadows, his hand wrapped around the hilt of his sword. He waited, straining to hear, but the only sound came from the gentle lapping of the Thames and the jostling of the wherries tied up at the water stairs at the end of the street. One of them would provide him with transport to Ashbourne House's landing and back again. The wherry's owner would be none the wiser in the morning when he returned to begin his day's work ferrying passengers up and down the river. By then, Nicholas would be safely back in Fox's room.

He continued down to the water, still gripping the hilt of his rapier. Unease settled into his stomach, or perhaps that was the lingering affects of the poison again. He continually checked over his shoulder, but there was nothing there except inky blackness. He untied one of the wherries and stepped in, pushing off with his foot.

He rowed up the river and was grateful for the lack of wind since his strength seemed to have deserted him. He'd rowed the same course easily and without breaking a sweat many times before but it seemed the poisoning had weakened him more than he anticipated. With the enormous stone landing at Ashbourne House in sight, he had to stop and rest. He withdrew the oars and allowed the boat's momentum to carry him along.

The soft splash of oars breaking the surface filtered through the darkness. Who in Hell would be rowing up river in the middle of a cold February night?

He squinted into the blackness, listening. The splashing drew closer but he could see nothing.

Someone was definitely following him.

Then let them follow. He continued on to Ashbourne House and tied up the wherry before sinking into the shadows of the stone arch that signaled the entrance to the stairs leading up to the gardens. Moments later another wherry pulled up and a hooded figure got out. The short blade of a dagger glinted in the moonlight as the rower tied up his boat.

Despite the cold, sweat dripped from Nicholas's forehead as he waited for the figure to approach. But time seemed to drag on forever and Nicholas's head felt like it had grown too big for his skull. He rubbed his temple, trying to concentrate and banish the dizziness and aches. He closed his eyes, just for a second, but when he opened them, the hooded figure was standing before him, dagger raised.

The blade suddenly descended and Nicholas just managed to dive out of the way as it sliced through the air near his face. He landed awkwardly on his side but rolled to a kneeling position near the water's edge, his rapier drawn. He started to stand but before he could get to his feet, the attacker flew out of the darkness and slashed.

Nicholas parried but was caught off guard and put a hand out to stop himself falling. Still on his knees, his body lay open and vulnerable for the seconds it took him to regain his balance.

Long enough for the attacker to kick him in the stomach.

Nicholas fell back, his head hitting the stones with a crack. His vision blurred, the familiar nausea returning with a vengeance. He had to get up, had to defend himself, had to...be sick. His insides were on fire, burning and heaving in protest. And why couldn't he get up? Why wouldn't his limbs work?

Above him, the hooded attacker came into view, the metal of his dagger catching the moonlight as it descended. With every ounce of strength in him, Nicholas tried to get out of the way, willing his body to move. He managed to roll.

But not fast enough. The blade struck deep into his side. White hot pain speared through him. His own shouts of agony filled his ears. He smelled blood and knew without looking or touching that it poured from his wound because he suddenly felt very cold and very tired. Too tired to keep his eyes open. He closed them and saw Isabel's beautiful face.

Isabel.

A fresh wave of pain ripped him apart, shattering the image. Then everything else began to slip away along with his blood until he was too cold, too empty, to feel even the pain anymore.

CHAPTER 13

*S*leep eluded Isabel the way Nick had eluded her questions. Would he ever admit he was a spy? Or that he was investigating her? The more she thought about it, the more she knew that to be the truth. Yet he still said nothing.

She sighed for the hundredth time and rolled over, being careful not to accidentally kick Lucy the maid. She tried to think of something other than Nick—her work, her customers—but that only led her to thinking of him again. How did he feel? What could she give him to make him recover faster? She smiled because she knew exactly what he'd say. And it was a medicine she would readily dispense.

But since they both shared a room with others and since he was still unwell, it probably wasn't a wise train of thought to follow. Especially since it made her ache for him. Her body craved his—to feel his warm skin, the curve of his back against her breasts, his heady scent...

She rolled over again, stifling a groan. It would be a long night.

Then she sat bolt upright at the sound of hammering on the front door. Who would want an apothecary in the middle of the night? Considering the occupation of many of her clients, it could be anyone. Ordinarily, she would leave Fox to deal with a late night caller but since she was already disturbed she saw no reason to wake the rest of the household.

She threw her cloak around her shoulders and tied it as she hurried down the stairs. The banging had grown more insistent and she opened the door with an irritable jerk.

"All right, I'm here," she said.

The man, dressed in silver and green livery colors, straightened and bowed. "I'm sorry, Mistress, but..." He broke off to suck in deep breaths. Sweat beaded at his hairline, a single drip slipped down past his ear. "But I come bearing important news. Are you Mistress Camm?"

A cold wind swept through the open door and settled into the pit of her stomach. She nodded, indicating he should come inside. He hesitated then complied, blowing on his bare hands as she shut the door behind him.

"Who do you work for?" she asked.

"Lord Ashbourne, Mistress. He sent me to bring you to Ashbourne House."

Lord Ashbourne! "Immediately? But it's the middle of the night. What's wrong with him?" The words tumbled over each other in her urgency. Something must be wrong with Nick's friend and he had sent for her. "Another poisoning? I'll need to know so I can pack the right potions—"

"It's not His Lordship who's dying, Mistress. It's Sir Nicholas Merritt."

She stared at him, her head suddenly feeling thick and she shivered. So cold. "But he's here," she said. "Upstairs. Asleep." Her voice trailed to a whisper as her breath escaped her.

The man spoke the truth. She didn't need to run up to Fox's room to see the empty pallet for herself because she couldn't feel Nick's presence in the building.

The man shifted his weight, clearly unsure what to say or do. "Lord Ashbourne wanted me to bring you immediately. I have a boat waiting."

"A boat?" Of course, the gates would still be closed. "I'll fetch my cloak."

"You're wearing your cloak, Mistress."

She looked down at it. "Right, so I am. My gloves, hat and bag of supplies then."

"And proper boots."

"Of course." Yes, boots. Where were her boots?

Only a few minutes later she was walking quickly behind Lord Ashbourne's man trying not to think of what he'd told her.

Dying.

When they reached St Paul's, she broke into a run. Her hair beneath her hat came loose and tumbled down her back but she didn't pause to fix it.

It's Sir Nicholas Merritt.

They reached a boat with the Ashbourne coat of arms stitched onto the canopy and climbed in. The servant helped her to a bench seat covered in cushions embroidered with the Ashbourne colors of silver and green then nodded at the two oarsmen. Moments later the boat sped down the river under the powerful pull of the oars.

Dying.

She closed her eyes, tried to still the erratic beat of her heart and regain some of the common sense that seemed to have left her. "Tell me what happened?" she finally managed to ask the servant.

"A few of us heard a shout coming from the landing. Woke us up. When we investigated, we found Sir Nicholas lying in a pool of blood."

"Was he insensible?" she heard herself ask. That must have been her apothecary instincts taking over because she certainly wasn't thinking clearly enough to ask such a rational question.

Nick...dying.

No, it wasn't possible. Not now. She shook her head and pulled her cloak tighter at her throat because she was so cold. Light rain had begun to fall and she was glad for the protection of the canopy.

The servant coughed politely. "If you don't mind me asking, Mistress, but are you some kind of lady doctor?"

"I'm an apothecary's assistant," she said.

The servant humphed. "Don't know what an apothecary can

do for Sir Nicholas now. His wounds are deep. Potions and oint-ments won't fix him."

Which meant Ashbourne must have fetched her because she was Nick's wife, not for her medical skills.

Oh God.

She tried not to think of that for the rest of the boat ride. Tried not to think at all, but images and memories of him kept recur-ring unbidden. Stolen kisses behind the Lyle House brewery before they married, long evening walks in summer, primal love-making after he returned from wherever it was he went.

The bump of the boat hitting the landing jerked her out of her thoughts. She swiped at a tear before being helped out by the servant. He held a blanket over her head to protect her from the rain but she hurried past him and up the stairs to the garden and the big house standing proudly at the end of the straight path.

The servant seemed to sense her urgency and directed her quickly through the maze of rooms. Isabel registered the opulence of the fabrics and furnishings but little else. Finally they stopped outside a closed door. The servant knocked softly and it opened immediately. A maid rushed past them carrying red sheets.

Red, bloodied sheets.

Isabel swallowed the emotions rising in her throat because Nick needed her to be brave more than ever. Nevertheless she ran to the bed, stumbling the last few steps and falling to her knees at his side. He lay completely still, his face white, the sheen of moisture covering his skin glistened in the flickering candlelight. He looked like a marble statue—perfectly carved yet lacking color. And life.

No, not lifeless. He breathed. The gentle rise and fall of his chest was evidence of that, but it was so shallow as to be almost non-existant. She brushed a damp strand of hair from his fore-head and bent to kiss him there. He felt cold against her lips. Too cold.

"My husband," she whispered, resting her cheek against his. It felt good to be near him, warming him, feeling him alive. "You'll live," she said, her voice stronger.

"That's not what I've been told."

She gasped and turned. "Lord Ashbourne! What are you doing here?"

"I live here." The earl stood in a shadowy corner untouched by the light of the fire and candles. He must have been there the entire time. He pushed off from the wall, never taking his eyes from her.

"Yes, of course you do." She watched as he paced around the room like a prowling cat, his gaze still on hers. "But I need you to leave the room now."

He stopped. His eyes narrowed. "Why?"

"I...need to speak to him alone."

"He can't hear you."

"Perhaps not but nevertheless, I want to be alone with my husband." She emphasized the last word to drive home her position.

"Estranged."

"Not anymore." Damn him, there wasn't time for semantics. Why did he argue with her now?

He straightened and folded his arms over his chest. He looked every bit the lord, not the easygoing man she had met earlier. "I summoned you because, as his wife, you had a right to be here. That is true. It is also true that Nicholas would have wanted you here for...the end. But I'll not leave this room. He was my best friend—"

"He's not dead yet." But he would be if she couldn't heal his wounds soon.

"As I said before, that's not what I've been told. The doctor just left. He gave Nicholas an hour, possibly two. There was nothing he could do for him. The wounds are too deep."

She clenched her fists, digging her nails into her palms in an attempt to stave off tears of frustration. "Please," she said, "please leave."

"No." He looked down at her, his eyes gleaming like two dark sapphires.

"Why? Don't you trust me?"

"No." But his gaze softened then faltered and he looked away as his arms dropped to his sides. "Nicholas trusted you. That's all that should matter now."

As if he heard his name, Nick coughed but his eyes remained closed. It signaled a change. His breathing quickened, interspersed with coughing fits.

"He's going." Lord Ashbourne suddenly appeared at her side, smelling of wine and sounding like misery.

He was right. She had run out of time. She couldn't wait another minute to begin the healing. The earl would witness her witchcraft but she would deal with the outcome of that later, once Nick was safe. His survival was all that mattered now.

She threw back the bedcovers. He was naked to the waist, thick bandages doing little to staunch the blood oozing from his side.

"What are you doing?" Lord Ashbourne asked, pulling her hands away as she began to remove the bandages.

"Stop! If you want him to live, don't hinder me."

His gaze locked with hers, fiercely protective. His grip tightened. "What are you doing?" he repeated.

Damn him, there was no time! A powerful surge of anger and other emotions shot through her like a lightning bolt. With a flick of her wrist, Lord Ashbourne flew across the room, slamming into a chair, shattering it. She turned back to Nick, ignoring the earl lying dazed on the floor. She placed both hands against the oozing hole at Nick's side and concentrated.

Her palms warmed, drawing heat and life from every part of her body into his. She concentrated harder, picturing him healed, whole, until her flesh burned. But she didn't let go. Not yet. She'd only healed twice before, and only once on a human, but she knew instinctively that the process wasn't complete. She squeezed her eyes closed, trying to shut out the searing heat in her hands, using her mind's eye to see his skin closed, the wound sealed, the blood flowing through his body not out of it.

Finally the heat lessened, the mad buzzing within her became a mere tingling vibration. She drew her hands away, not wanting to look at the burns on her palms. Instead she inspected Nick's side. New skin, pink and shiny, covered the gaping hole that had been there moments before. Whatever damage had been done to his insides would also be repaired. She knew as much from her experience with the horse on the Kent estate. Its broken leg had knitted after she placed her hands over the injury.

That first healing experience had been an accident, discovered while inspecting the animal after it fell. The second experience, on a small child who'd fallen from a barn roof, had been done out of sheer desperation and instinct. The child would have died by the time a doctor arrived. She'd had no idea if she could heal people, or anything more than a broken leg, but she knew she had to try.

Except for her own minor cuts, she hadn't used her healing powers since.

"Why didn't you tell me?" Lord Ashbourne's soft voice sounded close behind her.

She didn't answer straight away. Couldn't. Her tongue felt thick, her throat tight. She watched Nick as a spot of color appeared on each of his cheeks. He would live. Relief made her weak and dull-witted. She couldn't think of anything to say to the earl. What should she say? I'm a witch. Will you have me arrested tonight or wait until the morning?

She pulled the bedcovers up to cover Nick's chest and then she just sat there, watching him. It was the most perfect sight in the world.

"Why didn't you tell me?" Lord Ashbourne repeated, no longer soft but with a hint of anger.

Without turning around, she drew in a long breath and let it out slowly. When she felt sure of her voice, she said: "I wanted to avoid it. Being a witch is not something I want everyone to know about." Especially a man with friends who made the laws that ensured her kind couldn't be left in peace.

"It would have made a difference," he said. "I wouldn't have tried to stop you if I knew how much it would have hurt."

She turned to look at him, a surrendering smile on her lips. "I'm sorry. Are you all right? Anything injured?"

"Just my pride." One corner of his mouth lifted in a returning smile then dropped again. "I'm sorry," he added. "I should have known that if Nicholas trusted you I should too."

"Apology accepted. He's a friend of yours. You were protecting him."

"He's my only friend," he said so quietly it was barely audible. He leaned down past Isabel to inspect Nick's face. "When will he wake up?"

She shrugged. "I don't know. I've never healed on this scale before." A sickening thought occurred to her—what if he didn't wake? She may have healed the wound but what if something vital inside him had been damaged? "Did he have any other injuries?"

"There's a gash at the back of his head. It stopped bleeding before we brought him in here but it looks nasty."

She gently turned Nick's face away from her. The hair at the back of his head was matted and sticky. Parting it gently, she saw the jagged cut and placed her hand over it. The skin on her palm still felt tender and raw but she didn't care. She bit her lip as the fiery power burned her, stripping her flesh. She let go only when she knew the process had finished.

"I'll have the maid bring something for your hands," Lord Ashbourne said, already moving away.

"No, they're fine." She closed her fists. The pain instantly eased and she could feel the skin beginning to heal.

The earl checked Nick's head and nodded. "The cut is gone. You're a good healer."

She pressed her fingers into her eye sockets, suddenly exhausted. It must be near dawn and she hadn't slept a wink.

"One of the apartments upstairs has been prepared for you," Lord Ashbourne said. "I'll have a maid take you."

"No." She stood, noticing the room for the first time. One wall was covered in dark oak paneling while the other three were decorated with cloth painted in a crimson and white floral pattern. The same pattern was reflected in the white plastered ceiling. Isabel had never seen a ceiling like it. Such detail and perfection. The craftsmen must have been very skillful indeed.

Apart from the canopied bed, an armchair, large chest, a pedestal table and two stools also occupied the room. The bed itself was a statement of opulence with its intricately carved corner posts and headboard. The quilt, curtains, valance and tester all matched the walls with the same pattern embroidered in gold on the crimson damask. Lord Ashbourne enjoyed displaying his wealth it seemed. Another characteristic that didn't match the impression she'd built up of him, that of unpretentious, carefree gentleman.

"That chair looks comfortable," she said, pointing to the armchair by the fire with the thick red and gold embroidered cushion. "I'll sit there until he wakes."

He nodded. "Very well. I'll have blankets and other comforts brought to you. Good night, Isabel." He paused. "By the way, your secret is safe with me." He turned and left before she could say anything.

* * *

ISABEL AWOKE WITH A SORE NECK, a tingling foot and a strange sensation of being watched.

"It's about time," Nick said from the bed. "I've been awake for hours." He lay on his side, one arm bent, his hand supporting his head.

She threw off the blanket and sprang out of the chair. "You're awake." And alive. She sat on the edge of the bed, too scared to embrace him in case his wounds hadn't fully healed. Instead, she gingerly brushed a strand of hair from his forehead and simply stared into his eyes. Eyes that twinkled back at her, full of vitality.

He caught her waist and drew her on top of him. "Give me a kiss."

Very much alive. She obliged, kissing him hard, needing to taste him, feel him. And he felt amazing—so powerful and real beneath her, his heart beating a strong rhythm. Their kiss softened, became more sensual and loaded with the emotions they had not yet voiced—relief, gratitude, desire. Always desire. She raked her hands through his hair as he fumbled with her skirts, bunching them around her thighs.

"Not here," she muttered, even as familiar heat pooled inside her. She kissed his chin, his throat, moving down to his bare chest, snaking her hand down beneath the covers.

"Then you'd best stop now." But he too continued, arching up to her, grinding his hardness into her stomach.

He was right. With a sigh, she pulled away and sat down next to him on the bed. "Let me look at you," she said, drawing back the covers.

"If you insist." He flung the covers off and stretched his linked hands behind his head. "Best be quick. Ash's maids are too efficient and I expect one of them to enter at any moment."

She tried to look anywhere but at his hardness, tenting his hose. "I want to look at your injuries," she said, giving in anyway and staring with unashamed hunger.

"Sure you do. Look as much as you want." When she swatted his knee, he sat up with a smile and lifted his right arm to show her his side. The skin covering his wound was pinker in color than the rest of him but there was no other sign that a blade had gored him only a few hours earlier.

She traced the outline of the barely visible injury on his skin. "Thank God." When her gaze shifted to his face, she realized he had been watching her. The mischievous grin had been replaced by a somber expression.

"Since I can't recall how I got here, I take it I was not looking very well."

"No." She didn't take her eyes off his. "Not very."

He nodded. "And you healed me."

She studied him carefully, looking for signs that he was wary of her powers even though he'd already declared he didn't care that she was a witch. There were none. "Yes. I healed you. You have Lord Ashbourne to thank for sending for me so quickly."

"And I will thank him. But first, I want to thank you properly."

He drew her down into an oh-so-tender kiss that tugged at her heart and brought tears to her eyes. His hands played with her loosened hair then massaged the back of her head and neck. When he touched her cheeks, ending the kiss, she sighed.

"Thank you," he whispered. "You're my guardian angel."

At the soft knock on the door, they both turned but didn't let go of each other. "Come in," they said together.

Lord Ashbourne entered. He stood in the open doorway, filling the width with his broad shoulders, and stared at them as if seeing a ghost. "You're alive," he said simply.

"Well, that was a resoundingly unenthusiastic response," Nick said. "At least my wife gave me a kiss."

"Pucker up."

Nick laughed. Lord Ashbourne broke into a boyish grin. He approached the bed and slapped his friend on the back before briefly embracing him. When he straightened, Isabel noticed the darkened sacks beneath his eyes contrasting with the unusually pallid skin. She wondered if he'd been asleep at all, or if the effects of too much drink had caught up to him.

"So it worked?" The earl raised a brow at Isabel.

"The wound is healed," she said, still wary. Old habits, borne from years of self-preservation, didn't vanish overnight. She looked down at Nick and couldn't resist touching his warm, rosy cheek with her fingertips. "He seems to be as good as new."

"Better," Nick said. "Even the poison finally seems to have completely left my system."

"That wasn't me."

"Perhaps it was the apothecary who tended to him then," Lord Ashbourne said. He smiled tentatively at her, as if sensing her distrust and wanting to allay it.

"She was one clever woman," Nick said with an overly theatrical sigh.

"But rather formidable," Lord Ashbourne said. "I don't think she particularly liked me."

Nick snorted. "A rare jewel amongst women then. Perhaps I should marry her."

"She's far too good for you," Isabel said, joining in. "But I'll offer myself in her place."

"Ah, I was hoping you'd say that. I thought I'd have a better chance with you since you're already here in my bed."

"On it." She swatted him but he caught her hand. His lips brushed her knuckles, lingering over each little bump.

Lord Ashbourne choked. "Enough, before I taste my breakfast again."

They broke apart but Isabel stayed close. She didn't want to be any further away from Nick than was necessary.

"Speaking of breakfast..." Nick said.

"It's on its way. You and your wife may enjoy it in here

alone." But instead of leaving he strode to the chair Isabel had slept in and pulled it closer to the bed. He sat down, stretched out his long legs and fixed a heavy-lidded gaze on Nick. He seemed to be waiting for something and it took Isabel a few moments to realize he was waiting for her to leave, or for Nick to ask her to go.

Well, she wouldn't. The two men were about to have a conversation that she very much wanted to hear. A conversation about who wanted Nick dead.

A servant entered and built up the fire which had died down overnight to a pile of ashes. He worked efficiently, unobtrusively, but all three sets of eyes watched him as if he were a fascinating creature from an exotic land. When he finished and turned round, his cheeks colored at the attention. Bowing awkwardly to all three, he hurriedly left the room, closing the door behind him.

Awkward silence again infiltrated the large bedchamber. Since neither man seemed to know of a polite way to dismiss her, Isabel thought she would put them both out of their misery. But not in the way they intended.

"So who do you think tried to kill you?" she asked her husband.

Nick shrugged. "I, uh, well, I don't know. A footpad?"

"A footpad who followed you up the river to the landing at Ashbourne House? A persistent fellow."

He shrugged again. "There aren't many fools out on a winter's night. Perhaps he thought I'd be the only available victim."

She nodded at the table on top of which lay his sword and a full purse. "He went to all that trouble and didn't take your possessions?"

"My men disturbed him before he had a chance," Lord Ashbourne said. "It was a footpad. If Nick had been fully recovered from his poisoning he would have easily beaten the vagabond off."

"If Nick had been in bed in Fox's room he would have easily avoided the situation altogether."

Neither man spoke. Ash held her gaze levelly until she turned to Nick. Her husband took her hands in his, rubbing her thumbs with his own in a soothing, placating caress. But the turmoil in his eyes said far more than his gesture. Not a man normally lost for words, especially around women, his struggle to think of what to say to her was almost comical. Twice he opened his mouth but said nothing, snapping it shut as if cutting off words before they escaped. Eventually he let out a low groan and lay back against the pillows as if too ill to go on. She knew an act when she saw one.

Men! What sort of silly fool did they take her for? She could forgive the earl's assumption of her lack of intelligence, but Nick? He should know better than to feed her such ridiculous lies about footpads. She glared at him and he gave a small shrug as if resigning to the inevitable.

But "I woke up and wanted some fresh air," was all he said. "Since I needed to speak to Ash about some business affairs, I thought I'd come here."

"In the middle of the night?" She stood, clicking her tongue at his lie, and strode to the fire.

"My door is always open to Merritt," Lord Ashbourne said. "The servants know him. They'd have let him in."

She stared at the orange-yellow flames, mesmerized by their dance. She tried to think of what to say next, how to bring the conversation back into her corner, but her tongue felt twisted. She had given Nick every avenue to answer her with the truth. All he had to do was admit he was a spy and together they could try to work out who had injured him.

Was it Ashbourne's presence holding him back from confiding in her? Did the earl forbid discussing secret court business with someone not in their network, even the spy's own wife?

She hoped so, because the alternative was too horrible—that Nick didn't trust her enough to admit he was a secret agent for the Privy Council.

The only sound in the room came from the hissing, spitting fire. It seemed neither man would say anything else, nor would Lord Ashbourne leave her alone with Nick. And since she couldn't ask the earl to step outside while she was a guest in his house, she decided to do the only thing in her power left to do. She would ask Nick outright if he was spy.

She turned, but the door opened before she could say anything and the same servant who tended the fire entered, bowing.

"A Tristram Fox is here to see Mistress Merritt," he announced to the earl.

"Fox?" Isabel blinked at him. How could her apprentice possibly have known where to find her? Lord Ashbourne, ever the considerate gentleman, must have sent someone to tell him what had happened.

She followed the servant out of the room and the door closed behind her with a thud. She imagined the earl moving closer to the bed and the two men discussing their secret business in earnest, going through the possible suspects based on Nick's current investigation. The investigation that involved her and linked back to her father.

She was led into a small parlor, furnished rather plainly compared to the rest of the house. Fox stood with his back to the window, the cap in his hands worked into a crushed ball. He looked relieved when she entered.

"Is everything all right, Fox?" she asked, remaining near the door. "Master Shawe?"

"Is well, Mistress." The cap twisted between his fingers as if he were ringing water out of it. "When you weren't in the shop this morning, I got worried." That she doubted. "But then I heard you were here so I thought I should make sure you were all right."

"As you can see, I'm fine." She turned to go. "Please take care of the shop until my return. I'll be here all morning."

"So...is His Lordship well?"

So that was it. He came for the gossip. The news of an illness to one of the queen's favorite nobles would make Fox a popular man in Bucklersbury Street, at least for the rest of the day. She saw no reason to let him know she was there for another person entirely. "Very much so."

He made all the right responses. She opened the door but he spoke again. "Oh, and you should know that Sir Nicholas left sometime in the night. His pallet was empty when I awoke this morning. Should I send one of the servants to his lodgings to make sure he arrived home safely and is well?"

"No, that won't be necessary. Thank you, Fox." She left him to the servant hovering nearby and walked quickly back the way she had come.

She stopped outside Nick's door, wishing it was thinner or slightly ajar so she could overhear the conversation inside. Then suddenly the door opened silently but only enough for a mere sliver of light from the chamber beyond to pass through. And words too.

"...to tell her," she heard Lord Ashbourne say.

"I can't." Nick groaned then swore, his voice muffled as if he'd buried his face in something.

"Because of your link to her father?"

"It's more than a link, Ash," Nick said, sounding clearer. "I killed him."

Isabel's heart stopped beating and everything around her ceased to exist except the slit of light beaming past the door which she must have unwittingly opened with her powers. He'd killed her father? No, it wasn't possible. He had gone mad. Her healing had confused him, made him spout ridiculous things.

Yet she knew that wasn't true. She took a step closer to the door but stopped herself as the earl scoffed. "You didn't kill him. Your actions may not have helped his case—"

"May not have!" Nick said. "There's no doubt my information on Samuel condemned him further."

Information? What did he mean? What sort of information?

And then it became clear, like the letters of a complex code separating and reforming in the correct order. Nick had been absent after their marriage because he was spying, that much she had already guessed, but at least part of that time he must have been gathering information on her father.

"You were acting under Walsingham's orders," Ashbourne said. "She'll understand."

"I'm not so sure." Nick sighed heavily.

"I don't understand you," Lord Ashbourne said gruffly. "You claim she loves you and yet you're afraid to tell her the truth."

"You're right," Nick growled. "You don't understand me. And I don't understand my wife anymore. She might leave me again if she knew."

Isabel covered her mouth to smother a gasp.

"Why would she leave?" Ash asked. "I thought everything was resolved between you now."

"That doesn't mean she wouldn't leave me again over this."

Isabel knew she should go in and tell him she would never leave him, never again. But she couldn't move. Her feet stayed firmly on the floor.

"Where would she go?" the earl went on. "She has no one other than Shawe here in London, and you. If she leaves, who would take her in? Any sensible woman would realize she is better off staying with her husband."

"She's not the same as other women," Nick said. The pause that followed felt loaded even from where she stood outside the room. She waited with her heart lodged in her throat for him to continue.

Then he did. "She's not the same woman I married."

CHAPTER 14

*N*ot the same woman I married.

The words haunted Isabel as she walked down Fleet Street past Temple Bar and over the stinking, oozing Fleet River. Her head felt like it was full of the mist that still shrouded the ditches and river. Her lack of concentration led her into the path of a cart rumbling through Ludgate and she had to hurry or be crushed beneath its thundering wheels.

Not the same woman I married. Nick's words pressed down on her like weights. Why would he say such a thing after their recent reunion? She had thought he loved her. Every word he spoke, every action and reaction of his body was a sign he loved her.

Weren't they?

It seemed his mind was rebelling against his body, overthrowing its desires with rationalities. Rationalities that clearly were not in her favor. Rationalities which even she could not deny. He was right—she wasn't the same woman he had married. That girl had disappeared in the last six years, replaced by a woman who knew her own mind, who knew how to keep shop as well as any man. A woman who could cure a cough or a toothache as well as any doctor. A woman who read widely and even planned to write her own herbal one day. A woman who kept suitors at arm's length with a few quick, witty words that ensured no man lost his self-respect. A woman who could form her own opinions, could exist on her own, without a man to guide her, keep her.

A woman who was a witch.

No, she certainly wasn't the same person he'd married. She liked this one better.

But did Nick?

What husband would want the kind of wife who didn't lower her gaze when spoken to? Who didn't bite her tongue instead of giving her opinion? What man would want his wife to contradict him in a discussion, or question his motives for...spying? Or confront him over his lies?

What man would want a woman whose strength was superior to his own?

None would, no matter how much he loved her or claimed to love her. Claimed—yes, that was what Nick did. He only claimed to love her. Lies had become second nature to him through his spying so now he even lied to her. The line between his work and the rest of his life had stretched so thin it had become easy to cross, easy to blur truth and lies until one couldn't be distinguished from the other.

But even as she considered these things, a niggling thought tapped away in her head until she finally let it out.

He's not the man I married either.

It felt like a kind of betrayal to admit it considering she still loved him. But it was true. The man she had married would never have lied to her about anything, never have kept his life secret from her.

He would never have spied on her father.

She stumbled over an uneven stone in the road, the jolt waking her as if from a dream. It had begun to rain and she hurried on to Bucklersbury Street, running past her neighbors' shops.

Fox looked up from the counter when she rushed through the door and made a sound of surprise. "You're back already," he said.

She pushed back the hood of her cloak but felt too cold to remove it. "I'll be upstairs. Is Meg back yet?"

He shook his head. "Hasn't come in at all."

Curses. Not that she was concerned for Meg's safety—her friend was used to finding a warm bed when she needed it—but Isabel wished she was there to talk to.

She checked in on the sleeping form of Old Man Shawe before turning to her bedchamber and closing the door. She sat on her bed and stared out the window. The room was too high up to see anything except endless gray sky but the wintry conditions suited her mood.

What to do now?

She couldn't think of anything. Couldn't think of what to say to Nick or how to act around him when she saw him again. She couldn't even cry. She felt too numb.

He must be wondering what had happened to her or perhaps he thought she had left Ashbourne House with Fox. Did he really care?

A knock on the door focused her attention. Could he have come looking for her already? "Yes?"

Fox entered. "You have a caller, Mistress."

"Who is it?" She rose.

"Mistress Merritt."

She sat down again. Constance. Isabel clicked her tongue, irritated at the intrusion. What could the old crow possibly have to say to her now? More threats? Whatever it was, Isabel didn't need another distraction. "I'll see her in the parlor," she said, sighing.

She kept her mother-in-law waiting just long enough to annoy her and not long enough to be rude, then entered the parlor with a smile on her face as if she were in love with a wonderful man who reciprocated her feelings unconditionally. She hadn't any idea how much of that was true but as far as Constance knew, and as far as Isabel wanted her to see, it was.

"This is unexpected," she said. It was the safest, most inane greeting she could think of.

"Where is my son?" Constance asked, her jaw hardly moving as she spoke. She stood with her hands behind her back, squaring her shoulders even more. She looked like a domineering school mistress watching over a particularly naughty student.

"Ashbourne House."

Constance looked surprised for a brief moment until she composed herself, tipping her head to look down her nose at Isabel. "What? Not here with you?" She spoke as if she'd won a wager.

Isabel ignored the bait. Let Constance think what she wanted. Isabel would not be drawn into giving her a more detailed answer. She dismissed the idea of telling her about Nick's midnight escape and injury. He was healed. There was no need to alarm his mother now.

"He and Ash had business to discuss. You might still find him there if you hurry." Go, leave me in peace.

"Never mind, I'm sure you can pass on a message for me."

The hairs on the back of Isabel's neck rose at the look of triumph still printed on her mother-in-law's face. The confident smile, the tilt of her chin, the hard eyes all sent warning bells ringing in her ears.

And still Constance kept her hands behind her back.

"You obviously have something to say that I won't wish to hear," Isabel said. "So get it over with. I have work to do."

"Work." Constance snarled. "You bring disgrace to your husband and the name of Merritt with your work." She almost spat the word at Isabel. Suddenly the smile vanished but her eyes only gleamed harder, like the gems in her rings. "You have become a common shop girl, debasing what it means to be married to a knight. Nicholas has worked too hard to further the Merritt name to have his efforts completely disregarded by his wife. People will laugh at him behind his back. They will mock the knight whose wife counts whores amongst her friends—"

"That's enough, Constance," Isabel said, very low. "I will not be insulted in my own home or have my friends insulted within my hearing. You may leave."

"I haven't finished with you yet."

"Yes, you have. If you do not leave then I will have Fox forcibly remove you. People will certainly laugh at you then."

"You are insulting and impertinent, and you will get exactly what you deserve." The smile had returned as she drew herself up to her full height and Isabel knew she was finally getting around to the real reason for her visit. "Since my son won't set you aside then I must do it for him."

Isabel barked out a laugh. "What are you talking about?" But even as she said it, despite her outward show of bravado, a sense of dread chilled her.

"The current Lord Mayor was a friend of my husband's. I have spoken to him about you."

Isabel's heart pounded against her ribs. "Why?" she asked, even though she knew the answer.

"He will send the Justice of the Peace to arrest you at sundown on a charge of witchcraft."

"Sundown?" she echoed, trying hard not to show her fear. "Why not now?"

"Because I told him I will give him the evidence to charge you then. And I will only give the evidence if you are still in London."

Of course. Yet another agreement. "You want me to leave Nick again." Even as she spoke she felt her blood turn to ice in her veins.

"It will convince him once and for all that you do not love him. He won't seek an annulment unless he can be sure of that."

Isabel didn't think he would annul their marriage, even now after voicing his doubts about his wife and even if he thought she didn't love him. He was too honorable to break the promise he had made to her on their wedding day. Too honorable and definitely too stubborn.

"Leave and I will not give evidence to the Lord Mayor. Your life will be spared," Constance said, steely determination making the lines around her lips deepen. She certainly knew how to make effective threats.

Isabel's palms stung from where her fingernails had bitten into the flesh. She flexed her hands but otherwise kept her movements controlled, in direct contrast to her inner turmoil.

"You must truly hate me," she said. "To condemn your own daughter-in-law to a horrible death..."

"Witches are hanged in this country not burnt at the stake.

Not anymore." She made it sound like a merciful gesture on behalf of the law makers—a gesture she didn't agree with.

"And that makes it less horrible?" Isabel drew back in shock, swaying a little at the thought of swinging from the gallows for something she had not wanted and never asked for.

"You are no daughter-in-law to me anymore. You are the devil's creature, an abomination against God. Death is too good for your kind."

Isabel stared at her, speechless. How could she argue against such ignorance, such blind hatred nurtured by rumors and irrational fears? It was an argument she could never win, no matter how hard she fought.

"You are not welcome in my family," Constance continued. "My son will realize it when he is freed from the wicked spells you have cast over him. Leave him. Leave London. Don't come back."

Isabel balled up the hands she had used to heal this woman's son only hours before, the hands that could just as easily push the old crow through the wall to the street below. She fought against the throbbing anger, not wanting to do something she would regret later, but at the same time wanting to hurt her very much.

"Do me harm and your death warrant will be signed now, not at sundown," Constance said, her gaze taking in Isabel's clenched fists, her shaking body. "Leave."

Slowly, with great effort, Isabel nodded. "I will go. But you will incur your son's wrath." She felt certain of it. Despite his doubts about the woman his wife had become, he would still want to remain married to her, he would still want her with him. Even though he didn't love her as much as he once had, he was not a man who liked being manipulated in such a bald way. Nor was he a man who liked to lose. Isabel's abandonment had been a blow the first time, twice would be humiliation striking at the very essence of his manhood. He would blame his mother, but he would also blame Isabel.

"I am his mother," Constance said with a toss of her head. "He won't be angry at me for long."

Implying he would be angry with Isabel forever.

Constance spun on her heel and marched out of the parlor but not before Isabel noticed the shaking of her mother-in-law's hands. From guilt? Fear? Or anger?

When she had finally gone, Isabel's knees gave way and she collapsed onto a chair, trembling uncontrollably. She had never witnessed such pure hatred in her life, and never dreamed it would ever be directed at her. She felt nauseous, dizzy and frightened. So very very frightened.

She pressed a trembling hand to her stomach, another rubbed her forehead, trying to massage away the thick fog in her mind so she could think. What shall I do? What shall I do? The words rattled over and over like a wagon's wheels across an endless wooden bridge. Terror gripped her like never before, crippling, blinding, and she sat frozen in the chair, unable to move or think. Even her tears remained unshed, burning the backs of her eyes.

"Isabel? What's wrong?"

"Meg?" The paralysis eased and Isabel stood. It was all perfectly clear now, what she must do. She ran to her friend and gripped her shoulders. "Meg, I'm leaving."

Meg swayed under Isabel's weight and put a hand out to the door frame to steady herself. "Izzy, you look terrible. Are you ill?"

"I must go," was all she could say.

"Go? Do you mean on an errand?"

"No. Leave London. Will you help me pack? I must go now. This instant." She had to be far away from London before sundown. Far away from the Lord Mayor and his Justice of the Peace and far away from Constance.

She had seen a hanging once. The ugliness of it had remained with her since. The violent, desperate kicking out, the eyes bulging in terror, the crack of the snapping neck. And the screaming, not of the victim, but of his family watching from amongst the crowds.

But she'd only face a hanging if she ever got to trial. She could die in a London prison first. She knew all about the walls that were always damp, the stones that were stained with blood and excrement, the cries of sheer misery from prisoners left to rot in the dark, stinking cells.

Her father had died in prison, alone and broken. She would not end her life the same way. She would fight to live. She must.

Meg held Isabel at arm's length and bobbed her head to look in her eyes. "Izzy, you look terrified. What's happened? What has your husband done to you?" Anger made her voice rise and her face mottled.

"Nothing. It's not him, it's..." No matter how much she trusted Meg, she couldn't risk telling her about her powers, about her mother-in-law's threats. The mere mention of witches made even good people fearful and vengeful. She didn't want to see Meg turn against her too. Although Constance had never really liked Isabel, she had never hated her with such venom as she did since her daughter-in-law had accidentally revealed her witchcraft that day six years ago.

No, Isabel couldn't risk seeing her friend's eyes become cold and her arms withdraw.

"I have to go," she said simply. "You can come with me if you want." The suggestion tumbled out before she even thought it through and she regretted it a moment later. How could she condemn her friend to a life worse than the one she already led? A life on the run from the law? And how could she keep her terrible secret from Meg if she did follow?

Surprisingly, Meg giggled like a young girl. "No, I won't. I'm getting married."

"Married!" For a moment Isabel nearly forgot her troubles. But just for a moment. She rushed past Meg, directing her to follow her to the chamber they shared with Lucy. "Tell me while I pack."

"He used to be a regular customer of mine," Meg said, closing the door behind her and plopping down on the bed as if she didn't have a care in the world. "Ever since his wife died a year ago, he's been visiting me for...comfort. He's always been nice to me, never treated me like a sewer rat like some of the others." Bitterness laced her words, but so did hope and something else. Love?

Isabel threw two clean shifts onto the bed. Meg folded them and packed them into a cloth bag. "I went to see him after our little talk the other day. Remember? You told me to take charge of my own life now that Biggin don't want me."

"I remember." Isabel tried to concentrate but her mind was still on Constance and her threats. And on Nick. What would he think? How would he react to the news his wife had left him again?

"Well, I took matters into my own hands," Meg went on, folding one of Isabel's underskirts. "I told John, that's my betrothed, that I'd take care of him in his old age, and in return he's to teach me his craft and sign his business over to me. He's a draper with a shop on Candlewick Street. He's got no close kin since his wife died. His only son passed on nearly thirty years ago."

"How old is he?" Isabel asked, gathering her pins and hair combs into a small leather pouch.

"I'm not sure but he's quite aged. And rather ill too." She sighed quietly then shrugged, as if dislodging something irritating her shoulder. "Not long for this world, I'd say. I just hope he lasts long enough to teach me. Do you think I'd make a good businesswoman, Izzy? Do you think I made the right choice? Only I didn't want to be a burden to good friends like yourself for the rest of my life, didn't want to have to rely on a man, just like you said." She smiled tentatively as she gazed up at Isabel from where she sat on the bed, her feet tucked under her like a girl in her mother's chamber. "What do you think, Izzy?"

Isabel managed to smile at her. How could she not give her approval? A more naive person would think Meg greedy and opportunistic. Isabel was acutely aware that the Isabel of old, the innocent newlywed, would have scolded her and directed her to marry for love rather than money. But Isabel was wiser and knew more of the world now. Meg needed the protection that marriage to a prosperous, respectable man would provide, and her John needed a woman to comfort him in his final years, a wife to bury him when the time came. His reward for her service would be to leave her the business so she need never again find herself without a home.

If they treated each other well, with honesty and respect as she knew the good-hearted Meg would, then what harm was there in their arrangement? "You did the right thing. Be good to your John. He sounds like he deserves someone like you."

Meg jumped off the bed and hugged her. "Oh, I'll miss you, Izzy. Write to me and I'll have my husband teach me to read your letters. I will need to learn if I'm to run the business, you know." The new delight and passion in her eyes dimmed and her smile turned to a frown. "Are you sure your husband ain't done nothing to make you want to leave?"

"No." But that wasn't entirely true. If Isabel was honest with herself, she was running from Nick too. He had been involved in her father's death, then he'd lied about it, lied about so many things, including hiding his disappointment at the woman she had become. If he had only been honest with her, she would go straight to him now and they could fight his mother's accusations together. If she knew without a doubt that he loved her then she would not bear to break his heart by leaving.

Yes, she was running as much from him as from his mother.

Again.

She held Meg's gaze. "If you happen to see him, tell him...I'm sorry. But this is how it must be for everyone's sakes."

Meg's eyes shone with unshed tears. "I don't understand."

Isabel clutched her friend's arms and squeezed. "It'll be all right. I have to go now." She scooped up the two bags crammed with as much of her belongings as she could carry. Everything else would have to stay behind. "Goodbye, Meg."

They hugged and Meg cried. Isabel left and hurried downstairs before she allowed her tears to spill. Once she had safely passed the open-mouthed Fox serving a customer at the counter and was out on the street, she could no longer stop them flowing.

* * *

NICHOLAS STOPPED PACING the bedchamber he'd occupied since the previous night and watched Ash stride through the door. "Well? Where is she?"

The earl shrugged. "No one seems to know for sure, but one

of the servants thinks he saw her leave not long after the apprentice."

"Not with him?"

"No."

Nicholas resumed his pacing. It didn't make sense. Why would she leave without saying goodbye? Surely if Fox had told her the shop needed her immediate presence, she would have left Nicholas a message with one of the servants. He stopped pacing and looked at Ash who frowned back at him. "And none of them spoke to her before she left?" he asked.

Ash shook his head. "Fox arrived, they met in the east parlor then he left. Some time later, she left too."

Nicholas started pacing again. "How much later?"

"Not long."

"And did anyone overhear their conversation?"

Ash looked offended. "My servants don't eavesdrop on my guests."

"Why not? Everyone else's do."

The earl sighed. "Merritt, you're wearing my rushes thin."

"I'm thinking," Nicholas said without stopping.

"Then think in a different pattern so you wear them out evenly at least."

Nicholas stopped long enough to glare at him. "You don't seem to be taking this very seriously."

Ash shrugged. "So she left without leaving you a message. Does it matter?"

"Yes. Why did she not leave a note with a servant if you and I were still talking?"

Ash picked up Nicholas's sword and full purse from the table and held them out. "Why not go to the shop and ask her?"

Nicholas took his belongings. "I was about to." He strapped on his rapier and pocketed the purse. He reached for his cloak but it was too bloodied and torn to be worn.

"You can borrow one of mine." Ash called for a servant. The man who'd announced Fox's arrival appeared at the door.

Ash told him to fetch another cloak, but Nicholas cut in before the servant could leave. "Are you the man who informed

Fox that Isabel was here?" Nicholas asked him. "How did he react to the news?"

The servant frowned and shook his head. "Informed him, Sir? No, not I."

"I sent no one to the Bucklersbury Street shop," Ash said after dismissing his servant.

"Then how did Fox know she was here?" Nicholas asked. "I assumed you had sent someone early this morning."

"No."

They stared at each other and Nicholas could see his friend come to the same conclusion as him at the same time. "He followed her," Nicholas said.

"In the middle of the night? Why would he do that?"

Nicholas shrugged. "Curiosity. He must have overheard her leaving the shop and decided to find out where she was going." But it didn't ring true. Why would Fox be curious about Isabel's comings and goings?

"Is he in love with her?" Ash asked.

"No!" But Nicholas's heart constricted. "I don't know." The servant returned with a dark blue velvet cloak and put it around Nicholas's shoulders, helping him with the ties and clasp. "I'm going to find out." Nicholas looked up at Ash when his friend said nothing. The earl looked thoughtful, confused even. "What is it?"

"If Fox heard Isabel leave the shop, then presumably he would have heard the knocking beforehand. My men told me they had to pound on the front door before she opened it."

"So the question is, why didn't he answer the knocking himself?" Nicholas said, finishing Ash's train of thought. Ash was right—it didn't make sense. Being the most senior able-bodied man of the household, Fox should have answered a knock on the door in the middle of the night. He shouldn't have left it to Isabel.

Ash held his gaze. "And the answer to that is—"

"Because he wasn't there."

"Precisely."

The servant left them to their stunned silence. It wasn't until the door closed that Nicholas spoke the question he knew Ash must also be considering. "So where was he?" But he already knew the answer, and he could see from Ash's darkening face that he did too.

"He was returning to the shop after trying to kill you." Ash's hand went to his hip where his sword would usually be if he was armed. "I'm going to kill him," he snarled. He made to leave but Nicholas stopped him with a hand on his shoulder.

"Wait. We need to tread carefully. If he's the one trying to kill me then he's most likely the Whitehall poisoner. I'd rather get him for treason, wouldn't you? But we need the evidence linking him to this plot, and Samuel's. I'll see what I can find out."

Ash looked like thunder. "He tried to kill you, Merritt! And now, after his meeting with Isabel, he must know you're not dead. Forget about gathering evidence, let's go and beat a confession out of him before he does more harm."

"You're as subtle as the rack, Ash."

The earl snorted. "Do you really want subtlety when a killer is in the same vicinity as your wife? Assuming they have both returned to the shop."

Nicholas shook off an involuntary shudder. "That's exactly where I'm going now. I won't be able to arrest Fox without evidence but at least I can warn Isabel."

And save her if necessary.

"She can take care of herself if it comes to that. I have the bruises to prove it."

Bruises? So Ash had learned about Isabel's powers the hard way. Normally he'd find that funny, but not with a killer after her.

"She doesn't know he's dangerous," Nicholas said. "She wouldn't be prepared. Besides, he might poison her or knock her senseless first while she's not looking." Speaking about it only made his heart pound faster, his throat dry up. His hand closed around his rapier's grip so tightly he thought he'd crush it. If only it were Fox's head.

"While I'm gone," he continued, "I want you to find out about the third apothecary from the Whitehall conference seven years ago. I have a feeling he's linked to this man Fox."

Ash nodded. "I'll do what I can. But be careful. Your near-death experiences are sending me to an early grave."

"Then you should consider giving up the drink," Nicholas said, sheathing his sword.

"I consider it every day." Ash grabbed Nicholas's arm and held it for a moment.

They gave each other a final nod before the earl let go and Nicholas strode out of the bedchamber.

CHAPTER 15

*T*he insipid sun struggled to burn off the mist clinging to the hollows and ditches. Isabel hunched into her hooded cloak, her head bent against the bitter wind blowing off Moor Fields and through Bishops Gate into the city. Her shoulders burned from the weight of her bags and her back ached almost as much as her heart. There was still so much further to go before she was safe. She must catch a ride in a passing cart if she wanted to be far away from London by sundown. She'd decided not to hire a horse for fear of being followed. A woman alone would stand out at the stables. The grooms would easily be able to identify her if her pursuers described her.

With the gate and the bleak buildings of Bedlam Hospital behind her, she dumped her bags on the side of the road outside the Swan Inn and hailed a passing cart. But it rolled by, the driver giving her only a sideways glance. One by one they continued on without stopping, even when she offered to pay for her passage. It seemed nobody trusted anyone in these hard times. With footpads of both sexes often colluding to rob ordinary folk it wasn't surprising.

Plopping down on top of one of her bags, too tired to even cry, she rested her chin on her hands and stared at the mud stuck to her boots. It was hopeless. She was exhausted after a sleepless night, her body stiff and sore. Perhaps she should see if the Swan had a room. She could pretend to be someone else, a widow or servant, and keep her hood low so no one would be able to describe her to the Justice of the Peace if he came looking for her. Or Nick.

No, she couldn't risk it. She would look suspicious if she didn't reveal her face. She had to keep moving.

She stood and dragged up her bags, lugging them over her shoulder and distributing their weight evenly across her back. Blocking out the aches, blocking out her misery and anger and fear, she trudged on. She tried to think of happier things and found Meg's smiling face came easily to mind.

She felt proud of her friend for taking up the reins of her life after everything fell apart. Her new arrangement might not be everyone's choice but it was Meg's and it suited her. On the death of her husband, she would have control over her own affairs for the first time in her life. It was a most exciting time for her.

So much the opposite of Isabel's own situation. The reversal in their fortunes struck her with a blunt force and her step faltered. Meg had made her own decisions and now she was rising above her terrible circumstances. Isabel had not made any decisions. She had merely reacted to someone else's, and so she had sunk lower than ever.

Clearly that had to change. It was time she took some of her own advice and followed in her friend's footsteps. She had to take charge again. Running away would never bring her peace, only loneliness and more anxiety.

Isabel turned around and headed back the way she had come.

She was going home, whatever the consequences.

She had a good life in London. A respectable, free life and she wasn't going to run away from it without fighting. Nor was she going to run from Nick. Not again. He didn't deserve it. The more she thought of him, the more her pace quickened.

Her Nick. With his easy smile, dimples and boyish mischief. His quick wit and ready words, something she hadn't liked when he directed them at other women.

But her jealousy seemed to have disappeared along with her

innocence in the last six years. She no longer worried that he desired anyone else. His soft kisses and hard erection was all for her. His words...well, they only meant something when reinforced by his actions. It was those very actions that spoke of his love for her more than his words ever would.

Not the same woman I married. More words, easily misunderstood. Just because she had changed didn't mean he'd stopped loving her. If nothing else, she owed it to him to hear his explanation. He had been devoted to her for six years, never giving up his search or his hope that she would return. If that didn't shout love then what did?

And Nick would know what to do about the charges against her. He might even be able to persuade his mother into withdrawing her testimony. She had to try. For Nick and for their love.

But most of all, for herself. She had to take control of her life or forever let life be in control of her. And she had come to like much of her life over the past six years. Having Nick in it would take it from good to perfect.

"Isabel."

The familiar voice made her look up. Fox hailed her and trotted over. As he drew closer, she could see the grim set of his mouth, the bleakness in his brown eyes.

"Fox? What are you doing here? What's wrong?"

She waited until he regained his breath. He must have chased after her, getting lucky that she had stopped, giving him time to catch up.

"Is it the shop?" she asked, impatience getting the better of her. "Or Shawe?" Oh no, not that, please.

When he nodded, her heart flipped. "He took a turn just after you left." His gaze slid away then back to her. "Meg said you were leaving London forever. But I thought you would want to know."

"Yes, thank you." She tried to think, tried to force her own problems from her mind. "Has someone fetched his son?"

He nodded, blowing on his bare hands and rubbing them together. He must have left in a hurry to have forgotten his gloves.

He must have closed the shop. Somehow that mattered, not because it would mean customers would turn to one of their neighbors, but because it would be the first place Nick would look for her. And if he spoke to Meg before Isabel returned...

She had to get back. Had to take care of Old Man Shawe and be with Nick so he would know she still loved him.

"Let's go," she said, striding off.

"Wait!" He caught her cloak and she stopped. "I have a salve to deliver to a customer."

"Out here?" Although they occasionally delivered to regular customers too frail to frequent the shop, she didn't know of any who lived as far as Norton Folgate.

"I was coming this way later after the shop closes anyway," he said, shrugging. "The man's servant came by earlier and asked if I could deliver it today. His master is ailing and is desperate for his potion."

She nodded. "You deliver it and I'll return to the shop."

"No". He caught her arm, his grip hard. "He needs some advice too. So his servant said. He probably won't trust me since I'm only an apprentice." He said it with a sneer, as if his status in life had begun to gnaw at him. If he'd been a better apprentice then perhaps he would already have become an apothecary in his own right. Perhaps it wasn't the best time to tell him that.

"Very well," she said with a sigh. "Let's be quick. Which way?"

He took one of her bags and led her off the main road and down a muddy lane. Not even the pale sunlight reached into the narrow space between the overhanging upper stories of the buildings lining both sides of the lane.

"Are you sure he lives down here?" she asked, wrinkling her nose against the stench of human and animal waste.

"Over there." He pointed to a door in the depths of the shadows and stepped carefully through the muck towards it.

Isabel followed, willing him to hurry so they could leave and return to the shop.

"Can you knock while I retrieve the potion?" he said.

She lifted her hand to the door but before she could knock something hard hit the back of her head. Pain ripped through her skull, down her neck and back. She tried to turn around, tried to speak, but everything faded to black and she felt her body collapsing, falling into the filth. What...? How...?

Fox.

Her last clear thought was of Nick and what he would do when he learned she had left him. Again.

* * *

As soon as Nicholas spotted his mother walking towards him along Cheapside, he knew something was wrong. She looked too...satisfied. These days when his mother was satisfied it meant she had managed to wedge another lever between himself and Isabel and was gradually forcing them apart.

He'd feel more inclined to speak to her if he knew why Isabel had left Ashbourne House without leaving him a message.

"Mother," he said in way of greeting.

"Son. I've been looking for you. I was told you were at Ashbourne House," she said, stroking the fur collar of her cloak.

Only Isabel or Fox knew where he'd been, which meant his mother must have been to the shop. "Have you seen Isabel?"

She nodded. "I have a message to you from her." Her mouth twisted in an odd smile.

Nicholas waited for her to go on, his heart thumping so hard against its cage he thought it would break out. "You might as well tell me, Mother, since you seem so eager."

She looped her hand through his arm. No, this didn't bode well at all. "Now, Son, don't be alarmed at what I'm about to say, just think of it as an opportunity—"

"Mother!" He withdrew and rounded on her. "Give me the message."

"She's left you," she said flatly.

The noise and activity of the busy street faded and he was once again in Lyle Hall, in the private chamber he shared with Isabel where he had first heard his mother say those three shocking words. Then, as now, he felt their force as if he'd been punched in the gut. Then, as now, everything stopped moving, stopped breathing, stopped existing except those three words.

Then, like now, he shook his head over and over. "No. It's not possible." He heard his denial, an echo from six years ago and yet not an echo. Real. Too sickeningly real.

But he knew it was true. His mother looked too triumphant not to be sure. And Isabel had left Ashbourne House without leaving him a message. That fact repeated in his mind, torturing him again and again. He pressed his fingers to his temples and tried to rub it away.

"Well, she has," his mother said.

"Why? What have you done?"

"She and I came to an agreement—"

"To the devil with your agreements, Mother." He spoke quietly so passersby wouldn't overhear but he could see by her flinch she had felt the sharp edge of his anger. "What have you said to her to make her leave? What have you done?"

"Nothing. That is," she added quickly when he grabbed her by the shoulders, "nothing new. We agreed that it was only a matter of time before her powers were discovered and she would be arrested, dragging you and the entire family down with her. Once we discussed it, she finally saw my point of view." She took his hands in her own but he snatched them away. Her eyes widened and he could see the uncertainty clouding them. "She left for your sake, Nick. So you could have the bright future you deserve." Her voice rose as she spoke so that by the end she sounded like a frightened little girl.

He knew she was lying. At the very least, she was leaving a vital piece of information out. But it didn't matter. There was something else which ate through his thoughts like a maggot through rancid meat. Even though his mother had virtually admitted forcing Isabel to go, the truth remained that she hadn't seen his wife until after Isabel left Ashbourne House.

So it couldn't be his mother's new threats which had made Isabel leave him that morning? Then...what could it be?

Whatever it was, it was something that combined with his mother's threats had been enough to drive Isabel away from him. Again.

"How long ago did she leave? In which direction? Was she on foot? Did she take any belongings?" The questions tripped over each other as they tumbled out of his mouth. To each of them, his mother just shook her head or shrugged.

"Bloody hell," he muttered and strode off in the direction of Bucklersbury Street.

"Wait!" She walked quickly beside him, her boots slipping on the wet stones as she tried to keep up. "What are you going to do?"

"Find her."

"She doesn't want to be found."

"I don't care. She's my wife. I'll find her and bring her back. She belongs with me." But even as he said it, he knew he had very little chance of convincing Isabel to do anything she didn't want to do. One thing he had learned since their reunion, she was not a woman to do a man's bidding, even her husband's.

What he had to do was convince her he loved her, that he needed her and couldn't go on without her. All of which was true but perhaps he hadn't made it clear in the past few hectic days.

Of course it all depended on whether she loved him enough to return. And that's what terrified him. He couldn't make her love him. In fact, he had no idea how strong her feelings were. She had fallen easily into his arms but that could have been from desire fuelled by six years of celibacy. Love was different. He might love her so much his heart ached when she wasn't near, but did she feel the same?

It didn't matter. None of it mattered if he couldn't find her and tell her how he felt. Even if she was to walk away again, he had to tell her.

"No, Son, you don't understand."

He stopped and turned on his mother. "What?"

"She can't be found."

The triumphant gleam in her eyes had all but vanished and that filled him with even more dread. "What. Have. You. Done?"

Her hands, grasping desperately at his, trembled. "The Justice of the Peace will be coming for her at sundown if she's still here."

Nicholas's throat went dry and his stomach roiled. No. No, this wasn't happening. His mother couldn't be so cruel as to alert the authorities.

But she had.

His fists closed into tight balls at his sides. He wanted to hit something, bellow out his rage to the world, but even at his worst he was too aware of the crowds that swarmed around them to show any outward sign of his anger.

Steady. Be calm. Think.

"You fool," he snarled. "You stupid old fool. Isabel is pregnant."

She reeled back in horror, her foot slipping. He caught her before she fell but she didn't seem to notice his steadying grip on her arms, even though it must have bruised.

"What?" she whispered, staring up at him. "What did you say?"

"She's carrying your grandchild." If his mother had been in her right mind she would have realized that couldn't be possible. Or perhaps she didn't know he'd been reunited with Isabel less than a week. Long enough to make a baby, not long enough to know. "You've just condemned the heir to the Merritt lands and fortune to death." The lie had been the only thing he could think of to shock her into understanding the horrible senselessness of her actions. Perhaps it would make her call off the dogs.

Her body shook under his hands. "I, I didn't know."

"And if you did, would it have made any difference?" He let go and strode off but she followed.

"Yes, of course."

But he wasn't so sure. His mother wanted an heir but only from a daughter-in-law she liked. One who would bow to her superiority as matriarch of the Merritt family, one who would do her bidding. One who wasn't a witch.

"Then you'll tell the Lord Mayor you were mistaken, since I'm sure you were the one who told him Isabel was...unique."

"Y, yes. Of course," she said, her long strides keeping pace with his.

"Then what are you waiting for! Go tell him before he sends the JP around."

Still she didn't leave his side. She was like a dog with a bone, unwilling to give it up until she'd stripped it of everything tasty. "But are you sure she wants to come back?"

"What do you mean?" he growled without slowing down.

"She agreed to leave quite readily this time. I would have thought, after her vehement denial at our last meeting, that she would have been more reluctant. Especially since you were so keen to keep her. Didn't you tell her you loved her?"

"Of course I did." But apparently the declaration hadn't been enough. "She must have been frightened by the prospect of going to prison. Her father died in Newgate. The threat of a death sentence can make up people's minds for them, Mother."

"That's another thing," she went on. "Do you want to forever be linked to a traitor? Surely if the queen or your friends knew about her father you would not be held in such high regard at court."

He had to laugh at that. If only she knew it was those so-called friends who'd coerced him into spying on his own father-in-law in the first place. "They already know."

"Then you must distance yourself from him, from his daughter."

"Mother," he ground out through a tight jaw. "I have had enough. Leave me now. I don't want to hear another word from you."

"Just one thing," she said and he bit down on the curses perched on the tip of his tongue. "As I said, she left quite readily this time. Little arguing or reasoning. I was wondering..." She stopped walking and he turned back to her, not wanting to hear what she had to say but knowing he needed to hear it anyway, in a perverse sense.

"Yes?" he prompted.

She sighed, as if what she was about to say genuinely concerned her. "Perhaps she's decided she doesn't really love you after all."

Grunting, he turned his back to her and kept walking. Already at the corner of Bucklersbury Street, he could see Isabel's shop. He focused on its door, willing Isabel to be on the other side, smiling, happy. Her arms wrapping around his middle and her lips closing on his in a soft, eager kiss.

But he knew she wouldn't be there. His mother's words repeated over and over in his head, becoming louder, clearer.

The sickening feeling that she might be right grew stronger. He had thought Isabel still loved him. Hadn't she said so?

Words. Merely words, easily spoken.

He put his hand to the door to push it open, and was reminded of another door, slightly ajar. It had seemed insignificant that morning when Ash had noticed the bedchamber door was open during their conversation and had got up to close it, but now Nicholas wasn't so sure.

What if Isabel had opened it?

What if she'd come back from her meeting with Fox and overheard him speaking to Ash about...what?

Oh God.

They'd spoken about his spying and his involvement in Samuel's case.

Then she had left. Without leaving a message.

And now he knew why.

She had learned he had lied to her, betrayed her in the worst possible way by helping send her father to prison. No wonder she wanted to be as far away from him as possible. She must hate him, possibly even fear him if she suspected he was also spying on her. Considering his actions, his furtive behavior recently, she most certainly would be thinking that.

Oh God.

He opened the door, still hoping, but Nicholas knew as soon as he entered the shop that she had gone. He couldn't feel her presence, couldn't sense her brightness. He was too late.

"Oh. It's you."

At the sound of the flat voice he looked up at the woman behind the counter. Isabel's friend, Meg, stood looking a little less unkempt than the last time he'd seen her. She'd dispensed with the wig and wore a demure caul over brown hair. She'd also removed the thick face paint and her clothes didn't hang like rags off her thin frame. In fact, the simple gown looked like Isabel's.

"Where is she?" he asked, trying to keep the edge out of his voice.

"Gone." Meg chewed on her lip and he noticed her eyes were red-rimmed.

"Where?" He strode up to the bench and half leaned across it to shake the answer out of her before restraining himself.

Nevertheless, she reeled back out of his reach.

"I'm sorry," he said quickly. "I'm sorry, I just..." He sucked in a breath to steady his speeding pulse. He didn't want to scare the one person who might know where Isabel had gone. "You're her friend, aren't you?"

"Yes." She curtsied awkwardly then blushed. "But I don't know where she went. She didn't tell me."

The same sickening feeling came back. If he knew Isabel, she would already be far away, and she would have made certain she couldn't be found.

"How long ago did she leave?" he asked.

"Not long. No, wait, it was a while." She shrugged. "I don't know. I've been busy here. I'm not allowed to sell anything but telling all the customers to come back later is hard work." Her eyes grew bigger as she spoke and she threw her hands in the air. "There's so many of them."

He frowned. "Where's Fox?" It seemed a lifetime ago that he and Ash had discussed Fox's possible link to the poisoning plots, both old and new. He almost didn't care anymore. Finding Isabel was more important.

"Oh, he left not long after Izzy. Said he had errands to run. I wish he'd come back. I've got to go see my intended. He's a draper. Has his own shop, you know."

Oh Hell. He knew with hideous clarity that Fox had followed her. The apprentice must be linked to the plots, it was the only explanation, and he had decided to get to Nicholas through Isabel. Fox knew it was the only way to make Nicholas give up his investigation.

He leaned on the bench, groaned and rubbed his hands through his hair. This was all his fault. If only he'd been honest with Isabel, told her everything...

"Are you all right, Sir Nick? It's just that you look really ill. And when you groan like that... Wait, I've probably got something here I could give you." He looked up to see her studying the rows of jars. "But I don't think Izzy sells anything for love sickness," she said. She plucked out a jar and placed it on the counter between them. "Maybe fennel. Izzy used to give me this all the time when I had pains in my stomach."

Nicholas swore.

"There's no need for that. I'm just trying to help."

"No, I'm sorry, I...I need to find Isabel. Is there anything you can tell me that might help?"

Meg suddenly looked serious again. She picked out something from the fennel jar, a fruit or berry maybe, and rubbed it between her thumb and forefinger. "No. Izzy's gone forever. She said she's not coming back." She looked up and absently fixed Nicholas with a brutal glare. "I don't know what you said to upset her so much that she had to leave all her friends."

"I didn't," he said, even as guilt made his chest tighten. It was all his fault. If she hadn't overheard his conversation with Ash... No, if he hadn't said anything to be overheard. If he hadn't spied for Walsingham in the first place...

So many ifs.

"Well, if not you then her." She nodded towards the door and he turned.

His mother stood straight as an arrow, severe as a thunderstorm. He hadn't realized she'd followed him all the way to the shop.

"You must be elated, Mother." He couldn't keep the harshness out of his tone, or out of his heart.

She blanched and her mouth crumpled. Suddenly she didn't look so hard. "I only want what's best for you."

"Then you'd better hope that I find her because there'll never be anyone else for me. Understand?"

"Good for you," Meg said. "So what are you going to do now?"

"Find her. Bring her back. And you," he said to his mother, "are going to the JP right now to tell him you were mistaken."

She stood like a statue carved from black marble. Eventually, she nodded, just a slight, barely perceptible nod, but it was an affirmation nevertheless.

The door opened behind her, causing her skirts to billow like a puff of black smoke. She stepped aside to allow the three newcomers to enter. A gentleman wearing trunk hose and a long furred cloak of dark velvet with a tall hat was clearly in charge, while the other two wore the simple clothing of regular Londoners. All wore stern expressions.

The bad feeling in the pit of Nicholas's stomach grew.

"I'm looking for Mistress Isabel Camm, also known as Isabel Merritt," the gentleman said.

"I am Sir Nicholas Merritt." He decided it was time to use his full title. "And you are?"

"Sir Henry Helpman, Justice of the Peace. I've come here to arrest your wife on the crime of exalting the law of the devil with witchcraft."

Nicholas glared at his mother and tried to accuse her of lying, again, but his throat had closed up and all that came out was a harsh, strangled gasp.

His mother's face turned white and she shook her head over and over as she stared at the three men. "No," she said. "No, I have an agreement with the Lord Mayor. She's not to be arrested until sundown. We had an agreement!"

"I know of no such agreement," Helpman said. He signaled his men to move forward with a jerk of his head. "Now, where is she?"

CHAPTER 16

"There must be a mistake," Constance said to Sir Henry in her haughtiest tone. "You can't arrest her until sundown and only then if she is still here in London."

The Justice of the Peace's pearl drop earring jiggled as he shook his head. "I know of no such arrangement."

"But the Lord Mayor was a friend of my husband's! He promised me he wouldn't do anything until sundown." Nicholas could hear the desperation in the high-pitched whine, so out of character for his mother.

At least she hadn't lied to him. She clearly hadn't expected to be betrayed by his father's old friend. Nicholas wondered how friendly they had been since he'd never heard mention of London's Lord Mayor before. But his mother still couldn't claim innocence in the matter considering she'd organized the witch hunt in the first place. His patience with her, with the whole damn lot of them, had worn gauze-thin.

He watched as the two men, most likely constables, quickly searched the shop, much to Meg's annoyance.

"She's not here," she said, hand on hip like a petulant child.

Nicholas caught her attention and shook his head slightly. She frowned back, mouthed "what?" and gave him a shrug. He desperately wanted to tell her not to give them any information, no matter how insignificant she thought it. The longer they could keep Helpman and his constables looking through the premises, the more time it would give Isabel to leave London and his jurisdiction.

Nicholas's only hope was that he could slip away and try to find her himself. Before Helpman. Before Fox.

"Search every room," Helpman ordered his men. "We'll flush her out."

"She's not a rat," Meg snapped as the men left through the back door.

"Worse," Helpman said without looking at her. "She's a witch."

Meg scoffed. "Don't be ridiculous. She's no more a witch than anyone else in this room. Except maybe her," she said with a nod at Constance.

"She's right," Nicholas said. "This is ridiculous. My wife is innocent."

Helpman crossed his arms and stayed near the door, not looking so smug with his constables out of the room. "We have testimony that says otherwise," he said. "That's enough to arrest her on suspicion of witchcraft."

"It was my mother's petty rivalry that led her to seek out the Lord Mayor and accuse Isabel. She wants to revoke her accusation, don't you, Mother?"

"Yes," his mother said quickly, still looking pale against her black gown. "It's all been a mistake. My son is right, the matter is a personal family one. I wish to end this now."

Helpman said nothing, just smirked.

"This instant," Constance said with a hint of her old ferocity.

"That isn't possible. There has been another accusation made against her."

"Who by?" Meg, Nicholas and Constance asked.

"I'm not at liberty to discuss such matters with you," Helpman said, sounding bored.

Rage flared within Nicholas, snapping every last remnant of self-control he'd been desperately trying to hold onto since he learned of Isabel's departure. He flew across the room and grabbed Helpman by the throat just above his enormous ruff. He squeezed, watching with a sense of satisfaction as the JP's face turned scarlet, his eyes bulging from their sockets. Sir Henry scrabbled pathetically at Nicholas's arms and chest, his feet kicking out wildly as he tried to free himself.

"Tell me who," Nicholas said, his voice sounding strange.

Helpman gurgled as his eyes rolled back and spittle foamed at the corner of his mouth.

"Nicholas! Stop! Let him go."

Constance's words penetrated Nicholas's dizzying onslaught. The rush of blood between his ears slowed to a steadier trickle, but still his heart beat loudly, his breathing came hard. He let go and Sir Henry fell to the floor, coughing and spluttering. He sat up and rubbed his throat where red welts were already forming.

"You'll pay for that," he rasped.

Nicholas took a step towards him and Helpman scampered back towards the door, bunching the rushes up behind him. "Tell me who else has accused Isabel and I'll overlook your intrusion here today."

"Overlook?" Helpman whispered hoarsely.

"I am willing to overlook your presence, however I will not overlook your rudeness. You insult me, my wife, you disturb the good people at Shawe's apothecary and you have the temerity to mess up their floor. Unless you want to be physically thrown onto the street, I'll ask you again," he said, very slowly so the idiot could understand, "who else has accused Isabel of witchcraft?"

Helpman had the good sense to look afraid and Nicholas even thought he might get an answer out of him, until the constables returned. They took in their senior officer's condition, looked at Nicholas and cracked their knuckles, undisguised pleasure on their faces.

"My son has the ear of Privy Councilors," Constance cut in through the charged mood.

Helpman and the constables turned to her. Nicholas didn't. Instead he watched the three men, weighing up which one to remove from the equation first.

"You wouldn't want to anger Sir Francis Walsingham now would you?" his mother went on.

That got Nicholas's attention. "Mother, enough," he growled.

"Walsingham?" Helpman said. When the biggest thug cracked his knuckles again, the JP held up a hand like a master controlling his hound. "In what capacity do you know the principal secretary?" he asked Nicholas.

"In a most secret capacity, Sir Henry," Constance went on, tilting her chin in undisguised pride.

Nicholas glared at her. Not so secret now. He'd always wondered if his mother knew he had taken over his father's spying duties. He'd never told her. It seemed she had known anyway, or guessed.

"Oh," said Helpman. He stretched his neck as if removing any lasting kinks. "Well, it changes nothing. Your wife is still under arrest, Sir Nicholas."

"She's not 'ere," one of the constables said.

"I can see that," Helpman said without moving his lips. "However, I see no reason to keep the identity of her other accuser from you." Again he stretched his neck and adjusted his ruff to try to hide the marks on his throat. "If the fellow comes to harm, I will of course immediately have a suspect." He flicked something off his sleeve but the sharp glares of the constables remained pointed at Nicholas.

"Just tell me," he said, his patience at breaking point. Isabel could be far away. Fox could have caught up to her.

Fox! Of course! It had to be him. He'd fatally wounded Nicholas and then visited Ashbourne House to expressly learn of his victim's fate. Fox must have expected to hear of Nicholas's death, only to have Isabel tell him he was perfectly fine. Did Fox realize then that she was a witch? Did he suspect her of healing the wound?

Or had Fox also been watching her over the years? Perhaps he'd seen her use her magic to move something when she thought no one was looking, or she'd invoked the seeking incantation within his hearing. If he'd been slyly watching her for his own devious purposes then he could have witnessed a small slip-up that gave rise to his suspicions.

Oh Hell.

Nicholas had to find her. Warn her. For whatever reason, Fox had switched his focus from killing Nicholas to getting Isabel arrested for witchcraft. It was a sickening new twist.

He had to get out of there and do something. Looking for Isabel would be like finding a single coin in the entire Treasury but he had to try. But instead of heading to the door, he stepped closer to Meg.

"Did you see which way she went?" he said. "Or Fox?"

"Uh, he went that way." She pointed right along Bucklersbury Street. "I didn't see Izzy leave.

"Thank you," he said with a wink. "Good day, gentlemen," he said to Helpman and the constables as he strode past them to the door.

The Justice of the Peace jumped back out of the way. "Don't you want to know?" he said as Nicholas opened the door. "It was her apprentice, the Fox lad."

Nicholas closed the door on them all.

* * *

ISABEL AWOKE in a bedchamber with a gag in her mouth and a pike through her head. At least, that's what it felt like. She tried to reach up and feel the damage but she couldn't move. Her hands were tied behind her. No, not exactly behind her, behind the back of the chair she was sitting in. Her feet were also tied to the heavy chair's legs.

She groaned and nearly choked on the gag stuffed into her mouth. The ensuing coughing fit increased the pounding in her head. Lord, it hurt. Not just her head, but her shoulders, her back, and her wrists and ankles where the ropes rubbed her skin raw. She squeezed her eyes shut and tried to will away the headache so she could clear her mind but she couldn't concentrate. Her head felt thick and full, like a mental gag had also been stuffed into it. Could the pain alone be slowing down her thoughts?

Or was something else causing the sluggishness? Her apothecary instincts told her she'd been given a potion, but in her confused state she couldn't say what. She couldn't even remember the names of the herbs that would affect her in such a powerful way. Everything was so...foggy.

Nevertheless, she tried again to concentrate, this time on the bonds tying her to the chair. She forced everything from her mind—the pain, the rising panic, the simmering anger—but nothing happened. Her witchcraft wouldn't work.

Had Fox known about her powers? Had he come prepared with a sleeping potion? He must have followed her with the intention of capturing her but for what reason, she couldn't say.

She might have been able to work out the answers if she wasn't under the influence of his herbs. The rat. When she got her hands on him, he would experience her wrath, and when she felt better, she would unleash all her powers on the swine.

She lifted her heavy head with difficulty and focused on her surroundings. She seemed to be in a bedchamber. The weak afternoon sun shone enough light through the window to cast long shadows over the bed. A jug and two cups occupied a small table. Her bags were nowhere to be seen. Nor could she see any food. Or anyone else. She was alone.

Raucous laughter filtered up through the uncovered floor and into her aching head. She strained to hear, fighting off the overwhelming urge to sleep, and heard the low rumble of people talking. A lot of people.

She must be lodged at an inn.

Perhaps it was the one just outside Bishops Gate near where Fox had attacked her. What was it called? The Mermaid? Whale? Something to do with water...

Hope made her heart race, but then she remembered Constance and the threat of arrest and fear made it race even faster. She needed to be further away from London. Much further away.

But Nick was in London. And her work. She should stay, fight the charges. Shouldn't she?

She shook her head, trying to clear it of the thick fog but only succeeding in increasing the pounding against her skull. It felt like the devil himself was building a house in there.

Her head slipped forward, too heavy to hold up, and her chin bumped her chest. With great effort, she raised it and kept her gaze on the window. She had to stay awake. Be alert. Listen. Think. Concentrate.

But she could feel the battle slipping from her grasp. Her eyes felt itchy, raw and her head just wouldn't stay upright. A moment before darkness finally engulfed her completely, she heard the door to the chamber open behind her and someone enter.

* * *

NICHOLAS'S HORSE jostled against the other beasts of burden traveling in the opposite direction into the City proper through Bishops Gate. His hired gelding must have been used to the crowds because the noise and activity didn't seem to bother him. Negotiating the traffic was painfully slow but once they'd left the City behind, he let the horse have its head while he kept his eyes peeled for Isabel. He couldn't be certain she'd left via Bishops Gate, but it was the fastest route out of London from Bucklersbury if she'd turned right out of the shop as Meg had said. He hoped she hadn't hitched a ride on a cart but was still on foot. That was the only chance he had of catching her. If she had been picked up, she could be anywhere. Within two days she could easily secure passage on a ship and leave the country altogether.

Or Fox could get to her first.

Fingers curled around his insides and squeezed. He had to find her. And this time it wasn't going to take him six years.

It was late in the afternoon and a group of weary travelers on horseback headed into The Swan Inn on his right to find rooms for the night. He wouldn't be one of them.

Nicholas spurred his horse along Bishopsgate Street Without and up to the liberty of Norton Folgate where any sort of pleasure could be bought. Being outside the City's jurisdiction, gaming houses, brothels and disreputable taverns filled the narrow, dirty lanes. Vagabonds and footpads lurked in the shadows and he shuddered to think that Isabel might have come this way on foot. He hoped she had found somewhere to stay for the night. Somewhere safe and warm and—

Isabel! He couldn't believe it. She knelt on the side of the road up ahead, rummaging through her bags. He'd recognize that deep green gown of hers anywhere with the white cuffs and distinctive embroidery on the bodice. It was the only gown she'd taken from Kent. He resisted the urge to shout. He didn't want to frighten her. He might be the last person she wanted to see. He kept the horse's pace slow when all he wanted to do was race up and embrace her.

Lord, he couldn't believe his luck. She hadn't gone far at all.

But as he drew closer, something didn't feel right. Her shoulders were too wide, her crouching position was too...masculine. And Isabel would be wearing her cloak over her gown and her hat wouldn't be a battered old thing with a broad brim like a man's.

"Hail!" he called out.

The vagabond, a crumpled fellow well past his middle age, looked up. "These're mine," he said gathering the bags to his chest. "I didn't steal 'em."

Isabel's belongings lay scattered in the mud like old rags. Nicholas's anger flared at the callous disregard for her things. He gripped the reins tighter to keep from leaping off the horse and squeezing the life out of the old man. Instead, he stabbed the vagabond with a glare.

"Where is she?" he growled.

The vagabond reeked of filth but amidst the grime, Nicholas couldn't see any signs he'd struggled with anyone. Perhaps Isabel wasn't harmed. Perhaps she'd simply had her bags stolen.

"Who?" the old man asked. No, he couldn't have harmed Isabel. She was too strong, too quick witted for this decaying piece of scum.

Nicholas flexed his cramping fingers around the reins. "The woman who owns these things."

"They're mine." The man gathered up the skirts and chemises and stuffed them back in the bags.

"Women's clothes?" On a different day, under different circumstances, Nicholas would have doubled over with laughter at the vagabond's appearance. Dressed in a gown with his own worn hat and muddy boots, he looked like a runaway player from one of the theaters up the road, and not a good one either.

But Nicholas had no laughter in him.

He tossed the man a coin. "Tell me where you found those bags and I'll let you keep the gown and your life."

The man scrambled in the mud for the coin. He bit it, nodded his approval then closed his fist around it. "Down that lane there." He indicated the narrow lane behind him.

Nicholas dismounted, his heart thudding wildly. He felt dizzy as he asked his next question. "The lady these bags belong to...is she...?"

"Dead?" The vagabond chuckled, revealing several crooked, blackened teeth. "I dunno now do I? Nothin' movin' in there 'cept rats."

Nicholas let out a pent-up breath. He put a hand up to the horse's warm neck to steady himself as the dizziness resumed. "Then where is she?"

"Like I said, I dunno. The bags were just sittin' there. I waited and no one came to get 'em so I thought maybe the lady didn't want 'em no more." When Nicholas didn't say anything he added, "If you don't believe me, go look yerself." When Nicholas started to walk off, the vagabond called after him, "Sure I can't keep the other stuff?"

"You got that gown, now get out of here."

The vagabond picked his skirt up out of the mud and left, muttering that the blue one would have suited him better than the green.

Nicholas tied his horse to a post and drew his sword. He strode into the lane, scanning the rubbish for signs of life. Apart from the rats gnawing at discarded animal bones, nothing moved. No one, alive or dead, lay amongst the debris and filth.

Relief gave way to hope. Somehow she had been parted from her belongings, but that didn't mean she was...dead.

There was only one reason she would have been separated from her clothing—her powers had been rendered useless.

The apprentice must have caught up to her. Knowing about her magic, he must have been prepared and somehow disabled her witchcraft and kidnapped her. It was the only possible explanation. With Isabel's powers, even the strongest footpad would come off worse in an attack. Fox must have duped her. What he might have done afterwards made Nicholas sick. He didn't want to think about the possibilities.

He untied his horse and mounted. For the first time since learning of her departure, the fog clouding his mind had cleared. He felt sharp, every one of his senses alert, his body ready for battle.

He looked up and down Bishopsgate Street Without. It was still busy but the traffic had lessened along with the sunlight. Soon the City gates would be closed and anyone on the outside would have to find lodgings at one of the nearby inns.

So many inns. If he had just abducted a woman who was probably unconscious, he would take her to a room in one of them. Maybe pretend she had fainted on a long journey and tell the landlord he needed a bed for her quickly.

That's what he'd do and he was an expert at deception. His gaze settled on the nearest inn, the Swan, and he urged the horse into the stable yard.

* * *

ISABEL AWOKE to the sound of hooves clacking on the stones outside the window. She tried to identify how many horses there were but everything kept fading in and out. It took her a moment to realize it wasn't the noise fading, but her.

The pain in her head had lessened a little but the ache in her shoulders had increased thanks to her awkward position in the chair. She wriggled to try and adjust the bonds but they were too tight. So she tried using her powers, concentrating on removing the ropes, seeing them untie in her mind.

Something moved. The knot at her wrists weakened and she could almost pull her hands free. She closed her eyes and focused, shutting out the background sounds of the inn. Every nerve in her body strained with the effort she put into releasing herself. The ropes loosened more. Almost there—

The tumbling of a lock broke her concentration. She opened her eyes and saw Fox enter the room. He closed the door behind him and watched her from a distance, his attention entirely on her, wary.

"Untie me now," she ordered him.

Her words seemed to release him from his stupor. He smiled and she couldn't believe she'd never noticed how sly it was. "No."

"What do you want? What have I done to deserve this?"

He crossed the room to the table and poured some wine from the jug into one of the cups. He had discarded the long blue robe that marked him as an apprentice and only wore loose gray trunk hose, leather doublet and a plain flat cap. "Let's just say I hate working for a woman."

She had no doubt he spoke the truth but it wasn't the rentire reason for the kidnap. "Then you should have sought an apprenticeship elsewhere. Now, are you going to tell me why you've abducted me or am I going to have to guess?" Her headache had returned like an angry warrior wielding a club around her skull. But she wouldn't let Fox see her pain. She wouldn't show the little rat any weakness.

"Let's discuss it over a drink." He held the cup to her lips. "Thirsty?"

The pungent smell of the wine roused her a little. She sniffed again. There was something else mixed with it. A bitter odor teased her senses, tingling inside her sensitive nose. If she'd been more alert, more like herself, she probably would have identified the herb but her head felt like it was wading through mud and singling out a single scent was impossible.

"What's in the wine?" She blinked up at a blurry Fox standing above her.

He cocked an eyebrow. "You can't tell? The great Isabel Camm can't detect what herb is mixed in with her wine?" He chuckled deep in his throat. "Just a little something to keep you awake."

"Liar." Whatever it was, she doubted he wanted her awake. "I'll not drink it." With renewed desperation, she focused again on her bonds. They were looser after her last attempt but not enough to free herself.

But with her pounding head and the extra distraction of

Fox's presence she couldn't concentrate, couldn't budge them. It was hopeless.

"Stop doing that!"

Her eyes snapped open at the menacing snarl in his voice.

"I know what you're doing," he said. "I know you're a witch and what you're capable of."

"Which is why you've drugged me."

He smiled that sly smile again. Just like a fox. Appropriate. He returned the cup to the table but kept his gaze on her. Then he moved behind her and tightened the ropes. "Couldn't quite do it, could you? How frustrating that must be."

She ignored his taunts. If she was going to get out alive, she needed to remain calm and in control of her emotions. It was the only way to find out what his plans were and then thwart them. But calmness eluded her—all she felt was a bone-shaking fear.

"Tell me why you've abducted me," she said, "and we'll come to an arrangement. Do you want money?"

"Money?" He sniggered. "Not anymore. I have enough money now. What I want is to have my life back. I want respect. I want what's owed to me—my apprenticeship."

She frowned but that only made her head ache more. "What are you talking about?"

He huffed out a breath and sat on the bed. "Where do I begin? Ah yes, with your father."

"My father?"

His youthful face turned hard, the mouth twisted. "He destroyed my father's life, and therefore mine."

Isabel blinked at him. "Did my father know yours? Was he a customer at our Winchester shop?" Perhaps it was all a misunderstanding and she could help clear up the problem before he did something they both regretted.

No, not even she believed that.

Fox burst into laughter but there wasn't a trace of humor in it. "You stupid bitch. My father was an apothecary too, just like yours. Better than yours. Until your father destroyed his reputation and his business. And my future."

Isabel's heart skidded to a halt. Now she understood. Fox's father was the third apothecary at Whitehall seven years ago.

Aside from her Papa, there had been Pullman, Shawe and... She frowned. No one named Fox.

"What is your real name?" she asked.

He looked surprised that she'd guessed that much. "Finch. I decided to use Fox when I came to London."

"And my father discredited your father in front of his colleagues. Isn't that right?"

"And the queen." He leaned forward on the bed, resting his elbows on his knees, but his casual position didn't fool her into thinking he was anything other than alert to her every movement. "So you know what happened at the conference?"

"I know," she said. "And I'm sorry for the way in which Papa confronted your father and the other apothecaries about their...questionable remedies. He should have had more tact. But Papa was a plain speaker and I can imagine his accusations must have wounded. Shawe was one of the others, you know."

"I know. And your apology is much too late." He screwed up one side of his face in a sneer. "I don't care anyway."

"About what?"

"About anything!" He stood. "My father died a poor, broken man because of your Papa. My mother was left with nothing." He stood over her and bent down so their faces were level. His eyes flashed in the dull light, either from tears or anger, she couldn't tell. "She worked herself to an early grave to feed me and my sisters. When we buried her, I vowed I would get my revenge."

She shook her head. "I don't understand. My father is long dead."

He straightened, nodding. "It was the best day of my life when I found out. I felt...free. I decided to start again. I wanted to re-establish the family business in London, earn back my father's good name and make a life for me and my girl, Betty."

Isabel felt nervous. If this had something to do with Betty breaking up with him then she was in trouble. Men could turn desperate when a woman they loved left them.

How desperate had Nick become when she left him?

But none of this told Isabel why Fox had abducted her. "A noble occupation for any young man," she said cautiously.

"Of course I needed an apprenticeship to open a shop in London. I applied to Shawe because my father had praised him after their meeting at Whitehall. Luckily he took me on." He laughed, the harsh snort reverberating around the room. "But just when everything's going so well, you turn up and the nightmare begins again. The old man loves you like a daughter." He strode from one side of the room to the other, glaring at her every time he passed. "You could do no wrong with him and the old lady, even though your father nearly ruined him. Then Mistress Shawe dies and he's ailing and you take over everything. Not me, who's been there longer, but you. A woman. A stupid, insignificant woman." He suddenly stopped pacing. "My apprenticeship came to a grinding halt. I'll never leave Shawe's at this rate. Never set up on my own."

It definitely wasn't the time to tell him he'd failed in nearly every component of his apprenticeship. Shawe couldn't possibly recommend him for membership in the Grocers Company. Without that, Fox would never be allowed to open his own shop in London or even to settle down as a paid journeyman. And without a good, reliable income, he'd never find a decent wife.

"Then my Betty left me," he went on. "Says she's got another man, someone with prospects."

Cold fingers of fear crept across Isabel's skin. His reasons for hating her were completely irrational. He blamed her for Betty's leaving—men had killed for similar reasons. "So you resent me," she said, carefully. "Why kill me now after all these years?"

"Kill you? I'm not going to kill you. You're going to be arrested for witchcraft." He looked like a delighted schoolboy waiting for a congratulatory pat on the head from the teacher. "I couldn't believe my luck when I found out you were a witch. I went to the Justice of the Peace straight away after my little visit to Ashbourne House this morning. But when you decided to leave London suddenly I knew I had to capture you and hold you until he could come. I've sent him a message. He's on his way."

Panic seized Isabel, paralyzing her. She tried concentrating on the ropes again but nothing happened. She couldn't focus enough to use her powers. What good were they if she couldn't use them when she needed them most!

"So you tried to poison the queen too then?" She had to keep him talking, had to keep him occupied until she had enough strength to use her powers on the bonds.

He shrugged as if it were nothing. "Lord Croxley came to me with an offer. Said he would pay me a lot of money to poison the sweetmeats. I had access to poisons and could make a delivery to the palace without raising suspicions." He shrugged again. "I got only half my money since the queen's stupid lady ate the sweetmeats instead, but half is still a nice amount."

His sanity was closer to the edge than she realized. She shivered at the coldness in his heart. If he could willingly commit murder and treason for money, then he would have no qualms about killing her if pushed. "And was it your father who tried to poison her seven years ago?" she asked, determined to continue talking to keep her own fears at bay.

"Yes." He smiled his slick smile again. "And he did it so your father took the blame. Very clever, don't you think?"

"Yes," she said wryly. "Very. So he got his revenge, and yet you still think you need more."

"Having your father arrested didn't stop my father's business from failing. It didn't put food on the table, or keep my parents alive."

She shook her head, genuinely confused. "So why try to poison the queen again? What could that possibly have to do with your vengeance against me?"

"You always think everything is about you," he sneered. "Well, it isn't. It had nothing to do with you. I needed money to set myself up for when I left Shawe's."

Finally she understood. "So all you needed to do was finish your apprenticeship," she said.

"Which I couldn't do with you in the way, always telling Shawe how lazy I was."

"So you tried to make it look like I did the poisoning. With me gone, disgraced, you could take my place and dupe Shawe into giving you the recommendation you need."

It hurt her aching head to take it all in but she thought she had worked it out. Fox must have suspected all along that Nick was a spy and so to deflect suspicion from himself and onto her, he must have planted the note from Lord Croxley in her Herbal. Good Lord, he was a scoundrel of the worst kind.

Rage quietly rose within her, a slow burning fire. She would not let him get away with it. "So were you attempting to kill Nick too?"

"Your husband?" He laughed as if that were a great joke. "Of course. He wouldn't arrest you like I planned, so I thought they'd send someone else upon his death, someone who would arrest you. Someone not under your spells." He shrugged. "Besides, it seemed appropriate. It's because of you that my Betty left me. So I decided to make you suffer like I did by taking away the one person you love. I couldn't believe it when I overheard you speaking in The Four Feathers. To find out he was your husband was a gift." He raised his eyes to the ceiling as if the gift had come straight from Heaven. "I decided then to kill him and watch you in pain. I already suspected he was investigating the poisoning, so eliminating him would serve two purposes."

"But you didn't kill him," she said, defiant. "He's too good to be beaten by someone like you."

"He had the devil's help from you," Fox growled. He was little more than a silhouette on the bed now in the waning light. She hadn't seen any candles or lanterns in the room so perhaps he would leave soon to get some. She hoped.

"But maybe its better this way," he went on. "He can watch you die on the gallows first." He lifted his face and she could just make out the twinkling in his eyes. "Maybe he'll die later, like your mother did. Pine away for his lovely, sweet wife." He sniggered.

"Whatever happens to me, Nick will make sure you don't get away with treason."

"You think they'll believe the man who married a witch? Especially when all the evidence points to the witch being the poisoner. No one will believe him when they find out his wife is a witch." He had it all worked out, every turn, every twist.

He was right. They wouldn't believe Nick after her arrest for witchcraft. Not even Lord Ashbourne could save her with so much evidence against her.

Isabel pulled against the bonds at her wrists with renewed desperation. She tried to concentrate and focus, picturing the knots loosening, the ropes untying.

"I told you before, stop that!" Fox leapt off the bed and came at her, his fist raised.

She didn't flinch, just saw the blow being deflected in her mind. It worked. But only just. In her weakened state, the punch still landed on the side of her jaw, hard enough to snap her head back but not hard enough to break any bones. Fighting against the pain and nauseating fear, she looked desperately around for him. But it was so dark and everything, even the shadows, had blurred after the punch.

So when the next blow struck, she was taken by complete surprise. She managed to keep her eyes open a moment more, just long enough to see Fox smirking and nodding to himself.

CHAPTER 17

*N*icholas slipped into the taproom of the Swan and surveyed the crowd from beneath his hood. Several people sat on the stools or at tables, drinking and talking quietly, weary from their travels. None of them were Fox.

He nodded at the landlord, an immense man with jowls that wobbled as he poured ales. "Drink, Sir?" he offered as Nicholas approached.

Nicholas shook his head. "I'm looking for a woman."

The landlord's bushy eyebrows spiked as his gaze scrutinized Nicholas from head to toe. "Didn't pick you as the type. But I can get you one if that's what you're after. What kind?"

Nicholas refrained from calling him vile names. He needed this man on his side if he was to find Isabel. "Not the kind you're thinking. I'm after a specific woman. Smallish, beautiful, golden brown hair, blue eyes." He could describe her forever but he kept it simple. "She might have come here looking for a room for the night."

The landlord shrugged. "Could be anyone." He moved off to pour an ale from the barrel. Nicholas waited with all the patience of a starved lion. Damn it, every minute that passed meant she could be further away. Or closer to death. Finally the landlord returned.

"She might have been brought here by a man." Nicholas

caught the landlord's arm when he started to walk off again. He ignored the scowl he received in return but let go. "She could have been unconscious."

The landlord's jaw fell like a slack drawbridge, making his jowls quiver. "I might have seen this woman of yours," he said, regaining his composure. He wiped a cloth over a tankard with an air of indifference.

Nicholas was familiar with this type of source. He pulled out his purse and handed over a sovereign.

The landlord pocketed it without hesitation. "A lad brought her in earlier. Said she was his sister and had fainted. Wanted a quiet room where she wouldn't be disturbed."

"What did the lad look like?"

The landlord chewed his fat lip in thought. "Brown hair, brown eyes." He shrugged. "Just like every other lad in the city."

"Which room?"

The landlord hesitated and Nicholas leaned forward and held his gaze. "I am Sir Nicholas Merritt and the lady in question is my wife." He spoke low so no one else could hear him, but the menace in his voice came through as sharp as a blade. "She has been abducted and if she is harmed in any way, I will kill the lad and then I will kill you if you do not tell me where she is. Now."

"Third door on the left upstairs."

Nicholas studied the stairs and produced another sovereign. The landlord tried to snatch it but Nicholas held it out of his reach. "I want you to send someone up to the room and lure the lad out for a while."

"How am I supposed to do that?"

"Tell him you've got a free meal for him then feed him." Nicholas shrugged. "I don't care how, just keep him out long enough for me to get my wife."

"I'll need more money for the meal."

Nicholas handed it over.

"How do I know you're telling me the truth?" the landlord asked.

"Because I'm paying you to believe me. And I'm very good with this rapier," he said, patting the hilt of his sword. He sidled over to the far corner of the room where the shadows were deepest. The crowd hummed around him yet he was oblivious to them. Their conversations and laughter belonged to happy people, not the world in which beloved wives were abducted or faced hanging for witchcraft. He flipped his hood over his head and watched the stairs, waiting.

A few minutes later, Fox came down looking like he'd won a prize at a fair. The landlord showed him to a table away from the stairs and the hostess presented him with a steaming stew. Fox tucked in with relish, slopping the stew down his doublet in his eagerness.

Nicholas took a candle and slipped up the stairs, almost running to the third door. He tried it and was surprised to find it unlocked. Fox must be confident no one would try to get in. Or that Isabel wouldn't get out.

He froze when he saw her slumped in a chair, her wrists and ankles tied. He placed the candle on the table then knelt before her and gently cradled her head between his hands. Her eyes were closed but she breathed. She was alive. Thank God.

"Isabel," he whispered. "Isabel, wake up, sweetheart." He gently shook her and she stirred.

"Nick?" she said the moment before her eyes opened. She looked towards him but he wasn't sure she could quite see him. "You're here," she said, wonder in her voice.

"I'm here. And you're coming home with me." He began to untie her ankles, still supporting her head on his shoulder.

"Home." She sighed, snuggling into his neck. She felt good, her breath warm against his skin, her scent filling him. He desired her, even now with Fox stuffing himself downstairs.

There would be time enough to sate that desire soon because he wasn't going to let her walk out of his life anymore.

"Can you hold your head up? I need to untie your wrists."

She nodded and lifted her head. The light from the candle played in the hollows of her cheeks and sunken eyes and picked out the bruise on her chin. He swore and gently kissed it, wishing he could make the hurt go away. She turned and her lips brushed his. She tasted good, sweet and familiar and he could have relished that kiss all night.

Not yet.

"Isabel," he whispered. "Are you all right?"

She nodded. "Hurry," she said, pulling away. She seemed more alert, holding her head up on her own and glancing towards the door. "Fox...where is he?"

"Downstairs. Eating."

She gasped. "But he'll kill you when he sees you!"

"Don't worry. I can take care of Fox."

"The Justice of the Peace is also on his way."

Nick swore. In his rush, he fumbled with the ropes. Fox had definitely tied them tightly.

"Nick!" she screamed.

He looked up just in time to dive out of the path of the dagger thrown at him. He rolled into a crouching position as Fox ran at him, another dagger drawn. Teeth bared, the blade held high, Fox growled like an animal as he came at Nicholas.

Instead of waiting for the lad to reach him, Nicholas rushed at him, low and fast, and caught him in the stomach with his shoulder. The tackle sent Fox tumbling to the floor, the impact causing him to let go of the dagger. It landed out of reach. Nicholas stood over him, sword drawn.

"I'll kill you," he snarled at the little whoreson. "I'm going to break every bone in your body first and then I'll kill you, slowly and very, very painfully." He raised his sword and Fox curled into a ball, his hands covering his face, whimpering.

"Nick, no," Isabel said from where she was still tied to the chair. "He's not worth going to prison for."

Anger crushed Nicholas's insides, making breathing difficult. But the JP would be there soon and Isabel was right. He sheathed his sword and picked up the whoreson by the front of his doublet. He had to do something to him, let the little toad know he couldn't go around kidnapping his wife—his wife, damn it—and expect to get away with it.

So he threw him against the wall. The entire room seemed to shake with the impact. Fox slithered to the floor like a wet cloth, mewling all the way.

"Nick! Look out!"

He turned, just in time to see Helpman's two thugs coming at him. The JP himself stood in the open doorway, his smug smile widening when he saw Isabel.

He clicked his tongue as if chiding a child. "I told you not to harm him," he said to Nicholas. The constables circled, their daggers drawn, ready to strike. "And now that you have...well, I have to arrest you too."

"He abducted my wife," Nicholas said without taking his eyes off both constables. It wasn't easy when they split up. He drew his sword and stepped back to keep them in his line of sight.

"On the contrary, he was holding her until my arrival. A commendable feat given her considerable powers, don't you think?"

"She is not a witch," Nicholas said, the lie rolling easily off his tongue. He'd tell a thousand lies if they could save Isabel. "And I will be damned if I let you arrest her."

"Nick, don't," Isabel said.

He didn't look at her, didn't want to see the plea in her eyes. He knew what she was going to say and he didn't want to hear it. "No, Isabel," he said. "I'm not losing you again."

"They'll hurt you," she said, her voice catching.

"I don't care."

"Listen to your wife," Helpman said. "We don't want to harm you, Sir Nicholas."

Nicholas snorted. The biggest thug moved forward but Nicholas thrust his sword towards him and the constable backed up. "If you want my wife, you have to kill me because nothing less will stop me protecting her."

"Nick, please," Isabel said. "Don't do this. You can't sacrifice yourself for me. I won't allow it."

"I can't let you go without a fight," he said. "How do you think I'd feel letting the woman I love be captured by this fool."

There was a pause in which Fox groaned. Nicholas didn't want to turn around to look but he hoped the little dung fly would stay unconscious a while longer.

"You do love me," she said weakly.

Having his back to her and his sword drawn on two cave

dwellers wasn't the ideal way to affirm his love but it would have to do.

"Yes." He readjusted his grip, ready to force his way out of the room. "Didn't I tell you? I never stopped."

"Yes, you did, but...never mind."

He smiled at the soft sound of her voice, wishing he could turn around and look at her, touch her, kiss her.

"How nauseating," Helpman sneered. "Now, step aside or my men will force you."

Nicholas beckoned them with his free hand. "Come on then. I can't stand around here all day waiting."

He heard Isabel's breath hitch and imagined her trying to get her powers working again. He hoped she managed to do it soon because Helpman was also drawing his sword. Three against one were tough odds. Thank God he had a sword and not a bow and arrows.

The big constable signaled to his colleague and they lunged at the same time. Nicholas easily parried one blow and dodged the other by stepping to the side.

"That was pathetic," he said. "My sister could do better than that."

The big one reacted exactly how Nicholas expected him to. He growled, drawing his thick brows together, and ran at Nicholas like a wild boar. Again, Nicholas easily parried the blade, but this time his sword point nicked the man's hand. He dropped his dagger with a yelp.

Nicholas had no time to admire his handiwork. The other constable came at him from the side but Helpman had also decided to contribute, waving his sword flamboyantly as he charged. It was almost comical. Nicholas expected three against one to be difficult odds but it was embarrassingly easy. If this was the city's finest law enforcers then it was amazing London wasn't infested with more criminals.

Nicholas kicked the dagger out of the constable's hand as he deflected Helpman's wild thrust with a flick of his rapier. But Helpman tried again and this time, whether by design or pure luck, the first thug also rushed at Nicholas again. As he was occupied with parrying Helpman's sword, the constable caught him in a headlock. Powerful muscles clenched around Nicholas's throat, cutting off his air supply. But still he managed to parry Helpman again and again. With his head ready to explode and his throat burning, Nicholas knew he only had precious moments before he blacked out.

When Helpman paused to gather himself, Nicholas saw his chance. He thrust his elbow back and up, catching the constable below the ribs. The big oaf's grip loosened just enough for Nicholas to suck in delicious air then flip his attacker over his shoulder. He also flipped the other constable when he ran at Nicholas. The two men lay groaning on the floor and Helpman stood to the side, his sword drooping, his eyes wide with alarm.

"Drop the sword or she dies." The threat came from behind him.

Nicholas swung round, terror making his heart stop.

Fox held a knife to Isabel's throat. He'd pressed hard enough into her flesh that a trickle of blood dripped into the top of her ruff. Isabel's eyes stared unblinking back at him, but she otherwise seemed calm. He'd never seen a woman so brave. And that just made her even more beautiful.

"Let her go," Nicholas said, hoping he looked as composed as she did.

"Make me," Fox said.

Nicholas's grip tightened on his rapier's hilt. He should have killed the little whoreson when he had the chance. He wanted to kill him now, but he couldn't. Not without Isabel getting hurt first.

He closed his eyes, tried to control his wrath. He wanted to hit something, hurt someone, make him pay.

Damn it, why hadn't he been watching Fox? Why had he let him get to Isabel so easily? The coward must have faked unconsciousness and Nicholas silently cursed himself for being duped by an old trick.

"It's all right, Nick," she said, soothingly. How could she remain so calm when everything around her, himself included, was in utter turmoil?

"It's not all right," was all he could say around his tight throat. Nothing will be all right until you are safe in my arms.

He had to do something. Had to, even if it led to his own death. If he could save her then whatever happened to him would be worth it.

"Put down your weapon," Helpman said. His men approached Nicholas cautiously, one holding a leather strap probably to tie Nicholas's hands together.

He had only moments in which to do something. He estimated the distance between himself and Fox. If he had a dagger instead of a sword he could throw it, but Fox was too close to Isabel to chance his arm with the rapier. His eyes darted to the ceiling, the walls, even the candles in the hope of finding something, anything that might work in his favor.

There was nothing. Just him. Just his rapier.

He would have to charge at Fox and hope to get to him before he inflicted a deep wound.

Something suddenly flew past his line of sight. Then Fox was on the ground, the constable's forgotten dagger sticking out of his eye.

"What was that?" Helpman hurried to Fox's side and checked his breathing even though it was clear from all the blood that the lad was dead. Helpman looked to his men. Both shrugged and shook their heads. The JP swallowed and his gaze shifted to Isabel.

She merely stared at Fox.

Nicholas groaned and closed his eyes. It was all over. He hadn't saved her at all. She'd saved and condemned herself by a single act of desperation.

"Witch!" one of the constables shouted, as if he'd not believed it before. He turned and ran out the door. His feet could be heard pounding down the stairs.

The other constable, the big one, stayed but he stared like a dazed animal at her. "Now what, Sir?" he eventually asked Helpman.

Helpman watched Isabel as she untied her own bonds. She must have regained her powers in the last few moments. "I... I..." the JP said.

"You leave," Nicholas said. "Now."

Isabel spared a passing glance at the body of Fox then rushed

233

to Nicholas. He caught her, crushing her to him so hard he thought he'd break her. He buried his face in her neck, breathed her scent deep into his body, but kept one eye on the men.

"Oh, Nick," she whispered. She caught his face between her hands and buried her fingers in his hair. She pulled his head down and gave him a brief kiss. She tasted like Heaven, sweet and warm. He wanted that kiss to continue, to feel her lips all over his body. But there was work to be done and he drew back. He caressed her cheek and gently touched the bruise on her chin.

She gave him a small smile before turning in his arms and pressing back against him, her head nestled below his chin. He kept one arm around her waist, his other still holding his sword although he kept the point down.

"We walk out of here and no one else will be hurt," Nicholas said to Helpman. He signaled the constable to stand near the JP so he could keep them both together on the far side of the room, away from the door.

He obeyed and Nicholas backed towards the door, Isabel in step with him.

"I can't stay in London," she said when they were out of Helpman's hearing.

"I know. We'll find somewhere to be together," he said softly. "Where no one knows us."

"No." She turned and looked up at him, her eyes wide. She looked more afraid now than she had when tied to the chair. "I can't let you throw away your life for me."

He pressed a finger to her lips and shushed her gently. "We'll discuss this later." But he had no intention of negotiating with her. They were going together and that was final.

Once outside the room, he slammed the door shut, grabbed her hand and pulled her after him down the stairs.

"You can get out of this," she said from behind him. "With your contacts—"

"Not now, Isabel, I'm busy."

"But Nick, this is the only chance we'll have to talk." She sounded angry and a little breathless. She'd been through a lot and was probably still suffering the effects of her abduction. He wanted to slow down for her but didn't dare.

"I'm leaving London as soon as we get out of here," she said. "And you're going home. Do you understand me? I'll not take no for an answer."

At the base of the stairs, he slowed his pace. "Neither will I." He turned and picked her up, lifting her unceremoniously over his shoulder like a sack of wheat so that her rump stuck out near his face. He resisted the urge to bite it since everyone in the main bar was looking at them. "I've just got you back after six long years. I am not letting you run off again. I love you, Isabel. You are mine and I'm going to keep you by my side no matter what, no matter where."

Two well-dressed gentlemen approached them, hands hovering over their sheathed swords. "Everything all right here, Miss?" one asked.

"Perfectly," Isabel said from over Nicholas's shoulder. "It's just a little marital disagreement. You know what it's like."

The one who'd spoken snickered. "That I do. Good luck," he said to Nicholas and they returned to their seats.

Nicholas nodded to the fat landlord, thought of telling him about the dead body upstairs then decided against it. Announcing that type of news would only hinder their escape. He pushed open the door and carried Isabel outside into the cold air. She'd stopped struggling so he let her down gently. It belatedly occurred to him that she could easily have extracted herself at any time if she'd wanted.

"Nicholas, I—"

"Be quiet, Wife," he said, unable to resist teasing her. "We've got to get away."

She put her hands on her hips, her eyes flashing in the darkness. "I will not. You don't understand what—"

He took her face in his hands and kissed her hard. He felt the tension in her body ease and she relaxed into him, soft and pliant. She felt so good. So right. So...his.

"We don't have time for this," he said, drawing away.

Isabel felt giddy from the kiss and the remaining effects of Fox's herbs. She tried to think straight, think of how she could make Nick understand that she would never jeopardize his life. And right now, he was in danger just as much as she was. But he could still get away and with Lord Ashbourne and his other important friends to protect him, it was possible his life would be spared.

Unlike hers.

The Justice of the Peace had witnessed her witchcraft first hand—there was no way he would let her walk away. She checked over her shoulder, expecting to see him racing out of the inn to arrest her. She had to escape before she did something terrible again. She didn't want to hurt anyone else. It was awful enough to have killed Fox, but to kill someone who was only doing his duty... No, she wanted to avoid that at all costs.

She had to leave now, slip into the dark lanes and disappear into the night. And she couldn't take Nick with her.

But Nick had other ideas. He pulled her by the hand into the stable yard, shouting at the lad to ready his horse.

"We'll travel as far as we can tonight, taking the lesser roads—"

"No!" She pulled him to a halt. "Don't make me render you unconscious, Nick. Please," she added when he said nothing. She couldn't see him well in the darkness but his seething anger reached her through their touching hands. He was furious.

"Doesn't my declaration of love mean anything to you?" His voice sounded raw, choked, and she wanted to kiss away the hurt and anger she'd caused.

Her tears spilled hotly down her cheeks and she swiped them with the back of her free hand. "It means everything to me." And she wasn't referring merely to his words of a few moments ago, but to his actions as well. He'd been willing to sacrifice his life for her up in the bedchamber and he was willing to sacrifice his future now by following her. He had thoroughly banished the doubts she'd harbored after eavesdropping on his conversation with Lord Ashbourne.

But she couldn't allow his sacrifice. She would do anything to keep him safe, and that included ensuring he didn't come with her. She held his face between her hands, taking one last look at the man who'd stolen her heart and wishing with everything she had that circumstances were different. "I love you, Nick," she whispered, the tears flowing like a waterfall down her cheeks. "Goodbye."

He opened his mouth to protest just as she focused on the rake leaning against the stables behind him. But her concentration was broken by shouting and the tool dropped to the stones with a clatter.

The shouting intensified, became a roar. It wasn't just one person but a lot of people.

Nick's gaze flicked past her. He swore and pulled her after him into the stable. She turned and saw the crowd coming into the yard, led by Helpman and his constable. He had raised a hue and cry back in the inn to capture them.

"There they are!" someone cried.

"Witch! Get the witch!"

Wielding swords, daggers, chairs and even tankards, the heaving mass surged. Not running, not hurrying, but steadily moving forward.

"Get up," Nick said, cupping his hands so she could step up onto the saddled horse.

"We won't make it." Panic pitched her voice high. "Nick, there's too many of them."

"You can use your powers. Sweep them aside to make a path."

She shook her head, even as she settled into the saddle. "There's too many. I can't—"

"Shh." He got up behind her and circled his arms around her waist. "Yes, you can," he said into her ear, his voice calm. "You can do anything, Isabel. You're amazing."

His confidence and powerful body soothed her. She could feel the strong beat of his heart at her back, his breath in her hair. He was like a solid shield behind her, protecting her. She felt safe. Whatever happened, they were together.

As it should be. It had taken her six years and a shocking ordeal but she knew that now.

He picked up the reins and rode the horse slowly into the yard. "I am Sir Nicholas Merritt." He spoke like a commander to his army and Isabel's heart swelled with pride. Her husband was an impressive man. "We are innocent of any crime. Step aside."

The mass hesitated, some muttered to their neighbors, but Helpman urged them forward with a shake of his brandished sword. "You won't be harmed," he called back to them. "We have God on our side. He will protect us."

Nick sighed and she felt him shake his head. "Ready?" he said to Isabel.

She nodded, focusing on the crowd, picturing them falling away to make a path, like Moses parting the Red Sea. She didn't know if she could do it with so many people, but she had to try. Had to get Nick to safety.

A familiar voice shouting above the crowd's hum broke her concentration before a single person was moved by her witchcraft. "Go back inside! On the orders of Her Majesty the Queen, these people are not to be harmed."

Then the crowd did indeed part, but not by Isabel's doing. Lord Ashbourne rode calmly through them on a white horse. A sizeable contingent dressed in Ashbourne livery followed him on foot. Using their swords, they hustled the crowd back inside the Swan.

"Not you," Ashbourne said to the JP. "You need to hear this."

"Hear what?" Helpman said. He looked towards the vanishing mob then to Isabel and Nick and finally to Ashbourne. He cleared his throat and straightened but he still looked small beside the mounted earl. "Who are you and by whose orders do you come here?"

"I am Richard Savoy, second Earl of Ashbourne and I am here on Sir Francis Walsingham's orders, on behalf of Her Majesty the Queen." He leaned down to look Helpman in the eye. "Do those credentials suffice?"

Helpman nodded quickly, swallowing again.

"Ash must be drunk," Nick whispered in her ear. "Either that or furious. Probably both." He chuckled and she felt the muscles in his body relax. He pulled her closer, kissed her throat near the cut inflicted by Fox. Already it had begun to heal without her even thinking about it. "I love you, Wife" he said.

She leaned back into him and reached up to rub the back of his neck. She turned her head and smiled as she kissed him, despite her lingering uncertainty. Whatever happened to her now, at least she knew Nick would be safe. Lord Ashboune would get him out of trouble.

"Am I to let them both go?" Helpman asked Ashbourne.

"Yes."

Isabel's heart rose into her throat. Could it be possible? Could she be free? Nick directed their horse closer to Ashbourne and Helpman. The four of them were alone in the dark stable yard, the slender moon providing little more than a faint glow.

"But I saw her with my own eyes!" Helpman protested. "She's a wi—"

"You saw nothing." Ashbourne pointed to the inn. "Get inside and be grateful you still have a job."

Helpman turned and strode off as ordered, running the last few paces until he reached the inn door. Ashbourne nodded at Nick then took Isabel's hand and kissed it.

When he lingered too long, Nick cleared his throat. "That's my wife you're kissing."

Ashbourne dropped her hand and Isabel was sure she could see his eyes shining before he glanced away. "You have all the luck with women," he joked without looking at them.

"Oh, does he now?" she said to break the strange mood that had engulfed them. "And here Nick tells me he's been thinking only of me these last six years."

"I have! Isabel, you're the only woman for me. Ash is being a—"

"Come now, Nick." She laughed and leaned into him. Amazingly, his erection pressed against the small of her back. She wanted to touch it, feel him inside her, feel the weight of his body on top of her, beneath her. She grew hot with need. Lifting and turning her head slightly, she pulled him down into a thorough kiss that lit a fire in her belly and dampened her inner thighs.

"I need a drink," Lord Ashbourne growled and Isabel broke the kiss, embarrassed. "Know anywhere good around here?"

"There's a little place right about, oh, here," Nick said with a grin. "Called The Swan. Mention my name to the landlord and he'll treat you how you deserve."

Ashbourne snorted and dismounted.

"And watch out for the dead body, third door on the left upstairs."

"Fox?"

Isabel and Nick both nodded. "He tried to poison the queen," she said. "And kill my husband." She looked at Nick, too afraid to think of what might have happened if he'd succeeded. She kissed him again, and Ashbourne made a low sound in the back of his throat.

Nick dismounted and clapped the earl on the shoulder. "You'll find yourself a woman of your own one day," he said quietly. When the earl appeared to ignore him, he added, "Thank you, my friend."

Ashbourne clasped Nick's arm in a strong shake. "I didn't do much. It's all thanks to you and your reputation with Walsingham. It appears you are indispensable. I'm just glad I got here on time." He winked up at Isabel. "Although I don't know if she's worth the trouble. A little stubborn for my liking."

"She's worth it all right." Nick led their horse out of the stable yard. Feeling daring, Isabel blew Lord Ashbourne a kiss. Without turning around, Nick said, "Stop flirting with my wife, Ash."

"I was framed!" Ashbourne's laughter followed them out to the street.

Bishopsgate Street Without was quiet, dark and freezing cold. Isabel shivered and Nick mounted behind her again and held her close against him. "Well," he said, nuzzling into her, "we can try our luck at the gate. They'll probably let us through if I tell them who I—."

Their horse reared when a dark figure ran out in front of them. Nick's grip tightened and he cursed the stranger.

"You're not going anywhere." Helpman! He must have slipped out of the inn during the chaos.

"You heard Lord Ashbourne," Nick snarled. "The queen—"

"She doesn't have all the facts." Helpman struck out with his sword, not at Isabel or Nick, but at the horse. The beast collapsed beneath them, its scream ripping through the night.

Isabel slid off but couldn't get away before the horse fell on her, its heavy body crushing her legs. Her own screams joined the beast's, and were echoed by Nick.

Oh God, not him too.

She managed to open her eyes, fighting off the unbearable pain shooting through her to see Nick charging at Helpman, his sword drawn. She couldn't see his face but she could feel his wrath vibrating across the air, and hear it in his battle-cry. He would kill the JP.

Isabel sucked in a breath and pulled herself free of the dying creature. Pushing the agony away, she pressed her palms to her legs. During the precious seconds in which her crushed bones knitted, Nick engaged Helpman in a sword fight. One, two parries, then he struck him with a blow to the stomach.

"No!" Her protest came too late. Helpman fell, clutching his bleeding side. "Not this way," she whimpered. Not another death.

Lord Ashbourne suddenly appeared and swore. He knelt beside a gasping Helpman and pressed his hands against the wound to stop the blood flow.

Nick looked down at the dying man and shook his head. "He would never have left Isabel alone. Not until she was dead."

"I have to do something," she said.

"Why? He would have killed you."

"I know but it doesn't matter."

He paused then nodded slowly. "I understand."

She knelt beside Lord Ashbourne and he removed his hands. She pressed her palms to the hole in Helpman's abdomen and felt the wound healing as her own flesh grew hot.

Moments later, Helpman blinked up at her, the sheen of shock making his eyes shine in the moonlight. "You didn't have to do that," he whispered.

"Yes, I did. I want no more deaths tonight."

Nick's hand rested on her shoulder, solid, sure. "I, on the other hand, have no such sentiments. Not for the likes of you. But my wife's heart is special, pure. You'd do best to remember that because she may not be around to heal you next time."

Helpman gulped as he slowly stood, keeping Nick in his line of sight.

"Very true," Ashbourne said. "And to help you remember, I'll be taking you on a little journey tomorrow to Whitehall. Some very important people will want to talk to you."

"I was only d d doing my job," Helpman stammered.

"And they'll define what that job is. Tomorrow." Ashbourne grabbed the back of Helpman's cloak and hustled him towards the inn.

Isabel turned to the horse and started the healing process on the animal's wound. She felt Nick move up behind her but he didn't touch her.

"I'm sorry," he said, voice low. "Your scream...I thought you were..."

"It's all right." The horse clambered unsteadily to its feet and trotted down the empty street before turning and trotting back. "I know why you did it." She touched Nick's face, tracing the hard contours of his cheeks, the soft line of his lips. "And I love you for it." She pulled him down for a gentle, sweet kiss which still managed to scorch her with its intensity.

"Now, we need to find an inn and stay the night. Not the Swan though."

"Definitely not the Swan." He caught the dangling reins in one hand and drew Isabel into his side with the other. He looked down at her. "I am going to make love to you all night, Isabel."

Delicious heat curled through her. "Is that a promise?"

"Absolutely. We've, ah, got some catching up to do."

"I know. Six years is a long time."

"It is, but that's not exactly what I meant. I told Mother you were pregnant."

"What? Why?"

"It felt like the right thing to say at the time."

"Well," she said with a theatrical sigh, "I suppose we'd best do something about it. I don't want to disappoint your mother."

He smiled and they walked off, Nick in the middle, the horse and his wife on either side. "Speaking of my mother," he said.

"Oh, dear." This time her sigh was for real. "Can't we talk about her tomorrow?"

He nodded. "In more detail, yes. All I want to say tonight is that Mother will be returning to Kent as soon as possible. But we're staying in London. And I want you to keep working at Shawe's. The old man needs you."

Now more than ever, she thought. She leaned into his warmth, relishing the feel of his powerful body. The anticipation of seeing it soon in all its beautiful nakedness quickened her pace. She felt safe, loved, desired. "I'm glad you finally see it my way."

"You're a persuasive woman."

She smiled. "Let's go make that baby."

Want more Isabel and Nick?
Available Now:
KISS OF ASH
The 2nd novel in the Witch Born series by C.J. Archer

Read on for an excerpt.

KISS OF ASH: AN EXCERPT

About KISS OF ASH

Pippa Ingleside will do anything to escape her ruthless uncle, but even she is surprised when her previously dormant powers aid her. Surprised and afraid. Her newly discovered abilities may have saved her but they condemn her at the same time.

Disguised as a boy, she travels to the home of Lord Ashbourne to find her one and only friend. To maintain her disguise and put a roof over her head, Pippa accepts a job as page of the wardrobe to Ash, a man as mysterious as he is dangerous. If he discovers her lie, he'll send her back to her uncle and her witchcraft will be exposed to the authorities.

As the lies build it gets harder for Pippa to maintain her disguise, especially when she falls in love with the man she must serve.

Her only hope is to find her friend. But when the friend is murdered, Ash investigates and where he goes, his page goes too. Together they uncover a web of secrets that could destroy Ash and condemn Pippa. But that's nothing compared to what happens when he discovers she's a woman...

CHAPTER 1

1583 – Berkshire, England

She would kill him.

Pippa Ingleside crumpled the documents in her fist and slammed them down on the desk, rattling quills and ink horns and her own fragile nerves. The swine! The thieving scoundrel! She'd known he was a black-hearted cur but to steal on such a grand scale was low indeed. She wouldn't have believed her uncle capable of it if the evidence wasn't written on those pages. And from his own niece too.

She flattened out the documents and scanned the figures on the first one again, then the second and third just to be sure. Anger rose with each page so that by the time she read the last one, she was almost blinded by sheer rage and the frustrating hopelessness of it all. It had been five years since she'd felt the same spirit-crushing emotions. Five long years that had slowly and consistently worn her down, drip by drip, until all that was left was a hole where something solid had been.

Then, as now, there was nothing she could do. That realization crushed her more than anything else. As Simon's ward she was completely at his mercy. As his prisoner, even more so. She could do nothing about his theft. She couldn't go to the authorities, couldn't appeal to another family member even if there were any.

Not long after her arrival, he'd locked her inside the confines of The Grange with only old Widow Dawson for company during the afternoons. But even that had been denied her after Pippa's two unsuccessful escape attempts. Although she'd never stopped looking for a means to get away, never stopped cursing her predicament, she'd always longed to know *why*. What did he gain by her trapped presence? He couldn't have been saving her for marriage because he never presented any candidates to her.

But now she knew. The documents had given her the answer.

"What are you doing in here?"

She stood so fast the chair she'd been sitting on fell back with a soft thud onto the rushes. Her uncle, filling the doorway with his bulk, glared at her. She gathered her wits and courage and prepared to confront him.

But he strode into the study and snatched the documents from her hand before she found her voice. "I said, what are you doing?"

He towered over her, anger making him seem bigger. He seethed with it. She'd never seen him so furious and her own rage subsided beneath the unnatural ferocity of his glare. Normally he did everything in such a controlled, cold manner. On the rare occasions he spoke to her, he never so much as raised his voice. He shouted at the servants regularly, even beat them sometimes, but to Pippa he was a silent, morose figure who avoided interacting with her. If it had been different, if he had funneled his infamous rages onto her, she could never have endured the last five years.

"Well?" His ruddy complexion had turned a violent mottled red, a stark contrast to the snow-white of his hair and beard. "Answer me, you stupid girl! What are you doing in *my* study?" He emphasized the "my" by smacking the rolled up pages against the palm of his hand.

"I, I..." Fear made her tongue useless. She watched the pages as they thumped into Simon's hand over and over, like a club he would use to hit something.

Hit her.

No, he wouldn't do it. He'd never laid a finger on her, even when she'd railed at him for weeks after informing her that she could never leave The Grange. Never receive callers, never receive friends. Never receive potential suitors. He hadn't used violence then and he wouldn't use it now, she was sure of it. For some reason, he thought physical force perfectly acceptable with his servants, but not with his niece. She supposed she should be grateful for small mercies. If nothing else, that knowledge gave her the courage to speak now.

"I was looking for some parchment for sketching." It was the truth. Or close to it. She *had* run out of parchment, but she'd been looking for the steward to ask him to fetch more when she realized her ever present guard was asleep and her uncle away for the afternoon. Ordinarily Widow Dawson never let Pippa out of her sight but she'd not turned up thanks to a chest cough that kept her abed. The sudden taste of freedom, and the yearning to discover the reason for her imprisonment, led her to her uncle's study.

"I found those instead." She nodded at the papers in his hand.

"You should never come in here. Ever!" He stepped closer, only an arm's length away. "This is my private study and these are my private papers. Do you understand me?"

"Perfectly." He must think her too dull-witted to have understood what she'd read. But then he had never taken much interest in her, before her father's death and especially after it. How could he possibly have known that her father had ensured his only child received a good education? And with nothing else to do during her imprisonment at The Grange, she'd devoured every book in her uncle's library, even the obscurest Greek poets. Widow Dawson had asked her friends and relations for reading material, but books were difficult to come by in Shelton. Simon's ignorance of his niece's education would prove to be his folly. She had a head for numbers and accounts, something her father had put to good use as his health failed in the year before his death.

"I understand that you have been stealing from me, Uncle." She would not let him get away with it. He might be her uncle and her guardian, but he was taking *her* money, her dowry. She might need it one day. She hadn't completely given up on being rescued by a knight in shining armor, although she had to admit knights, like books, were thin on the ground in Shelton.

"Stealing?" Simon snorted. With his round face and broad nose, the sound made him resemble a pig. "I'm merely taking what I am owed. Keeping you in the manner to which you have become accustomed is a costly business."

"Nonsense! It is clear from those figures that you are taking more than that. Much more. I demand an explanation. No, I demand every last penny be returned to me. With interest." Ha! Let him see what this stupid girl was capable of.

He stared at her. Then he burst into laughter. "Or you'll what?"

She flexed her fingers as an odd tingling sensation warmed them. It seemed to be emanating from deep within where her rage surged like a tide. She forced herself to remain calm. Anger would not solve this situation. It required clear thinking and calculated words. "I will get out of here one day, Uncle. And I can assure you, when I do, I will retrieve everything you owe me."

"With interest?" His laughter ended with snorts. "My girl, you know nothing of the world if you think you will ever get away from me. You seem to forget, you have nowhere to go. No family, no friends, not even the Widow Dawson would help you. She's too afraid of me. Everyone is too afraid of me in this county." He smacked his palm again with the papers.

"You are mistaken," she said with deliberate effort to keep her voice calm. "I have friends. You forget I had a full life before I came here. There are people who would gladly help me." But even as she said it, she could think of only one.

Georgiana. Sweet Georgiana Dale had never given up trying to contact her even though all Pippa's correspondence, in or out, had been confiscated. Nearly two years ago, a sympathetic servant had risked a great deal to smuggle in a letter from Pippa's elderly friend. But it was the only one. There had been nothing since.

"If you manage to get out of The Grange," he went on as if she'd not spoken, "I can easily hunt you down and drag you back here. You will never leave. You and your land are mine."

The pool of rage surged again but this time she didn't check it. Couldn't. It was too fierce as it rushed through her body, along her arms and burst from her fingertips like bolts of lightning. She wasn't sure how it happened but suddenly the papers in her uncle's hand caught alight.

With a yelp, he dropped them onto the rushes and tried to stamp out the flames with his riding boots. But the pages scattered and Molly the house maid hadn't changed the rushes in too long. They were dry and the flames quickly spread across the floor.

"Fire!" her uncle shouted. "Fetch water! Fire!" He removed his cloak and swatted at the flames but it only served to fan them towards the curtains. "You witch," he yelled at her. "You did this. I'll see you hung for witchcraft, you filthy bitch." He returned to swatting the fire but fell back when the flames swallowed up the curtains.

Pippa watched in a kind of trance but her uncle's accusation was as good as a slap to her face. Oh God. She *had* caused the fire. She knew it as clearly as she could feel its heat on her face and smell the smoke.

But how...?

There was no time to consider the answer. The fire was rapidly consuming the study. Servants handed pails of water through the door but their efforts did nothing to dampen the flames. Her uncle had given up trying to put it out and was frantically rummaging through one of his coffers, its edges already smoldering. He shouted orders, barely heard above the roar of the fire, for valuables to be rescued. Servants abandoned their buckets and ran to either do his bidding or save themselves.

The thick smoke stung Pippa's eyes and filled her nose and mouth. Her chest ached. She couldn't breathe. She had to get out.

The door was wide open. Some servants remained to help Simon with his papers and books but most had vanished. No one seemed to take notice of her.

She ran. Out of the study, down two flights of stairs, past scurrying, hysterical servants, to the front door. She would leave through the main entrance this time, no backstairs with her guard on her heels.

No one on her heels at all.

She fled to the stables where grooms led horses out and away from the rapidly spreading fire. She could probably take one in the confusion but she wasn't dressed for riding and she'd not ridden in five years anyway. No doubt one of the frightened creatures would throw her before she even left the estate.

She would have to flee on foot. She changed direction and ran towards the gatehouse, hampered by her skirts. She lifted them and kept running. The steep pitched roof of the gatehouse loomed closer. People from the village streamed past her, carrying buckets and blankets. They jostled her but didn't seem to see her. She was dressed plainly and most had never even met her—no doubt they thought her a frightened servant fleeing to safety.

"Stop her!" Simon's command rose above the confusion.

She looked back. He stood near the stables, his arms full of ledgers and papers, his white lace ruff and cuffs blackened by soot. He kicked one of the serving boys racing past but the lad was too scared or too occupied to stop. Simon swore at him then looked around for someone else but no one seemed aware that their master needed them. Behind him, black smoke billowed from the study windows and two of the adjoining rooms. Servants threw valuable tapestries and painted cloths out of the other windows, but most got trampled beneath frantic feet.

Pippa continued running towards the gatehouse and the arched entrance to the estate. Almost there. Even though she knew Simon could recapture her beyond the gates, she still desperately wanted to reach them, wanted to taste the air on the other side.

"Stop!" Simon again, his voice hoarse. "Get back here, Witch!" When she didn't stop, he shouted, "I'll send the Witch Hunter after you."

She stumbled and fell, tearing her hose and scraping her knee. Simon's threat lingered in the air with the ash and smoke. Despite the warmth of the day, she felt cold to the bone.

Witch.

No. Not her. Surely not.

Yet she had caused the fire. She'd felt the force of it gathering within, felt the heat and power flood her body and blast from her fingertips.

Her stomach lurched. She wanted to throw up. There was no doubt—she *was* a witch. But...how?

She had no time to consider the answer to that. Two fat hands clamped down on her shoulders and drew her roughly out of the dirt. She looked up at her uncle and shrank back from his crazed glare. His fingers dug into her skin where shoulders met throat. A little higher and he would strangle her.

Pippa fought down panic and tried to control her breathing. "Let me go!"

"Allow my dear niece to abandon me?" He sneered, as if that were amusing. "Foolish girl." Without warning, he slapped her.

She gasped at the sting but refused to rub her cheek or check if he'd drawn blood with his rings. She wouldn't show weakness. Not to Simon. He fed on it. He wanted it. Her fear only made him feel more powerful and she would rather die than give him what he wanted.

"That was for running off." He raised his hand, laughing like a madman when she flinched in anticipation of the pain. "And this is for burning my house down." His hand curled into a fist.

Instinctively, she lifted her arm to block his blow. But she did more than merely stop him hitting her. With an explosion of power that seemed to emanate from her core, her arm connected with his and he flew through the air, landing some distance away on his back.

Dusty, sooty and sprawled in the dirt like a beggar, he stared up at her, fear imprinted in every feature. He was afraid of her.

Good Lord, the giddiness of it. The sheer pleasure of knowing that *she* could make a man like Simon Rowe afraid. It was intoxicating, heady and thoroughly exhilarating, like riding extremely fast in rough terrain.

But also very, very dangerous.

Thankfully no one had seen but she needed to be more careful in the future. If she didn't learn to control these strange new powers, she would find herself at the end of a noose.

Simon pointed a finger at her. "You...you...!"

"Witch?" she offered after making sure no one was within earshot. "*Now* will you let me go?"

He licked cracked lips. "Go if you dare. But I will set the Witch Hunter onto you. He will find you no matter where you go, and when he does, I'll not stop him from doing his job."

She backed away from the sheer venom in his voice. The Witch Hunter's self-appointed job was to kill witches. Kill them and obliterate every trace of them as if they never existed. Legend said he knew how to negate a witch's powers, making it easier to capture them. No one knew how he did it and no one knew what he did to the women afterwards, but rumors were rife. Some said he tortured the accused before killing them, others said he took his perverse sexual desires out on their bodies first.

Pippa swallowed and backed away. Simon stood and dusted

himself off, watching her all the while. Despite wobbling legs, she turned and ran.

"You'll never find peace again!" he shouted after her. "He will hunt you down. You can't hide, my girl. He'll find you and your kind. He always does."

The sound of his mad laugh dogged her heels. She had to get away, had to run far enough and hide somewhere that not even the Witch Hunter would find her. But where? The man was said to be omniscient. He could find witches anywhere in England.

She tried desperately to think of somewhere and of someone who could help her. But she knew of only one person—Georgiana Dale—and one place. With a silent prayer of thanks to Georgiana for her kindly offer in that final letter, Pippa ran through the gatehouse and didn't look back.

* * *

2 Days Later

Even dressed in boys' clothes and perched half way up a tree just outside London's ancient walls, Pippa didn't feel safe. She wouldn't until she reached Ashbourne House and Georgiana Dale. She needed some of her mother's friend's calm wisdom to help her get far away from Simon. And the Witch Hunter. Especially the Witch Hunter.

Now, if only she could climb down, she could complete her journey. Without stiff skirts and a bodice, climbing the tree had been easy. Getting down was a different matter entirely.

She tried stretching her foot to reach the lowest branch but it was a few inches beyond her toes. How had she managed to get up in the first place? She'd taken no notice of her progress, too intent on climbing high enough to see over the row of buildings lining the northern side of The Strand. Her tree stood in a large field behind those houses and gardens. Ashbourne House lay beyond them on the other side of the busy thoroughfare into London proper.

She looked down again and tried to determine the best route

for a safe descent. With a sigh, she realized it was the one she'd already attempted.

Curses. No fifteen year-old boy would find himself stuck up a tree. That fact was of more concern than her current predicament because it meant she wasn't completely immersed in her disguise, even after two days in it. She could not let her concentration or her disguise slip, even at this late stage.

She blew out a breath. She could do it. Or more to the point, *Pip* could. She lowered herself again, this time holding onto the trunk for balance and—

Crack!

The branch snapped under her weight. Pippa grappled at leaves, twigs and then emptiness in vain. With a cry, she crashed to the ground, landing with a thud that bruised her rump and stole her breath. But any pain she felt was forgotten when an unearthly screech ripped through the air. She looked up to see a huge beast rise above her, its hooves threatening to smash her skull. She screamed, drowning out the creature's snorts.

The front legs descended. She rolled out of the way. Fear made her fast and she scrabbled backwards to the base of the tree. The creature, one of hell's beasts for sure, reared again. She gathered her strength around her, inside her, drawing on the well of heat at her core and feeling it surge down her arms to her fingers. In the two days since setting fire to The Grange, she'd grown accustomed to the new sensations building whenever her fear or anger rose. But in that time, she'd also learned to control it.

"Easy, Devil," a man's voice boomed over the snorts of the beast. Except the beast was nothing more than a horse. A very large horse, but still not the hellhound she'd thought it to be moments ago. "Easy now," he said again, his voice more soothing.

Pippa quickly stood and suppressed the magic until it was no more than a tingling warmth in her belly. The horse whinnied and shied away from her, its nostrils flaring, its big head jerking fiercely. The rider held the reins in one hand and leaned forward to stroke the horse's neck and murmur in its ear.

She stared at them and tried to control her galloping heartbeat. It took a moment of forcing herself to think rationally to realize horse and rider hadn't suddenly appeared from nowhere like some supernatural spirit. They must have emerged from around the small hill alongside her tree. She'd been so intent on getting down, she'd failed to notice their approach.

When the horse grew calm, the rider dismounted and fixed a glare on Pippa that made her wish she possessed the power to vanish as well.

"What kind of foolish prank was that?" he blasted. "You could have been killed!" He raised his hand and she put an arm up in defence, but instead of striking her, he merely pulled the hat off his head and wiped his brow.

"It was no prank," she said, hearing the tremor in her voice and not liking it. She had no reason to be afraid. Not here on the edge of London where no one knew her. She hadn't been followed—she'd made sure of that. She was safe.

Unless this horseman decided to thrash her.

He looked quite capable of doing it too, with his large hands and broad frame. He had the sort of shoulders used to hard work and breaking bones.

Yet she was quite capable of breaking bones too—something she'd discovered when the highwayman tried to rob her only the day before. Still, it wouldn't do to draw attention to her...abilities. Her situation was precarious enough. It would be wiser simply to stay silent.

"Then what were you doing jumping in front of my horse?" His deep blue eyes brimmed with anger. "Well, lad?" he said when she didn't answer. When she still didn't answer, he growled low in his throat. "God's teeth, what a bloody foolish thing to do! You're lucky Devil didn't crush you to death."

Devil—how appropriate.

She stared up at him, a hundred retorts racing through her mind. She swallowed them all. *Easy, Pippa,* she told herself using the same tones the rider had with his horse. Best to let the man get his anger out of his system then she could be on her way. From her earlier vantage point in the tree, she guessed Lord Ashbourne's house to be at least another half hour away. It had been easy to spot amongst the other grand houses stretching from The Strand down to the riverfront, thanks to Georgiana Dale's detailed description.

The rider grunted again and turned his attention to the horse stamping at the ground with a hoof. He rubbed its neck and shoulder until the muscles stopped quivering and the horse quieted. When the man turned back to her, his face had lost some of its hardness and his eyes were more like deep, still lakes than stormy seas.

"Are you injured?" he asked.

"No." Except for the bruises. And her pride. She went to tuck her hair behind her ear only to remember it had been cropped short. She adjusted her cap instead.

The man swept her with a brisk gaze as if satisfying himself of her wellbeing. No, not *her* wellbeing, Pip's. The rider only saw a boy standing in front of him. She hoped.

"Well?" he asked, one eyebrow raised.

She frowned. "Well what?"

"Are you going to tell me why you thought it would be amusing to startle my horse?" Irritation threaded his words, even though his stance relaxed somewhat. He held the reins with one hand, the other clutching a piece of paper at his side which she hadn't noticed before. Had he been reading it when she dropped out of the tree? That would explain why he hadn't seen her fall.

"Amusing?" she said. "Am I laughing?"

His eyes locked on her mouth which suddenly went dry under his direct gaze.

"I didn't startle your horse on purpose," she continued. "And if you'd been watching where you were going, you'd have known that."

One corner of his mouth lifted, but not in humor. She had thought him quite handsome at first, not in a fashionably pretty way, but with unconventional roughness that couldn't be smoothed away by a mere improvement in his grooming. Now she thought him quite ugly. He was much too dark, too sharp of cheek, and too big. Far too big. Anyway, he looked to be well over thirty.

"You're quite forthright, aren't you?" he said, his voice low and dangerous. "Considering you don't know who I am or what I'm capable of."

She suspected he was capable of a lot of things, snapping her in half being one of them. However, she didn't think he would hurt her. There'd been genuine concern in his expression when he'd asked her if she was hurt. As to who he was, well, he dressed like any other traveler. Dirty boots, simple black cloak over black riding doublet and breeches. A rapier sat like an old friend at his hip, the hilt worn smooth as if he'd had it for years —and used it well. Not a shiny, gold-hilted weapon like her uncle's, but a real blade. How many people had he killed with it?

At least the dark rider didn't seem like anyone of importance, although he didn't have the same bearing as an artisan or simple villager either. He held himself erect, his broad back straight and his gaze shrewd. He didn't carry any bags so he was most likely a Londoner out for a ride, and London was no village. She'd seen it sprawling like a multi-legged beast across both sides of the river from her tree. She wondered if all Londoners were as arrogant as this one.

Again, he raised an eyebrow. Definitely arrogant. "So you just happened to jump out from behind a bush at the same time I passed?" He rolled his eyes. "Don't lie to me, lad. I'm an expert at detecting them."

"I am not lying! And furthermore, I don't like the accusation that I am."

There was a heavy pause in which Pippa's heart stopped beating. She really should have kept to her earlier decision not to say anything. But something about being in disguise so far from home made her feel safe. And adventurous. A dangerous notion that, and one she needed to suppress. She might be free but adventuring could end her freedom too soon.

"I see," was all he said. He studied her for a long time and she felt the familiar swell of fear overtaking her anger. Then the man blinked and began to chuckle. The chuckle turned to a laugh, crinkling his eyes and softening his features. "Then tell me your version of events."

She hesitated, not trusting his sudden change of mood. "I

didn't jump, I fell." She pointed to the tree canopy above her. "From there."

He looked up then back at her, his gaze lingering like hot summer sunshine on her chest. Her cheeks reddened and she moved instinctively to cover her breasts but stopped herself when he looked at her face again.

"Are you sure you're not injured?" he said. "That's quite a fall."

Pippa shrugged then winced at the pain in her shoulders. "I'm perfectly fine. Thank you. I must be going." She picked up her satchel, still resting against the tree trunk where she'd left it, and walked off. Her hip felt a little sore but not enough to make her limp, something to be grateful for.

"Wait!" The rider joined her, leading his horse which followed meekly. "It seems I owe you an apology."

"Yes."

"Right." He coughed. "I'm sorry."

She inclined her head in acknowledgement.

"What's your name, lad?"

She glanced at him sideways. "Pip." It couldn't hurt to give him the false name she'd been using at inns between Shelton and London, and would continue to use at Ashbourne House.

"Where are you heading? Perhaps I could give you a ride. Devil can hold both—"

"No!" Good Lord, she couldn't sit behind this stranger! Her breasts may be small and easily hidden beneath her oversized cloak and the thick leather of her jerkin, but squashing them against his back was a little too risky. How could he fail not to notice them? He was a man after all.

He looked taken aback. "Are you sure? You've just had a fall. And a fright, if the expression on your face when Devil reared is anything to go by."

"I'm unharmed. And I've not far to go."

"You're going to The Strand?" He nodded in the direction they were heading.

She said nothing and kept her eyes on the worn dirt path.

"Very well," he said, tartly. "I can see you're not one to forgive easily."

"No, it's not—." She bit her lip to stop herself talking. Best to let him think her still annoyed.

He mounted and Devil began to prance as if sensing his master's urgency to be away. "You'll want to arrive at your destination before nightfall, lad," the rider said with a nod at the sinking sun. "London's not safe after dark." He urged Devil on and the horse charged off before Pippa could politely thank him for his advice.

She blew out a breath, relieved to see the back of him. If all Londoners were as unsettling as that man, she was in for a challenging time ahead.

* * *

Lord Ashbourne's steward regarded Pippa closely before turning away as if bored. The quick change in his manner made her uneasy and she held her breath waiting for him to speak, hoping he didn't see through her disguise.

"Would you care to sit?" he asked.

"No thank you, Sir." She preferred to stand near the door to make escape easier if necessary. A new habit, borne of two days fleeing in disguise.

"I understand you were enquiring after Mistress Dale?" he said, idly brushing his long fingers across the back of a chair. Checking for dust?

The chair was one of only two bracketing the fireplace in an otherwise bare chamber near the kitchens. Clean rushes covered the floor but the walls and chairs were unadorned. Not even a cushion offered comfort. The steward, Fallon, had directed her to the room after she asked to speak to him. The servant who'd let her in through the kitchen entrance hadn't been any help at all. He'd told her he'd never heard of Georgiana Dale. Thankfully Fallon didn't seem so ignorant.

"She was my mother's friend," Pippa explained. "She wrote telling me I would find her here."

"You won't," he said, rubbing his fingertips together to remove the dust. His attention seemed to be completely on his task. If he wasn't speaking to her, Pippa would have thought he didn't even see her. "She's gone," he went on. "She left Lord Ashbourne's service two years ago." His gaze met hers, direct and uncompromising. "As her *friend*, you would have known that."

Pippa swallowed around the lump in her throat. Gone? And soon after her last letter by the sound of it. "My mother died some time ago. Mistress Dale wrote to me saying that if I ever needed her, I was to come here."

Fallon's brown eyes grew softer as he took in ever inch of her from her newly cropped hair to her dirty boots. "I cannot help you. I'm sorry."

"Do you know where I can find her?" Please let it not be far. The sun was almost set and she needed somewhere to stay for the night. What little money she'd taken with her had run out after she'd paid for the previous night's room. If she left immediately, she could probably make it through the London gates before curfew.

"Haverford," he said.

"Is that nearby?"

"About half a day's ride from here."

"Ride?" she said weakly.

He nodded and glanced past her to the door, looking eager to be gone himself.

Pippa wished she'd taken up the offer of a chair. Her legs suddenly felt too weak to hold her. "Haverford," she said to no one in particular. "Oh."

His sad, bloodhound eyes regarded her again with cautious curiosity. "Mistress Dale was a friend of your mother's, you say?"

"Yes." She rallied under his sympathetic gaze. She had come this far and would not crumble at the final stage. All she needed was a bed for the night and then she would somehow complete her journey tomorrow. "Great friends but I believe it was mostly by correspondence. I've never met her." It was the truth. She had found during the years lived under her uncle's roof that it was best to keep to the truth where possible. It made it easier to keep track of the lies.

He nodded thoughtfully. "It'll be dark soon. Do you have somewhere to stay, lad?"

"No. I was hoping Mistress Dale would accommodate me here with the servants until she found me employment." Another lie, quickly formed and not very well thought through. She held her breath and watched the long, straight face of the imperial steward as he considered her words.

"Employment?" he said. "As what? A pageboy perhaps?"

"Yes." What did it matter now? Georgiana was gone and Pippa would say anything to get a room for the night.

"Good. Then you can start immediately."

"Pardon?" She blinked at him.

Fallon inclined his head. "Last week the page of the wardrobe received news of his father's illness and had to leave unexpectedly. You can take his position until he returns. I'm sure Geor...Mistress Dale would approve."

Pippa's fingers tightened around the strap of her satchel. "Page of the w, wardrobe?"

An almighty clatter from the kitchen made her jump. Fallon looked irritably past her. "It is a great honor," he said, distracted.

"B, but I simply want to find Mistress Dale. She will help me—"

"To find employment, yes? Well, you don't need to travel all the way to Haverford only to have her send you back here to be page of the wardrobe." He looked at her as if she was a dullard.

She snapped her mouth shut when she realized it was open. "Are you sure I am the most suitable person?"

The noise from the kitchens returned to the dull hum of earlier and his attention returned to Pippa. "And why wouldn't you be?"

Because she didn't want employment, she only wanted a night's shelter. And because she would have to see Lord Ashbourne naked! She would be required to help him dress and attend to his most personal needs. No, she couldn't possibly take the disguise that far.

"You require employment," he went on, not hiding his impatience, "Lord Asbhourne requires a page of the wardrobe."

"I've never been a page of the wardrobe before." Never served anyone in her life although she had been around servants since she was born and knew the duties each performed in a major household.

"You seem a well-bred boy, if a little travel-stained, and his lordship would dismiss me on the spot if I turned away a friend of Mistress Dale's." His eyes twinkled unexpectedly. The effect was rather delightful.

She longed to ask why his lordship would dismiss Fallon but refrained. She would ask Georgiana herself when she saw her. That's if she got through the night safely at Ashbourne House. But not as the page of the wardrobe. Certainly not.

"Is there some other service I could undertake, Sir? In the kitchens perhaps? It's just that I don't think I am suited to be page of the wardrobe."

"Nonsense! There's nothing to it. You simply do as his lordship requests. Besides, you're much too skinny to be of use anywhere else. Don't worry, Gertie will help you settle in. His lordship isn't expected to return until the morning anyway so you'll have all evening to familiarize yourself with your tasks."

Not expected until the morning? Perfect. She'd be gone by the time he returned. "Then I accept. Thank you, Sir."

"Good! I'll send Gertie to show you to the master's apartments." The steward moved past her, his stride brisk and purposeful.

"Just one question," she said and he stopped in the doorway. "Where will I sleep?" As a male servant, she would normally share a bed with one of the other male servants. It may be for only one night but that was long enough for her secret to be uncovered in the close proximity of a bed. However, her uncle's page had slept in a separate room within hearing of his master's shout. Hopefully the setup at Ashbourne House would be the same.

"You'll have a room adjoining the master's chamber," Fallon said. He gave her a brief nod of dismissal and left.

Pippa didn't let out her breath until the quick steps of the steward had disappeared. She drew in another and the delicious scent of cinnamon from the kitchen made her stomach rumble. She hadn't eaten since breaking her fast that morning.

She sat on one of the high-back chairs, clutched her satchel on her lap, and waited.

A few minutes later, a plump girl of about seventeen arrived and introduced herself as Gertie, one of the maids. She eyed Pippa from head to foot, lingering on the groin area. Pippa quickly stood and placed the satchel over herself before the maid found her lacking.

"You the Pip boy?" Gertie asked.

"Yes. I'm the new page—"

"Of the wardrobe. I know," the maid said cheerfully. "Come on, let's go." Gertie smiled and her entire face smiled too, from her brown eyes to her protruding front teeth.

"You new to London?" she asked, leading the way through the kitchen, two larders and a scullery.

"Is it that obvious?" Pippa wondered what had marked her as different. Her clothes? Her manner?

"You don't speak like one of us," Gertie said. "Where you from?"

"The west," Pippa said vaguely. "Tell me, what is Lord Ashbourne like?" She needed to keep the maid talking to stop her asking too many questions.

"He's a good master," Gertie said as she led the way up the back stairs. "Never raised a hand to any of us, even though Ralphy deserved it when he pinched the countess's necklace. *She'd* have had Ralphy flogged but his lordship would hear nothin' of it. Dismissed the little dog turd with full wages, so I heard."

Pippa followed Gertie up the next flight of stairs to the second floor. "I'll get lost in this place."

"You get used to it. Just remember these stairs lead straight to the master's lodgings and you can't go wrong. Only the servants use them." She paused and waited for Pippa to join her. "And sometimes the master, so mind he doesn't knock you over if he passes you in a hurry. These stairs aren't wide and you bein' so slight and him bein' so big...well, you'll come off worse." She laughed and continued up.

"Why would his lordship come this way?" The backstairs were built to provide access for the servants between the master's lodgings and the kitchen, larders and cellars. Why would the earl want to traverse through such an undignified passage?

Gertie shrugged rounded shoulders. "Who knows why he does anythin'? He's...what's the word? Unperdickable. Yep, that's it."

"Unpredictable," Pippa corrected.

"That's what I said. Unperdickable. He comes and goes when he pleases, no matter the hour, and..." she lowered her voice, "his visitors sometimes come and go at strange hours too. Even in the middle of the night when they think we're all asleep."

Pippa's eyes widened. "What sort of visitors?"

"All sorts. Men, women—"

"Women!" She bit her lip when Gertie shushed her with a finger to her lips. "Oh, of course. Women," Pippa said simply. Why wouldn't the unwed earl have dalliances? It was only natural. Wasn't it? She really had no idea.

"His lordship's not in," Gertie said, opening a door at the top of the stairs. "This is the master's wardrobe." She swept her hand wide to encompass the daybed, large cupboard and coffers beside it and the fireplace surrounded by three stools. Although the room had none of the embellishments Pippa was used to in her own wardrobe—not a single embroidered cushion, Turkey carpet or wall hanging—it didn't feel cold or uninviting. The embers in the grate still glowed, effusing the room with warmth, and the last pale rays of daylight reached into even the furthest corner thanks to the large windows. She ran her hand along the top of one of the coffers, enjoying the feel of the cedar, worn smooth from years of use and polishing. The scent of cloves and something spicier lingered in the air.

"Is this where I am to sleep?" Pippa asked, wondering if she would be required to lie on a pallet on the floor. She was so tired she wouldn't mind curling up near the enormous fire as long as the straw mattress was clean.

"No, your room is through there." Gertie pointed to a door beside the stairwell entrance.

Pippa peeked inside. The room was tiny. A small trestle bed was pushed up against one wall and an oak chest squatted opposite. A single stool was situated to take in the view of the knot garden from the window.

"Peter's things are still here," Gertie said, opening the chest. She pulled out a garment in the Ashbourne colors of silver and green and held it up against Pippa. "He was about your height so his livery should fit. Everything'll be a bit big in the shoulders and legs but they'll do." She pulled it away but continued to scrutinize Pippa. "Get some of Cook's food into you and you'll soon be filling these out. His beef broth'll put hairs on your chest, mark my words."

"How...appetizing." Hairy chests notwithstanding, she'd been tall and slender ever since she'd reached womanhood and she didn't think she'd thicken out no matter what Cook concocted.

"Now," said Gertie, whisking Pippa out of her new room and back through the vast wardrobe, "through that door is the master's bedchamber."

Pippa nodded, growing curious about the earl even though she would never meet him. It must be the close proximity to all his things that made her wonder about their owner. "Can I ask you something?" she said.

"Of course." Gertie paused at the door to the master's chamber and crossed her arms in a way that pushed her large breasts up and out. Then she winked. "You can ask me anythin', Pip."

Pippa cleared her throat. Somehow she felt more in danger with this girl than she had in two days. "Is he feeble-minded? Or ugly? Or is he both perhaps?"

"Who?"

"The earl."

Gertie threw her head back and laughed, a high, nasally sound that ended with a snort. "He's very clever and one of the handsomest devils in London if you ask me. Why?"

Pippa shrugged. "Curiosity. He's not married and he's past the age that most men of noble birth are wed for the first time. Well past it, I believe."

"That is his lordship's business, not yours or mine, Pip," Gertie said with a wag of her finger. "Best not to wonder how your betters conduct their affairs. They're a mystery to me, especially this one." She stuck her thumb at the door leading to the backstairs.

At precisely that moment, it opened. Gertie gasped then quickly bobbed her head as she tucked her offending thumb into the folds of her apron. "My lord! You're not expected! I mean, I didn't know you were here."

Pippa froze as a man entered. Not just any man. *Him*. The rider. The one she'd angered in the field. And of all the cruel twists of Fate, it seemed he was the Earl of Ashbourne.

"My business finished earlier than expected," he said.

Pippa choked back her anguish. *Dear God, I promise to attend church twice every Sunday if you strike me dead now!*

Perhaps he wouldn't remember her. He was an earl after all, and she nothing but an ungainly youth. But when he looked at her, recognition flared.

"You again!" He made a sound—half grunt, half laugh, all humorless. "It seems our paths have crossed once more."

"So it would seem, my lord," she said, bowing low to hide her face which ran hot and cold.

"Are you going to fall in front of me again, lad?" he said. "Because you look quite ill."

"This here is Pip," Gertie said, nudging Pippa forward. "He's the new page of the wardrobe."

The earl cocked an eyebrow. "Really? Well, lad, I'm sorry."

"My lord?" Pippa dared to ask.

He smiled. "You'll see."

Pippa felt sick. Her stomach rolled, her skin felt cold and damp and she had to grip the back of a chair to steady herself. With any luck she was dying and her misery would soon be over.

But her luck had run out because Lord Ashbourne's smile broadened, leaving her with no doubt he was aware of her discomfort and enjoying it.

She had the distinct feeling her day was about to get a whole lot worse.

KISS OF ASH is now available.

A MESSAGE FROM THE AUTHOR

I hope you enjoyed reading HONOR BOUND as much as I enjoyed writing it. As an independent author, getting the word out about my book is vital to its success, so if you liked this book please consider telling your friends and writing a review at the store where you purchased it. If you would like to be contacted when I release a new book, subscribe to my newsletter at http://cjarcher.com/contact-cj/newsletter/. You will only be contacted when I have a new book out.

ALSO BY C.J. ARCHER

SERIES WITH 2 OR MORE BOOKS

After The Rift

Glass and Steele

The Ministry of Curiosities Series

The Emily Chambers Spirit Medium Trilogy

The 1st Freak House Trilogy

The 2nd Freak House Trilogy

The 3rd Freak House Trilogy

The Assassins Guild Series

Lord Hawkesbury's Players Series

Witch Born

SINGLE TITLES NOT IN A SERIES

Courting His Countess

Surrender

Redemption

The Mercenary's Price

ABOUT THE AUTHOR

C.J. Archer has loved history and books for as long as she can remember and feels fortunate that she found a way to combine the two. She spent her early childhood in the dramatic beauty of outback Queensland, Australia, but now lives in suburban Melbourne with her husband, two children and a mischievous black & white cat named Coco.

Subscribe to C.J.'s newsletter through her website to be notified when she releases a new book, as well as get access to exclusive content and subscriber-only giveaways. Her website also contains up to date details on all her books: http:// cjarcher.com She loves to hear from readers. You can contact her through email cj@cjarcher.com or follow her on social media to get the latest updates on her books:

   BB